# THE SWAN KEEPER

Milana Marsenich

Open Books

Published by Open Books

Copyright © 2018 by Milana Marsenich

Cover image "Feather 2" © by Jim Champion
Learn more about the artist at www.flickr.com/photos/treehouse1977/

ISBN-13: 978-1948598033

To the Montana Waterfowl Foundation, the Confederated Salish and Kootenai Tribes Wildlife Management Program, and all who have worked so hard to reintroduce the trumpeter swan to the Flathead Indian Reservation, Montana, Wyoming, and North America.

When the fall air came in crisp and fresh, the bare-bone leaves sang to Lilly. She tilted her ear to the wind and listened. Aspen leaves floated down to the forest floor, reminding her that life is precious, it comes and it goes, reminding her of that cool Montana night when she climbed a game trail toward the pass and ran away from her father's killer.

Moisture from the night's rain salted the air and mixed with the sweat on her twelve-year-old forehead. Wild air tumbled around in her lungs as she moved up the trail, away from the wetlands. She was transforming, her supple neck stretching, her body both round and smooth. She followed the game trail through dried bear grass, up the mountainside. Wind whistled through the rocks and hoot owls called across the gully. The damp smell of cedar receded where dark larch and fir trees hovered. Gurgling sounds of creek water reached across the forest and encouraged her.

Run. Run. Fly.

Bushes scratched Lilly's ankles and grabbed her trouser legs. Night flies swarmed down from the larch branches and buzzed around her head. The ground, muddy from the fall rains, squished up over the edge of her shoes and down under the arches of her feet.

She charged forward, bone light and frail, her chest beating hard where her heart should have been. A partial moon peeked between the clouds, over the mountain, and opened its brilliant mouth to the trail where she saw the white carcass of a dead swan. It must have flown too low, hitting a tree, or was perhaps carried up here by a bear. Suddenly she was back in the marsh of radiant white trumpeter swans. The gunshots rang out and, one by one, the birds fell, standing or in flight, turning the swamp a bright mix of crimson and pink.

A phantom swan swept in beside Lilly, pulling her back to the trail, and moving her swiftly up the mountainside. The dense timber thinned and lightened, the moon passed west, and the sun came up over the eastern ridge. A feather fell into her hand, a quill for words written on the sky. She put it safely in the pocket of her trousers, next to the photo of her father with his fists clenched at his sides. The phantom swan flapped her wings and pulled Lilly into them, the down soft and warm, the last vestiges of night cool to the touch.

# White Swan

# 1

Lilly told three lies to go with her father one stormy afternoon when she was ten, the afternoon that she first learned about the swan killer. She said she'd done her chores, she forgave Pa for fighting with her mother, and she wasn't afraid. She was afraid. Not even Lilly's fourteen-year-old sister Anna could blame her for cinching her arms at their father's waist when the brown mare reared at the raucous trumpeting coming from the Cattail Marsh. It was a natural thing to keep from falling. Any girl would dig her heels into the mare's flanks like Lilly did, tilting her body into her father's back. She smelled the horse's fear. She tasted her own fear in her throat and relied on her father's courage. Sam Connelly turned the mare into the wind and snow. The horse galloped down the stage road, across the field toward the noise.

Through the bushes, at the edge of the water, a young trumpeter swan sat trapped on the bank. Nightshade wrapped around his ankle and each time he tried to fly, the relentless red-berried vine pulled him back to the spot where water met dirt. The fledgling tried again to fly, gave up, settled down and, before Lilly could throw her braids over her shoulders, he flailed his wings another time, spreading them wide as Lilly was tall, going nowhere. Sleet lined his head like cake icing. A mean wind blew his feathers up and away from his body in a way that made Lilly shiver in spite of the heavy wool coat she wore.

Her father dismounted, his bad leg coming up short when he hit the ground, and left Lilly sitting on the brown mare, face into the wind. Its sharp edges stung her cheeks.

"Lilly, come here. I've got a job for you," her father called from the marsh. He walked toward the bird, looking at it from different angles, tilting his wide cheeks first one way and then the other. "I want you to wrap your arms around his wings and hold him tight."

Lilly looked hard at her father with two good eyes, all heart and vision mixed together. Sam Connelly was a short man, with big shoulders, and a kind smile. His brown hair hung long and his winter beard hid his chin. He'd been taking pictures of swans since before Lilly was born, pictures of swans surrounding a meadow at the end of a calm pond, swans nesting on a great expanse of twigs and grasses, swans protecting their eggs, swans foraging for food, swans teaching their young to eat, swans paddling to shore.

There were pictures of cygnets peeking out from under their mother's wing, following their pink bills in circles, and, when they went out to feed, tipping their tiny tails to the air as they dipped their heads to eat the duckweed that grew on the pond. There was a picture of a single fierce swan pointing his silken black bill at the sky, and one with his elbows turned back, black eyes staring at her, strong and ready to fly.

Pa wasn't there the moment Nell gave birth to Lilly but he always said that he knew the second she entered the world. He had been out on the marsh that night taking photos in the lunar light. With a full wind lifting the water, two large swans danced on their tail feathers, wings held out to the rocking glow, trumpeting to the wild moon. When he saw them dancing like that he knew his Lilly had arrived. He mounted the brown mare and rode for home to greet her.

This swan was caught tight in the nightshade. He was not dancing and he scared Lilly. She looked at the young trumpeter, neck splaying out, claws scratching the water, his huge wings flapping, giving Lilly second thoughts. She wished more than ever that she hadn't lied, that she'd just stayed home with her mother and Anna where she belonged. The cygnet's narrow pink bill snapped and she thought sure it was at the crazy sour smell in the air. That swan and Lilly agreed on this much: she wasn't going anywhere near him.

"He's too mean," she said to her father, throwing her voice across the marsh. "He'll hurt me."

"He'll just go limp in your arms." Sam spoke loudly, above the trill and trumpet of the swans and the loud thunder of wings circling the marsh.

"I don't think so."

"It's easier than you think," he said.

Pa believed her when she said she wasn't afraid. And the truth was that she couldn't bear to disappoint him, not now that he was off the whiskey for a week and needed her, but she couldn't wrap her arms around those wild wings. Tears spilled out and froze on her cheeks.

"He'll lie down quietly on your lap." Her father softened his voice in a way that might have made her brave at any other time. "I'll help you."

When she was nine, Lilly climbed mountains and trees. She swam in the ice-cold waters of the big lake up north and refused to get out until she couldn't move her arms, numbed and deadened by the cold, laughing as she shivered to shore. That was nine. At ten she lied. She lied to get to do things she wanted to do and she lied to get out of things she didn't want to do. She lied to be liked and to act like she knew something. She lied to get others to do her bidding. Mostly, she lied about not being afraid. Lilly was afraid of so many things: storms that set fire to the forest, nights when guns went off, grizzly bears that walked through their yard, swans tied to the earth.

"Now, get off that horse," her father was saying. "Tie her to that branch and come over here. You can do this."

She got off the mare and tied her up but she stayed next to her, feeling the horse's warm breath on her neck, frozen in place.

Her father came over and knelt down beside Lilly. She stared at his bad leg twisting off to the side. He had injured it in a mining accident in Butte, a fortunate accident in Lilly's mind, an accident that turned her father into a better photographer. Before Sam Connelly injured his knee, he photographed the inside of tunnels, landslides, and the results of several mine explosions. He photographed the miners and their injuries, a missing leg, an eye turned grey and clouded over, the humped shoulders of a miner with bad lungs. When he left the mines for good, he turned to nature, to mountains and trees, fox or bear, and Lilly saw the world as a beautiful place.

"Remember Horse Child, my friend who died in the mines in Butte?" her father asked.

"Did you read my mind?"

"I saw you looking at my leg. You remember me talking about him?"

She nodded. He had a photograph of Horse Child that he pulled out and looked at on cold winter nights. He talked about his good friend often, especially after he'd been drinking and something dark swelled out of him and spilled into sadness and regret. At those times Lilly could see the wish in her father's eyes, to have made a move, to have changed something, and she wondered if she would regret it if she didn't help him now. She squinted her eyes, holding her tears, silently begging that he'd just cut the bird free without her. He was big enough to do it himself.

"Horse Child told me that in the old days, before the allotments, when the northern tribes traveled the land and the sky reached out for everyone," Pa said, "those tribes left the sick and dying behind. The tribe's survival was the most important thing to each person. Everyone was important, yes. They all had their jobs. Yet staying back during bad conditions to take care of the dying would kill the whole tribe and everyone knew it. They felt deep sadness and fear when they left people behind. They cut their hair, or slashed their faces, and moved on. It was the only way. Swans will do the same thing. The flock will leave the sick and injured behind. They

4

won't want to, but they will." He paused, looked at the fledgling and back to Lilly. "This little one will die here in this marsh, if we don't cut him free."

Lilly wiped a tear from her eye and took in a deep breath.

"Even the Queen of England has a swan keeper," he said.

"A swan keeper?" She couldn't imagine anyone keeping one of these creatures.

"Someone who watches over and protects the swans. You're natural born to it, with your blond hair and fair skin. You're nearly half-swan yourself. This cygnet won't have a chance unless we get him out of here. Will you help me?"

Against her better notions, she nodded.

"OK," Pa said. "I'll take hold of him and then I'll pass him to you. I've got to cut that nightshade from his leg. If he stays bogged down here, the marsh will freeze over and he'll starve to death. The rest of his family is ready to go. See how they keep skimming the water and taking flight? Only to come back, waiting for this one? They'll wait as long as they can, but they won't endanger the flock."

Lilly nodded again. Shame filled her chest. She couldn't talk. He'd asked a simple thing of her and she had let him down.

He went behind the young trumpeter and spread his arms wide catching the bird's wings as they came in close to his body. The swan dropped his head toward the water and sat quietly in her father's lap. Her father hadn't lied. He spoke the truth, not the mean drinking truth, but the natural truth. The swan lay perfectly still in his arms. Lilly drew in a breath, a small bit of courage growing in her.

"I'll take your knife and cut the grasses away from his feet," she suggested.

"No, Lilly. You hold him." She knew Pa was too smart for her. Those webbed feet could hurt her. "Come here now," he said. "I wouldn't ask you to do something impossible."

But he had asked her to do something impossible, hadn't he, all those nights when he came home drunk and fought with Nell, and told Lilly the next morning to forget what she'd heard the night before, as though it was no concern to her or her sister. He told her to think only of the beautiful sun that rose over the Mission Mountains, or the snow piled high at the base of their cabin, or the wild lupine in the spring. Lilly could hold a trumpeter swan more than she could forget about her parents fighting. Even Anna would agree with her there. When their parents fought, the house got loud and a mean smell spun around the small rooms, stealing everyone's breath.

Lilly walked slowly over to her father, the wind pushing her, choosing sides, the wind Pa's friend and not hers.

"Good. Slide in here between the cygnet and myself. Slowly. Now put your arms under mine. That's it. You've got his wings tucked into your hug?"

Lilly nodded. Her whole body shook.

"Clasp your hands in front, near his chest. Be firm but gentle."

She closed her eyes and did as Pa said. When she opened them she held a trumpeter swan in her lap, a young one, about four months old. His gray feathers rested against her arms and he bent his neck around her head, as if hugging her, reassuring her that he didn't mind her holding him. His body went completely still. She thought about her name: Lillian. She knew what her name meant. It meant Elizabeth, which in turn meant God Has Sworn, which really meant God Has Promised. Lillian. Elizabeth. God Has Sworn. In that moment she felt God's promise like a prayer, one given just to her.

Like the swan, her body went limp and careful, afraid to even smell the wetlands. She was sure that even the hairs on her head stayed perfectly still, resisting the wind. The trumpeter dropped his head forward, shifting his neck into the shape of a tear. His weight hurt her legs. Nell said that Lilly had frail bones. She said that a four-month-old cygnet weighed nearly half as much as Lilly did. Ignoring the pain, Lilly closed her eyes and, for a moment, felt the magic that lived inside of the large bird, and there, then, with the weight of the bird on her legs, she wanted to be a swan keeper.

If the world could reverse itself and turn upside down, she'd lay flat on the trumpeter's back, stretch her arms like wings. He'd flap his gray feathers against the wind and soar across the marsh. Lilly would ride along and see every hawk nest from the Cattail Marsh to the great lake up north. She felt the flight ready to push through those wings, ready to push the air out from under them.

The world had not turned upside down. The swan sat quietly in her lap while her father cut the vine away from his ankle and freed him. Her arms were now the only things holding the young trumpeter to the earth, his big body in her lap, his tear shaped neck quiet as winter.

"When you're ready," Pa said, "I'll come take hold of him, and you let him go." He must've understood finally that he had asked too much of her. He must've understood that she was a girl who could do some things, but not all things.

"I'm ready," she said.

He sat in the wet marsh behind her. "OK, easy now. That's it. Give him over to me. Good. Now slip out from between us and go stand by my horse."

Lilly looked at her father across the pond where he moved away from the fledgling. "How did you do that?" she asked.

"Do what?"

"Make him stay still?"

"Easier than you'd think."

"You didn't shoot him."

Pa burst out laughing. "No. I just counted on his natural impulse. When a swan senses danger he plays dead. Fawns do it too. It's one of the ways that animals protect themselves."

The young swan stayed motionless on the bank until her father crossed through the weeds and stood at her side. With the way clear, the cygnet perked up and swam across the swamp, the wind rustling his frozen feathers. The other birds came near, put their bills down close to him. They circled and splashed the water and slid across the pond, as though trying to pick him up with their wings. Yet, the young swan wouldn't fly.

The cygnet swam in slow circles, his wings splayed out across the water, looking like Lilly felt when she'd ridden her bicycle too long and all her muscles hurt. The wind blew the smell of duckweed past them, and Pa waded back into the cold water. The swan now looked as if the pond had frozen him before he had the chance to take flight. At first that's what Lilly thought had happened—the bird had quickly frozen to death—until she noticed the blood on her coat.

"This bird's been shot." Sam Connelly spit the words out between his teeth like bitter, unwanted seeds. He captured the bird a second time—which looked easier than the first, since the cygnet had no strength left—and carried him to the bank. He told Lilly to climb up on his horse. She pulled herself up and sat stiffly behind the saddle. "Take a blanket from the side bag," Pa said, "and lay it across your lap and the back of the saddle."

She did what he said. Not knowing what he had in mind, she waited quietly.

"Good thing you're experienced at holding swans," he said. Without waiting for an answer, he put the swan in her lap.

He hooked his foot in the stirrup, and, careful to avoid the swan with his free leg, he mounted the mare. As they loped across the field the wind stung Lilly's cheeks and she hung on firmly to the young swan, gripping the mare's flanks with her legs to keep them both from falling. She held the fledgling so close that she tasted his feathers in her mouth. She felt the faint rise and fall of his chest, and maybe his heartbeat, as the bird fell limp against her belly. It will live, she thought. If I hold it close to my heart and pour all of my love into it, it will live. She held her breath and conjured up all the love she had ever known—Pa, Nell, Anna, the beautiful mountains, the way that the clouds rolled across the sky in every season, the smell of warm pine and damp cedar, the iced smell of winter snow. She even included the sound of the coyotes at night at the edge of the mountains, the owls in the trees in late fall, the mourning doves.

She breathed all that love into the swan's heart so that the swan would live. Lilly would reverse bullets. Even as the swan lay limp in her arms, she would protect it, save it. She could save it, being natural born to it, she could save the trumpeter swan.

They rode across the flatlands to Charlie West's ranch as the snow began in earnest. By the time they got there, the rise and fall of the swan's chest was so faint Lilly could barely feel it. Still. Hope crowded out the darkness that stuck in her throat. Charlie came out of the house, unshaven and half-dressed in brown pants and a long work coat. He was much taller than Pa and bean thin with kind green eyes. Charlie West was the county sheriff, and though he gave people the benefit of the doubt, he had no qualms about locking up the guilty. He took the young swan from Lilly, held the bird carefully and walked toward a fenced pond where another swan watched from across the water.

"He's gone," Charlie said to Lilly's father, placing the bird in a shed with hay and warm water. "You're both sopping wet, gotta be ice cold. I've got an extra pair of trousers in here. And Jerome's got a pair Lilly can wear."

Pa shook his head no and followed Charlie into the shed. He shut the door, shutting Lilly out. She stood on the other side of the shed, close to the door, stunned and disbelieving. Gone. How could the swan be gone? She had filled him with love. She had gathered light from all good things and poured it into him. He couldn't be gone.

"Drake did this." She heard her father's voice through the door. "Someone needs to stop him."

Lilly didn't know this Drake, but from the sound of her father's heavy boots on the wooden floor, she knew he must be a very bad man and it scared her. She'd only heard Pa this mad after he'd been drinking and he'd fought with Nell and spanked Anna for no good reason. That night Lilly's mother kicked Pa out and told him to come back when he could behave, and keep his hands off her girls. He left and came back calm and never hit any of them again.

This time, though, her father's anger would turn on him and Lilly knew it. She could feel it in her cold hands where she'd just let go of the dead swan. Suddenly all of her own bitter anger about Pa's drinking and fighting with Nell vanished. He'd trusted her to hold and save a trumpeter swan, a four-month-old cygnet, and she had let him down.

"I'll stop him," she said, bursting through the shed door. "I'll stop Drake, Pa." Jerome West, just two years older than Lilly, stood in the corner, his eyes wide, his dark hair long and falling in his face, shaking his head. "A man can't just go around killing swans, not trumpeters," she said to Jerome. "It's a miracle this flock of swans is even here. Trumpeters are mostly all dead."

Jerome shook his head again and moved toward her like he wanted to keep her from making a grave mistake. Lilly wasn't wrong though. She knew her swan history.

"Aren't they, Pa? They've mostly been killed off for stupid things, like women making themselves pretty, or soft beds for selfish people. In Chicago they paid ten dollars for one egg at the turn of the century. The trumpeter swans are all gone now. Except this one stubborn flock."

"Lillian, wait outside," Sam said, his eyes as cold as the mountains.

"But it's freezing out there." She was shivering wet in her pond clothes.

"Go."

She looked to Jerome for rescue but he only took her hand and led her out into the snow. She leaned in close to the door again so that she could hear every word they said.

"How can you be sure it's him? He's been helping down at the fire hall and the men like him. They say he's a hard worker," Charlie said.

"Working hard to deceive others."

"You've said he's no good," Charlie said.

"He's got a bad head on him. About the only thing he loves more than hunting wild animals and leaving them to rot is hurting others."

"You can't accuse a man just because you think he did something wrong. You have to know something, witness his wrongdoing, have evidence of some sort. Let it be and I'll sort it out. Time has a way of making the truth clear."

"I can't let it be. There are too few trumpeters left. Lilly's right. This is a rare flock. I can't sit by and let him shoot them for sport. He left a wounded trumpeter to get tangled in the swamp weed and die. He didn't even stop to make sure it was dead, and at least finish the job and eat the meat. And he won't stop, not till he's good and sure they're all gone."

"Especially if he thinks you have a stake in it, right? I'm not saying I agree with you Sam, but don't go borrowing trouble. If he is what you say he is, he'll come after you."

"Let him," Pa said. "You should be on my side." He paused and continued. "It's against the law to kill trumpeter swans."

"You can't prove it's him killing the swans. Go after him and I'll have to arrest you," Charlie said. "You know that, don't you?"

Lilly didn't like the hatred that she heard in her father's voice, but even more, she hated the idea of him being put in jail. She pulled against Jerome's grip just as the wind kicked up. He pulled her back and she turned her face into his shoulder where he covered her head with his coat.

"The man killed a trumpeter swan," she said, speaking into his chest, her teeth chattering. "He shouldn't have done that."

"Our fathers will take care of it," Jerome said.

"It's illegal."

"It's the law's problem, not ours."

Lilly quieted then, letting her head warm on Jerome's chest. The snow piled on her father's saddle and gathered in the brown mare's mane. The wind whistled through the valley. The wind, now Lilly's friend too, talked to her. It told her that she had a job to do. Help your father, it said. Stop the swan killer.

# 2

Lilly's mother told her own story of Lilly's birth. She said that the night Lilly was born a storm brewed in the distance. The clouds shielded the earth from the light of the stars; lightning lit the wetlands and the swans danced on the water. Lilly had pale white hair and a moon white face, the daughter of a swan. She said even as an infant Lilly twisted her lips into the shape of a bill. Later, she said it kept her from saying "Ma" and that's how Lilly came to call her mother by her given name. Nell said it with a soft pitch to her voice, confidential and full of secrets, not liking it and wanting to be called "Mom" or "Ma" or any variation of "Mother" but accepting "Nell" nonetheless.

That evening, after leaving the dead swan with Charlie West, the temperature had dropped below freezing and snow covered the land. Her mother pulled her close and patted her hair with a soft hand. Lilly leaned into her, enjoying the warmth of her soft lap. She thought about her mother's story and the cygnet that had died in her lap. He would never use his bill again, or lean quietly into his mother's feathers, like Lilly resting in her mother's arms. He'd never call out to any of his flock or share another secret.

The next day she was still thinking about the cygnet—his heart quiet, his feathers cold, Charlie West's final announcement that he was gone—as she watched her father stare at the day-old storm. The snow had stopped but the land had frozen up and she couldn't get the feel of that dead swan out of her hands. Her hands were bitter cold and blue, as if all the failed love had spilled out of them to save the young swan. She wouldn't mind blue hands, if only it had worked and the swan had lived. But the swan died and she just couldn't let it go by.

When Pa dressed for travel and Nell begged him to stay home and take care of his cold, Lilly crawled under the kitchen table to hear what they said. The rough pine floorboards rubbed at her knees as she moved closer, her heart beating fast in her throat. Pa would send her out to the woodpile if he caught her eavesdropping. He'd remind Lilly that she was a child and had no business in his business. Never mind that she had helped him cut free a trumpeter swan just yesterday.

His face looked like Lilly's hands felt, blue and frozen, clenched and tight. He looked like the wind had settled into his bones, edged its way into his chest, and made his lungs hurt. Nell said that a fever lingered there, waiting to swell and grow and pull him into its heat. The last thing she wanted him doing was going back out to the marsh and feeding his sickness.

She leaned close to Pa, pulling her brown skirt tightly around her legs, leaning into the soft material as if she wanted to wrap Lilly's father in it and put him to bed for the day.

Sam Connelly didn't ignore her or move away, but he didn't take her up on her offer, his mind clearly somewhere else. "I have to make sure that all of the swans have flown off to their wintering grounds," he said. "Otherwise, they might be in trouble."

"It's nature," Nell said. "Swans die in the wild."

"Nothing natural here," he said. He rubbed the sweat from his forehead with the back of his hand. "Dean Drake is out there waiting for any stray trumpeter."

"You're sick." Nell flung a piece of wood into the stove and slammed the oven door shut.

"I'll talk to him, see what he knows."

"Did you see Dean?" She asked, shoving her hands into her apron pockets. Her skirt clung to her legs where her work boots ended, lonely, dejected. She said Dean's name like it was a well-worn sweater, something comfortable and old.

"He's out there. I can feel it," Pa said.

"You usually need something more than a feeling to condemn a man."

"I'm just going to talk to him."

"Sam. Stay home. Yesterday's tromping through pondweed has made you sick and weak already. You're burning up. I'm sure you've got a fever. If it is Dean out there shooting swans, so what? He's just doing what any man does to survive." She stood nearly as tall as Pa, and her hair had come out of its bun in small tuffs, wild and rebellious, her jaw held tight and certain.

"Except," Pa said with an edge to his voice, "any normal man doesn't shoot a wild animal and leave it to die without taking the meat. Plus…"

"Plus what?"

"He's not all you think him to be," Pa said.

Nell shook her head and the muscles in her neck tightened. "You've no reason to be jealous."

"I'm not jealous. He's cold-hearted. I've seen him at his worst."

Nell narrowed her soft eyes. "Hmm. Cold-hearted? At his worst? Sounds like a close cousin to jealousy. Let Charlie West take care of it, whatever it is."

Sam Connelly shook his head and put another piece of wood on the fire. Smoke from the open stove door escaped and attacked him, throwing him into a coughing fit. When the cough let loose of him he said, "How can you defend him?"

"He helped me when my parents died." Nell dropped her head like she hid her tears, or maybe it was shame. From under the table Lilly couldn't tell.

"Helped you after ignoring their danger," he said in a quiet voice.

"It wasn't his fault," Nell said.

"That's not all."

Pa coughed and Nell waited until he caught his breath. "You know he'd like nothing more than a good reason to come after you."

"That makes us even. He's already gotten away with too much." Sam turned to face Nell. "I'm tired of looking over my shoulder."

Nell furrowed her eyebrows and her large forehead wrinkled, disapproving, a look Lilly knew by heart. She looked out to the mountains that rose up halfway to heaven, her brown eyes squinting in the sun that glared off the snow. She pulled her sleeves tight over her fists and crossed her arms.

"Charlie said he's been showing up in town at the fire hall." Sam sucked in a breath and held it, cautiously looking at Nell. "Have you seen him?"

"You accusing me of something? You..." She stopped like she'd lost her breath.

A small ripple of air walked up Lilly's spine and landed at the base of her neck, sensing the crash of the pan before she threw it. The frying pan hit the wall and clanged to the floor. Nell put her hands to her face, covering her cheeks, pulling back her sudden burst of anger.

"You taking lessons from him?" Pa asked quietly.

Lilly didn't think that her father meant for his words to be mean. Nell was good and loyal to all of them, even when she was mad. Even then the aroma of her bread in the oven wafted up and promised a good end to the fight. But Sam Connelly's anger grew too, and he seemed sure to let it spill.

Under the kitchen table, Lilly held her breath, afraid to move.

Nell turned her face away, picked up the pan, took kindling, and stoked the fire again, the heat filling the room, an avoidance no one tried to name.

The wood crackled in the cook stove and the warm, doughy smell of the bread pulled at Lilly, dragging her out to the edge of the table, nearly into view of her parents.

"Me and Dean, we grew up together," Nell said. "You don't know him like I do. He helped around the ranch when he was young. He's had hard times."

"Tell you what," Pa said, containing his anger. "I'll talk to Charlie and let him deal with Drake." But Lilly knew what her father was doing. He was playing dead. He just wanted to calm Nell, change the topic, and get out of the fight in her good graces, and then do what ever he wanted to do. Lilly had used this strategy herself countless times. She'd already heard him talk to Charlie West about Dean Drake. With Lilly's own ears she had heard Charlie tell him to let it be. There would be no talking to Charlie West. Pa already knew his opinion.

"Or just let it be," Nell said as if reading Lilly's mind, proving that she did hear thoughts inside her head, which made Lilly's lying much more difficult.

Sam's lip quivered as he turned and saw Lilly watching them from under the table. She didn't mean to have tears in her eyes when he saw her. She didn't mean to cry about him lying to Nell like that. After all, Lilly lied. She didn't want to cry about lying. She wanted to be brave so that he'd take her with him when he went back out to the Cattail Marsh.

His voice softened. "I'll be careful," he said. "Of me and of him. I just want to get him away from us." Lilly's father tilted his head toward her and winced as if all the pain he held in his head slid to one side. It made him look sad and ill. He stood close to her mother and motioned for Lilly to come out from her hiding spot.

"Lillian Grace Connelly," he said, calling her by her full name. His voice sounded like the kind of nice that's only pretending and working way too hard to be pleasant. "You've got no business in our talk."

Lilly opened her eyes wide at him and the tears fell down her face.

Nell swooped in to the rescue. "Your legs are getting a wee bit long for such small spaces. You can nearly tie them into knots under that table."

Lilly wiped her eyes and felt her face blush. "At school they call me spider legs," she said, hoping to change the subject.

Nell reached down and her skirt fell toward Lilly, an invitation to hide there in the safety of her lap. Her arms tightened and held strong as she lifted Lilly from under the table and helped her stand. A sweet lavender smell drifted off Nell, slowing Lilly's heartbeat, soothing her tears, and calming her in a way that only her mother could. Nell looked at Sam, laughed softly, and shook her head, denying him what, Lilly didn't know.

"Spiders have great, fast legs," Nell said, brushing a bit of flour from her face. "Your legs are simply finding their way to their true beauty."

"Just like the young trumpeters." Pa's tone was kinder now. "They grow into beautiful white swans. Your legs will keep their strength and gain their grace."

"When you turn eleven, your magic legs will be at your command," Nell said, as if just saying it made it true. "Now quit hiding and go tend to your chores."

"I'm going," Lilly said, calmed by her mother's now quiet way.

By then the bread had stayed too long in the oven. Nell opened the oven and angry black smoke floated out. Lilly tasted that bitterness of the forgotten loaves. Its singed smell followed her, a dark omen, as she went up the stairs to where Anna, her sister, sat reading.

Anna shook her head at Lilly, reminding her to mind her manners, a lesson repeatedly lost on Lilly.

"This grudge you hold against Dean," Nell said, pulling out the ruined bread, her stilted words floating to the upper floor of their small cabin, "it's wrong. No good can come of it. I married you, not him. He's the one with a bone to bury."

"Things you don't know," Pa said, his face mean and tangled.

"Sam, there is no justice to be had here. For Lilly and Anna's sake, forget the past. We're here together, you and me and the girls. We have our family. He has his mule and not much else. Let the man be. Love us."

Sam just nodded. Lilly could see his next move in her mind, her father riding his horse out to the marsh, scouting the waters, so she grabbed a jacket from her room, climbed out on the roof, and jumped down into the snow-covered grasses below.

Lilly watched in dismay from behind the stacked bales of hay outside the barn as Pa strapped his shotgun to his horse and Nell placed dried meat in the saddlebag. She had a blanket wrapped around her shoulders, the one she had knit for Anna when she was Lilly's age. She folded her arms in it. Her hair fell across her wide forehead and down, against the ribbed edges of the blanket, her bun completely failed, looking as if she'd forgotten to get ready for the day.

A warm smile started at the corners of Pa's mouth. But then, as if a crow flew in and turned a leaf in his brain, he turned on her with suspicion, a wicked worm of distrust. He rubbed his beard. Lilly could smell the sour edge of their new fight beginning.

"Deer meat?" He asked. "Where did you get deer meat? I haven't been out hunting."

"Left over from early season." Nell shifted from foot to foot.

Lilly could tell by the low slant of his shoulders that he didn't believe her. But, unless Lilly came from a long line of liars, which she was starting to half believe, why would her mother lie?

"Drake didn't bring it by?" her father asked with raised eyebrows, looking away from her mother, cautious.

"Sam, you're throwing fits with no cause." Nell looked at the valley, a dark cloud rolling across her face. She turned her head toward Lilly and Lilly ducked further behind the hay, scraping her knuckles on the dried edge of the feed and trying not to make a sound. She wanted to tell her mother she understood being in trouble for no good reason, and she didn't like it any more than Nell probably liked it. But Lilly was too much on Pa's side to say anything comforting to her mother.

"Lilly." She turned to see her sister, who narrowed her brown eyes at her. Anna stood shivering on the thin layer of new snow, snow that had come too early in the fall. Anna's brown ponytail pulled her face tight. Her simple tan skirt fell to her calves and she tugged gray sweater sleeves over her fists, looking like she meant business. The sweet smell of rose water wafted off her, a smell designed for George James King, even though Lilly still enjoyed it.

"I'm gonna tell," Anna said.

"Shhh. They'll hear you. How long have you been standing

there?" Lilly shielded her eyes from the sun.

"Long enough to know you're up to no good." A mischievous grin rolled across her face.

"You tell and I'll tell George that you don't care for him." Lilly raised her eyebrows in a dare. Anna had been daydreaming about George James King for the last four years.

"That's a stupid lie, one he'd never believe if a million know-it-all ten-year-olds told him." Anna shook her head. "You better stay out of this. It's between Mama and Pa."

"Pa must be right, though. I heard him talking to Charlie West last night. Who else would shoot and leave a swan to die without at least taking the meat? Pa knows what he's talking about. It's a miracle…"

"Yes, yes, I know, it's a miracle that a flock of swans even comes to the Mission Valley, given that they all nearly disappeared years ago. I've heard Pa say it a dozen times."

Lilly pointed her chin stubbornly. "Well, it's true. Name another modern miracle if you're so smart."

"The miracle will be if Pa doesn't whip your bottom," Anna said, turning to lean against the hay bales so that Lilly didn't have to look into the sun.

"Pa wouldn't whip a flea," Lilly said. The cold fall air picked at her skin. A bitter wind whistled across the land, kicking up tufts of dried hay and dislodging spider webs bogged down with old leaves. "This man needs to be stopped from hurting the swans. You could help us. Pa won't turn us back once we're out there with him."

"And hurt Mama? This man is someone that she cares about."

Lilly bit her lip, her world shifting and changing in a way she didn't like. "She thought about taking up with him instead of Pa?"

"Thought about it, didn't do it. She can care about a man, like a brother. And he's probably a good guy if she cares about him and if she's willing to fight with Pa on it. All I know is it's no good you going out chasing after him too."

"You mean chasing after Pa or the swan killer?"

"Either one, little sister." She put a protective arm around her.

"I don't want you to get hurt."

"And Pa?"

"He can take care of himself."

She felt the cold tremble in Anna's arm and she knew that she'd been out in the cold longer than she'd wanted. Anna liked warm spaces like the one next to the kitchen fire. She'd bake and cook all day long if it kept her from a chill. The wind whistled hard through the trees, knocking the leaves down, pushing fall out of the way for winter.

"OK," Lilly said half-heartedly, letting Anna win. That settled her easily and Lilly watched her go back in to bake and dream about George James King.

When she turned back toward her parents, Pa was turning his horse toward the wetlands, so she waited for Nell to go back inside with Anna, got her bicycle out of the barn, and went after him.

# 3

Through the years, trumpeter swans had been killed and sold at trading posts for their meat, eggs, skins, and down. The feathers were used for bedding, ladies' powder puffs, and fashionable hats. The eggs were sold for delicacies. By the time Lilly was ten, trumpeter swan harvests had gone from thousands a year to a few hundred a year. Their demise had been duly noted. In 1918, the year Lilly was born, a federal law went into effect, making it illegal to kill a trumpeter swan.

Lilly imagined what it must have been like before they dwindled to near nothing—when the mass of great white birds filled the waters and then took flight, lifting from the wetlands and turning the sky into a shiny bright heaven. The loss of swans filled her heart with a sadness that weighed her down as she followed her father and the brown mare through the forest to the Cattail Marsh where a stubborn flock of swans nested each spring. She knew they'd find the wetlands empty that day, but she figured if Pa wanted to double check it she was happy to tag along, even if she wasn't invited.

At the marsh her father slid down off his horse, his legs looking weak from his illness, his bad leg turned sideways and off kilter. He gazed over the marsh. Using a thick stick for support, he limped near the water. Cattails rustled behind Lilly and she turned to find nothing there. She parked her bike and went after her father, stepping quietly through the swampy land. The pond had a thin layer of ice.

On her end of the swamp she smelled something rank, like a well-lived-in bear-hide and it sent a chill through her. Looking around for the animal she found instead a man dressed in dirty brown trousers and a thick leather coat. He sat on a large mule, not ten feet away. Pa had told her that men rode mules because they were good in the mountains. Although she had never seen this man before she knew instinctively that he was Dean Drake. Her head throbbed in her ears when he narrowed his green eyes at her. Her heart darted off to a mountain peak, far from his dark stare.

"Ma'am," he muttered. To Pa he said, "Looks like you're in a terrible mess."

"Dean Drake, I figured you for the damage done to that swan yesterday." Pa stood up straight, pressing his weight down on both feet.

"I've been nowhere near here till today, when I saw you dragging your little girl out in this cold," Drake said, his voice the voice of liar. Lilly knew lying.

Pa glanced over at her and shook his head. "Lillian, get over here by me."

Although she couldn't see the harm in staying put, she rolled her bicycle over near the brown mare. The mare threw her head and stepped sideways away from the rubber and metal creature.

Pa turned a placid face to Drake. "You shouldn't be killing swans."

"Not even if they bring a pretty profit on the black market?" His smile dared Pa to come at him. The wind blew against Drake's face and turned his cheeks red. Lilly had seen the same red blotches on Pa when he drank too much whiskey.

"Except you didn't sell it. You left it to suffer and die, for the bears and coyotes to scavenge. You leave the swans alone. Go on back into the mountains."

Drake shrugged, his teeth clamped tight. "You still have those pictures?"

"That was a long time ago," Pa said, glancing at Lilly, seeming to tell the man on the mule not to talk about it in front of her. "Stuff gets ruined."

She held tightly to her bicycle. Her hands felt frozen to the handlebars. The chill went through her whole body now. She could see her father working to stay calm by focusing on the jagged peaks that rose up and zig-zagged across the sky, cradling snowfields, some that were impossible to see from the valley floor.

"But they didn't get ruined, did they? They'd be the one's you'd be holding onto with bad intentions. Those photographs, they could hurt a man."

Lilly saw such fury in Dean Drake's eyes that it tightened her chest. Her mother was wrong about this man. Something had turned him cold, leaving nothing good in him.

"The film got ruined, got left in a tailings pile outside of Butte. The way I see it, the whole thing ended there and there it'll stay. Here, in the Mission Valley, that's a different matter."

"Always looking for trouble, Connelly. It's no business of yours. That swan coulda got killed a million ways. No man's been hurt."

"No. No man's been hurt here." Pa waited, letting his meaning sink into Drake. "It's simple. Leave, go back across the mountains, and you can keep your peace. Otherwise, not saying those photographs still exist, but you never know what might show up in Charlie West's office one day."

Drake threw his gaze out toward the rock wall that sat to the side of and slightly lower than the big snowfield in the Missions. "Well, sure. Still, I do hope I don't mistake some pretty little girl with blond braids for one of those blond bear cubs some day. That would be a real shame."

Lilly shivered as icy shards went right through her.

"You're threatening my family?"

"Just anger talking. Forget it. I'll take care where I aim my gun and you do the same with that camera. Let our feud be over."

Drake waited a while, staring at the mountains, his mule looking tired and bored.

Finally Pa nodded. Revenge has a sweet bitter flavor, and Lilly could taste it in the cold air. Her father would have said she was too young to know much, but she understood him. She could see the grudge spilling out of him like the smoke from Nell's burned bread, harsh and pungent.

Drake turned the mule north and rode off.

Pa shivered, his hands blue where he gripped the stiff leather reins. Without looking at her, he mounted and turned his mare toward the house. Lilly trailed behind on her bicycle. The sun had disappeared behind the clouds and the wind was picking up. She hoped they'd get home before their hands froze shut for good.

Twisting his wrist like it might crack, her father turned the mare away from home, slowed the horse slightly, and waited for her to catch up.

---

They followed a deer trail into the mountains to Pascal Joseph's hunting camp, Pa on his horse, Lilly on her bicycle, her fingers finally warmed by sheer determination to keep up with her father. Gold and brown leaves whistled in the wind and a thin layer of yesterday's snow dusted the ground. Smoke rose up next to the wall tents ahead. The camp was very quiet, which probably meant that the men were out hunting. Children ran and hid behind the large canvas tents, a pack of dogs following them. Two women scraped hides. Others sliced meat and laid it on a rack to dry near a fire. One of them looked up, nodded, and motioned with her head to a nearby lodge, the lone tipi in the camp.

Sam thanked the woman, his face serious, full of intention. He lifted the leather flap to the warm inner circle of the lodge.

"Two Sons," Pascal Joseph said with a great smile, using Pa's Indian name.

"Father," Pa said, calling him by an endearment. Pascal was the man's Anglo name. Running Bear was his other name, his name that held power and touched only the lips of those he knew with trust and honor, the name Lilly's father used when he talked about him.

Running Bear was a tall man with husky shoulders and dark hair. He wore a colorful ribbon shirt over his trousers, and wrapped a blanket around his shoulders. He had raised Pa from age five to seven, after Pa's mother died in Running Bear's care. That was before Sam Connelly's uncle found out that he was living in the woods with Indians, and brought him back east to a civilized life.

When Pa was fifteen, he left the east for good. The first thing he did, he'd told Lilly, was return to Running Bear's camp. While he was there two things changed his life: Running Bear gave Pa his mother's camera, the camera she had left for him when she died; and he became best friends with Running Bear's son, Jimmy Pascal—known by Lilly's father and those who loved him as Horse Child.

"Come sit," Running Bear said.

They sat on the ground close to the flames, where the smoky hides held the heat from the fire. Pa crossed his legs and sat up tall. Lilly did the same. Bedding was piled at the outer edge of the tipi. A small pile of wood lined another part of the circle. A pot of coffee sat in the fire, and Running Bear poured a cup for Pa.

"This is my daughter, Lilly. She helps me with the swans. We found a young trumpeter tangled in the weeds yesterday and she held the bird while I cut it loose. But the swan couldn't fly. It had been shot. We took it out to Charlie West's ranch, but it didn't make it."

"Men are hungry," Running Bear said. His quiet voice sucked the air out of the lodge and the sweltering heat crawled up Lilly's legs. He handed Pa his coffee. Slowly turning his head, he looked right through Lilly and she felt herself turn into a ghost and disappear. Running Bear commanded the lodge from the deer hide where he sat. He demanded her silence. She was too hot. Her stomach boiled like the coffee. Her hands grew a mind of their own, digging at the bare earth near her knees and flipping pebbles into the fire. One hit the coffee pot, pitching a high note into the air. Running Bear looked through her again, evicting the ghostly Lilly out of his lodge.

A blind shiver went through her. Pulling at Pa's sleeve to go, she got up so quickly she tipped his coffee. The hot rocks sizzled where the brown liquid spilled on them. Steam lifted up off of the rocks and they quickly dried. The fire crackled and spit out a warning, and, having jumped out of her own skin, Lilly couldn't make out the nature of the warning, couldn't tell if the fire was friend or foe.

Running Bear poured more coffee into Pa's cup. Obviously Lilly's father had no intention of leaving until he was finished. He sipped quietly until she sat back down.

"That swan wasn't shot for food," he said, staring into his cup before taking another drink. He swallowed hard, took a breath, and let it out. "He was shot for sport and left to die."

"You want our help," Running Bear said.

"I think it's Dean Drake. If any of your hunters see anything…"

"You want us to tell you."

"He threatened my family."

Running Bear's eyebrows shot up at Lilly and suddenly she did exist.

"He wears a thick leather coat," she said. "He smells like bear." Out of nowhere, courage boiled up in her and she found her voice. She wanted to throw water on it and knock it down again, but it was too late. Words had already flown out her mouth, mixed with the smoke and filled the lodge, too loud, too harsh to be hauled back in. "He's really mean."

"I will tell the men to watch for this swan killer," Running Bear said.

"That will be good." Pa tossed the last of his coffee on the fire.

# 4

"You were a small, frail baby with halo-white hair," Nell said in her story-telling voice, "and I worried every day that you might not live to see another. I'd pray St. Patrick's Breastplate—'Now I put on the power of heaven, the light of the sun, the radiance of the moon'— and I'd hold you close to my heart, believing that if I could just fill you with enough love you'd live. It worked. Just think, you're almost eleven."

Lilly nodded and watched her mother gaze at the flames in the stone fireplace, waiting for her to go on. They were both ready for bed and Anna had already disappeared into the upper room. Lilly stood and pushed her chair closer to Nell. Her mother pulled Lilly on her lap, her lavender scent soothing and sweet. She felt her mother's warmth through the flannel of her own nightgown.

Lilly had heard the story many times before. "If you could save me, why couldn't I save that swan?" she asked.

"Some things want to leave the earth and go beyond the clouds, over the mountains and into a fragile light."

"Like heaven?"

"Yes, like heaven."

That gave Lilly pause. Heaven. She watched the flames dance. Little wisps of smoke swirled up the chimney. It seemed to Lilly that those beautiful white swans already lived in a fragile light, a light that came down to earth to meet them, creating a bridge to another world.

"Maybe swans have their own heaven," she said.

"Oh, I think swans have a special place beside the angels."

"How old was I when I learned to sleep on my own?" She knew the answer, but she loved the sound of her mother's voice. Plus, Nell wouldn't send Lilly to bed as long as she was talking about her or her sister.

"I had grown used to sleeping on my back, with you in our bed. But your father didn't like it. He said a child should sleep in her own bed. And he was right." She laid her palm on Lilly's cheek and held it there before continuing. "I couldn't stand being away from you. I loved feeling your heart next to mine. Finally, when you were six months old, I agreed to put you in the cradle Pa had made. He'd worked hard on that cradle, sanding it, painting tiny trumpeters on it, and polishing it until it glowed in the lamp light."

Lilly could've told the rest of the story herself. Pa had been out to the swamps photographing the swans that day and wasn't due home until after dark. Nell had rocked her in that cradle and sung, "Hush little baby don't you cry." But Lilly cried and cried and finally fell deeply asleep, her white hair matted to her head by tears, Nell and Anna sitting watchfully by her side. When Pa developed the photos of that day, a picture of Lilly's downy white head sat next to the photos of the white-headed cygnets.

"Those were good days," Nell said, looking out the window. The wind blew a rank smell through a crack in the door. Lilly thought she heard a large animal come close to the house. A wild, cautious look crossed Nell's face and Lilly wondered what her mother feared. Like Lilly, maybe she sensed something, pacing the ground, tracking the family, putting a scent out, marking territory. Lilly was a girl, without the experience of her mother, but she knew, deep in her heart, that it was the swan killer. She knew then that he was out there, watching, stalking, a mountain lion crouched on a rock, waiting from the blind to take his prey. She could feel him in the way that the breath caught in her throat, and the hair curled on her arms. He was there and something was wrong.

"You're thinking of the swan killer, aren't you?" Lilly said.

Her mother sighed and looked at her, close and deliberate, closed her eyes and opened them. From a nearby table she picked up two lemon drops and offered Lilly one. When Lilly nodded she put it gently in her mouth. Nell's fingers tasted sweet and full of goodness. "Don't call names," Lilly's mother said. "He's just confused. He means no harm."

Outside tree branches cracked in a harsh wind. Overhead Anna walked around their room, perhaps putting away her schoolwork and turning back the yellow quilt.

"Time for bed," Nell said, all memory and longing gone out of her voice.

Lilly nodded and didn't say anything else. But she knew her mother was wrong about the swan killer. She knew it like she knew the migration pattern of the swans, like she knew the wind tearing through the valley, like she knew the sweet, sour taste of her mother's fingertips. Her skin ached with knowing. The swan killer meant to hurt them.

———————

For the next three days Lilly's father struggled to get out of bed, and then crawled back in. His cold had turned into pneumonia and it flattened him out like the old sweater that hung heavy on his shoulders. When he finally found the strength to sit at the breakfast table, Nell made pancakes he wouldn't eat. She gave him the last of the cheese she'd made that week. His face was gray as the boulders at the edge of their land, and Lilly could smell his sickness from under the stairs where she watched him slowly chew the goat cheese.

What could make her father's soul fly out the window and sit on the rocks for three days? She heard sounds out there, like a man walking around, not inside the fence but at the edge of the mountains where the trail rose up over the pass. The footsteps paced back and forth, mostly at night when she tried to sleep. Finally, she went out to call Pa's soul back to him, to say he's up eating now, you don't have to be afraid anymore.

She saw the boot prints there in the snow, climbing partway up the trail, crossing in and around the boulders, Pa's spirit waiting for Pa to get rid of the sickness.

By the time Pa finished the cheese, the pancakes left to leather and dry, the gray was gone from his face. Lilly could see that he had returned to himself. He left the table to feed his horse and put the goat out to graze. She sat in the chair he had just deserted and ate his abandoned pancakes. Then she washed the dishes and went to the window, waiting for him to return.

The next morning he rode for the mountains.

In a quiet voice Lilly told Anna that she was going with their father. Anna pinched her lips and duty flared in her cheeks, and Lilly knew that she was right. Anna would tell Nell. If she got lost, or stayed away too long, Anna would tell their mother and Nell would send someone looking for her.

Windblown pine needles stood at attention where they were caught in the white-crusted snow. Even as the clouds hung low on the mountain peaks and the November air smelled like winter, Lilly pulled her bicycle out of the barn and hoped for good weather. She had lived through most of her tenth year and ideas cut into her brain with a curve they'd never had before. She noticed every nuance in the weather. Clouds rumbled overhead, coming in and moving out again, the chill breeze sweeping her hair back. A light layer of snow sparkled on the ground and the last of the autumn leaves shivered and fell.

Her father had gotten quite a head start on her, so she pedaled hard to catch up, straining the muscles in her legs, gripping the handlebars with a fierce might. A late morning wind stung her face and pine trees crowded toward the game trail, needles shading the icy snow. The forest was thick and dull, the mountain steep, and massive. It sucked the air right out of her lungs. When she left the smell of frozen pines and entered the cedar forest, moss draped off the branches. Silky fibers reached out for her. Large tree trunks climbed up out of the smooth forest floor, a place a dark creature could live comfortably.

She saw two large piles of bear scat, steam rising off of them, so green they were nearly black, and filled with seeds. She thought she heard the deep, rough sound of bears breathing, and the woods turned frightening. The trees creaked and moaned as the wind blew through them. Branches dropped and ghostly mountain lions shifted on their haunches. Wolves lapped the stream around each corner, only to disappear before she could spot them. By the time Lilly left the cedars for the red foliage of the huckleberry bushes, her heart beat a thousand times a minute.

She leaned her bike against a tree when the game trail became too steep to ride. Grabbing at the last remnants of bear grass, the white flowers turned brown with the high mountain freeze, she pulled herself up the steep mountain. Ahead of Lilly the wind had already blown most of the new snow off the mountainside, revealing bare ground and patches of starved grass scattered between the rocks.

Her wool pants caught on a bush and she fell, catching herself with her palms, leaving tiny red welts to spot and bleed. Rocks shifted under her boots and rolled down the mountain. She winced, not from the pain where her hands were scraped raw, but at the sound. If her father heard, he'd be impatient with her disobedience and turn them both around, abandoning his mission up the pass until late in the day. And that would mean him climbing the snowfield in the moonlight, which was dangerous, especially with the pneumonia lingering in him.

Lilly spotted the brown mare tied to a tree. Cold air circled her nostrils like tiny ghosts. Her father sat on a boulder next to the dried bones of an elk or a large deer. A gust of wind blew over the open face of the mountain and larch needles danced across the dead animal's bare ribs. Pa wore a heavy wool coat with a fur collar. His boots came up over his trousers to keep the snow out. His lips looked blue as he ate a piece of jerky. After a minute or so he leaned forward, his head hanging out over his knees.

"You might as well come on over here," he said, turning toward Lilly. "I know you're there. Your mother's going to be worried sick. Have something to eat and I'll take you home."

Lilly came out from behind the dried huckleberry bushes and climbed to within an arm's distance of him, her belly fluttering as she caught her breath. The mouth of an abandoned mine tunnel opened in the mountainside behind Pa. She focused on it to keep from meeting his eyes. "I want to go with you," she said, pulling her mittens tight against her knuckles.

Sam shook his head. "Not a chance."

"Please, Pa. I won't be any trouble. I can climb. It's an easy hour back to the house. Besides, Anna will tell Nell where I am. She won't worry."

"Too dangerous," he said. "The other side of this snowfield stretches over a thousand feet straight down to the lakes on the other side. One wrong step and you're drowned, or served up cold to the grizzly bears. They'd probably like a little bite of girl pie, but I'm not the one to give it to them."

His voice sounded too fragile for a man on the side of a mountain, and Lilly wanted to help him. She could hear in his voice, his breath, that he was still sick. She didn't want to leave him alone out there. Plus, she knew in that growing part of her brain that whatever he was doing up there had to do with the swan killer.

"The sun won't last forever," she said.

"Answer's no."

"I brought a rope. You could tie me to you. I mean, for safety. You're going after him, aren't you? The swan killer."

Pa looked suspiciously at the pack he had cinched to the mare, like someone had stowed a secret in there, something put away where it couldn't hurt a fly. He looked back at Lilly and pointed to the valley. "You see those little dots of blue down there? Mixed in with the green?"

The sun had come up over the spine of the mountains, fought its way through the clouds and lit up the valley floor. Snow scattered across the land, leaving bits of grass and water to peek through.

"I see them," Lilly said.

"Home of the trumpeter swans. Every year a handful of them come to nest and lay eggs. Baby cygnets will be hatching right around the time of your birthday."

"Can we go see them again?"

"On your birthday we'll go. I heard the angels say you'll be eleven. The most important birthday of all."

"You can't talk to angels."

"No, but up here, I feel like I can. Eat something and I'll take you home."

Lilly nodded, but she didn't mean it. She sat next to her father on that mountainside, looking out across the valley. She sat away from the cured skeleton, on the side where he had tied his camera to his waist. "He's a bad man, the swan killer," she said. "Nell doesn't think so, but I do."

"She's got her reasons."

Something, as deathly still as the white bones on the other side of Pa, crawled into Lilly's chest. She couldn't believe he stood up for that man. "He's bad and I know it," she said, looking up at her father, watching the twitch in his eye, his lips ready to move and stopping. He shook his head, but Lilly went on undeterred. She'd find a way to help him stop the swan killer. "If you won't let me go with you, I'll just go home on my own. You can keep going."

She could see him thinking about it. The sun had already inched out to the middle of the valley, spinning away the short hours of daylight. "You won't come back today, if you take me home," she said. "Something tells me you are doing something really important." Her mind worked double time in that sharp curve of her brain that she had somehow just stumbled upon. She counted to ten, then turned and looked at him, wide-eyed. "I saw two big piles of bear scat in the cedar forest."

"Grizzly. I just took a couple photos of one."

Lilly nodded.

It wasn't a fair fight, with Pa still sick and barely recovering, his sickness still showing in him. He looked confused and then, like the sun, absolute clarity crossed his face.

"Touché," he said, and smiled. "Great try. Finish your jerky. Bear or no bear, we're going home."

Before Lilly could finish chewing the dried meat in her mouth, voices floated up from lower on the game trail, something she hadn't expected.

"Give me that rope," Pa said, doing a complete about face, "and I'll tie it to you."

---

Sam left the mare tied to a tree far off the trail and they started up the snowfield just as the clouds crowded back into the sky and the first snowflakes fell. The wind turned the snow into tiny pellets pounding their faces.

Lilly wore a wool coat, a scarf she wrapped around her face and thick trousers. She was warm enough and, more than that, she felt strong. Her spider-thin legs fortified by each step up the pass. She could soar across the mountain into the wind. She could spin wildly in that wind, looking down on the valley floor to the Cattail Marsh, landing lightly back on the snowfield leading to the top of the pass. From this high up, anyone climbing the cliffs could either fall to the rocks below or fly straight up to heaven.

She did neither. Her father kicked solid steps into the snow pack, creating giant white crevasses for her feet. Lilly stepped lightly and confidently into them. This was no time or place to disappoint her father. When they reached the top of the pass she looked out across the valley and saw the wetlands where the swans lived, and the tiny mission town where she went to school. The valley crawled north to the great lake and south to the bison range. Turning the other direction she saw a lake at the base of the mountain and another range that stretched on forever.

The rope tightened around her waist as Pa pulled her close. "Carrying you will be safer on this side of the pass," he said. "If you lose your step as we go down, I don't know if I'll be able to hold you and we'll both become grizzly bear fodder."

"I won't lose my step," Lilly said, standing tall. She wanted her father to have faith in her, to know that she could hold her own, and could, in fact, take care of herself.

"I know you won't," Pa said as he hoisted her up. "Because I'm holding onto you."

He made his way down the snowfield with Lilly tucked into his hip, her knee banging against his backpack, bumping against something hard. He kicked his heels into the snow to secure his footing as they descended and, even with the lingering pneumonia and his bad knee, he stomped solid steps. The way was slow and he was very careful. No voices followed them. Whoever had been on the other side of the pass must've turned around.

Crows cawed from the trees and Lilly heard a nearby owl. The Indians talk about owls as omens of death. Yet there was no death there. They were very much alive. In fact, Lilly had never felt so alive, mountain climbing with her father, the wind pelting her face, the clouds racing in to coddle them in a dark cocoon. And best of all, Lilly's father had promised they could go see the big birds in the Cattail Marsh on her eleventh birthday. Swans, it seemed to Lilly, were the exact opposite of the owl, calling out for the beauty of life.

"Do you hear that owl?" She asked her father.

He stopped and turned his ear toward her, twisting his body toward the sound. His bad knee slipped out from under him and they went down. Lilly slammed hard against the snowfield and Sam's pack flew open. They slid toward the lake at the bottom of the cliff, but caught on a thick band of young trees sticking up out of the snow. A silver pistol lay there at Lilly's feet. Below it, an empty box lay in the snow, shiny bullets flung far down the slope. Pa put a nearby bullet back in the box and put the box and the pistol back in his pack. He shook his head at the trail of bullets far below them and shrugged.

"You hurt?"

"I'm fine. How about you?" Lilly's hip ached something terrible, but she wasn't about to tell him.

"Just a little embarrassed." He gave a shy smile that actually made her hip feel fine. "I shoulda heeded the owl's warning and taken more care putting my feet down."

Lilly smiled back. She didn't blame her father. He could do no wrong.

Behind them a long gully of gray snow marked their sudden drop. They were at the bottom of the snowfield and the mountain had leveled out a bit. Sam didn't bother to pick her up again. They walked away from the gully through the grove of trees to a place where the snow receded and loose shale rock covered the eastern side of the mountain. The sun bullied through the clouds again and turned the shale rich shades of red, gold and gray, the afternoon light glowing and happy, wild, proud of itself for breaking through the gray barrier again.

They followed the rock field and turned back up the mountain to an opening in the stones. The stones and boulders looked dangerous, like they could come crashing down at any time.

Sam led Lilly to the cave and sat her on a rock. "Stay there and don't move," he said as he walked into the black hole. He rummaged around behind a large boulder that sat heavily just inside the mouth of the mountain.

"But I won't be in your way." Lilly did not want to sit anywhere this high on the mountain, this far from home, without her father.

"You'll stay put!"

"But I can help you." She inched closer, kept the fear out of her voice.

"No. You shouldn't be here in the first place. Your mother will already have my neck for not turning around and bringing you back to her. Now sit still."

She did as she was told—for a good two minutes. Then the light shifted, cautious and gray. Clouds wrapped around the sun. A wolf howled in the distance and a squirrel raced up a tree. She heard something crack in the woods and smelled that foul odor of bear. That musty rank odor spilled through the trees, toppled over boulders. A warning.

She heard voices again, on this side of the mountain. Her heart jumped out of her chest and ran for cover. The hair on her arms quivered and rose, sending her to the mouth of the cave.

"Pa!" She hissed. "They're here!" When he didn't answer, something bitter swirled down her spine, a dark dirty animal. She crept into the great darkness where her father had disappeared. It was sweaty and cool, a moldy tang lifting off of the dirt floor and walls. Lilly turned back toward the opening in time to see Dean Drake and another man cross in front of the cave. She couldn't make out their words but she could hear the rhythm of their voices swelling and faltering. The other man was much shorter than Drake. He wore a brown tailored coat and a round-rimmed hat.

Her shoulders shivered as she crept out of the cave to hide behind a tree, fear filling her mouth. She watched them pick their way through the rocks, the cold air trailing them, their voices a barbed rasp. Something was wrong. A mistake. No good here. No, no good could come from them.

Lilly slipped back into the cave to wait for her father. Light wandered in as her eyes adjusted, and she spotted the top of Pa's head above a large rock inside of the darkness. She wanted him to look at her. She would tell him about Dean Drake and the other man. They might come back. She'd be in trouble when Pa saw her there, but then both of them would be in trouble if Drake found them. She didn't know how she knew this. But she knew in that very deep part of her heart that even trouble fled Dean Drake's wrath.

Sam's whole head and body finally emerged from behind the boulder, and he walked over and picked Lilly up. He was so solemn coming out of that dark cave that she decided to wait until they were back home to tell him about the swan killer. Her father tied her to his back, in place of the pack he'd carried earlier. Lilly guessed he'd left the gun buried somewhere in the cave. Back up the slope Sam tromped, kicking new steps into the snow.

Exhausted, and rocking slightly to the steady rhythm of his steps, Lilly fell asleep there on his back. He carried her all the way to the mare, and she barely woke as they rode back to Nell. By morning, when they went back to get her bicycle, she had completely forgotten about the swan killer.

# 5

Sam spent the long, slow winter educating Lilly about swans. Anna and Nell focused on cooking. None of them mentioned the swan killer.

"Swans can live up to thirty years," Sam said one evening as he put his photos into a box for safekeeping. "A swan that escapes the dangers of bear, cougar, muskrat traps, bad weather and any number of other evils will be around to fly over your children."

Lilly laughed at that, the idea of her having children. At ten she was far more interested in frogs than babies.

"Hunters don't understand the danger they pose to a swan," her father said. "A hunter can kill a slew of ducks one season, and the lead pellets from his shotgun can kill a swan twenty years later."

"How can that be? Are they magic bullets?" She wondered if she'd be safe riding her bicycle out there with stray bullets flying around. They might mistake her nearly white braids for swan feathers.

"They are pellets, sweetheart, not bullets," Pa said. "Nothing magic about it. The shotgun shell spreads the lead pellets across the pond. That's how the hunter kills the ducks. The spread catches any bird in its path. The lead pellets then settle through the duckweed to the bottom. Years later, a swan lights down and dips its long neck into the pond, searching for feed. He stirs the sludge, frees up the lead pellets that have been resting there for years, and eats them along with the duckweed. The lead poisons the swan and the swan dies. The hunter has no idea that his pellets have killed a second set of birds. He cooked and ate his ducks and figured that was the end of it."

According to her father, the swan's greatest blessing was the knowledge that only beauty waited on the other side of life. "That's why the swans' last song, the lovely lilting song that they sing as death approaches, is their most beautiful." His words filled the room with warmth, but his eyes were sad.

When winter finally passed, a day arrived with a brilliant blue sky, the clouds breaking into a thousand small puffs and dissipating. The cool wind lifted and shed pine needles in a playful spray. The snow melted out of the mountains and flooded the valleys, turning the grass rich green and mossy.

Lilly rode her bike around the swelling waters out to the marsh. She wore trousers and a dark coat that drew the sun to her and she dwelled in its warmth. The pond shone like a smooth silver mist, and she instantly smelled danger. That rank smell of bear or something worse was in the air.

She inched closer to the marsh. White feathers poked out of the mud. She dropped her bike and raced over to them. Three dead swans lay in the grass, their heads full of muck and their necks tangled up in each other. Fear gripped her throat and squeezed. Wind slapped her face. She leaned into it, turned slowly to see if the swan killer was hiding in the cattails like he had been last fall.

Suddenly the wind calmed, an erratic creature, stilted by rage, finding its way. The green stalks moved slightly in the breeze, a gentle, natural motion. He wasn't there. Lilly pulled the swans out of the mud and arranged them neatly on dry land. After another look around, scouring the long grasses, following the pond bank to the horizon on the other side, she said a prayer for the swans.

She wondered if they'd had the chance to sing their last song, their swan song.

She rode like a high mountain blizzard back to the house and found her father sitting at the kitchen table. Her mother worked at a blue sweater, her knitting needles clicking in the silence between them. Yarn spilled across her knees, a temporary blanket from the cool spring air. Anna sat by the fire reading a book. They all looked up as she burst through the door.

Before she could tell them about the dead swans, there was a knock on the door. Jerome West stood there, his hair a mess and a worried look on his face. His dark canvas coat and boots were covered with mud, and his trousers were soaked up to his knees.

Jerome, who Lilly thought enjoyed acting like a grown up, looked at her like he had say-so over her, like she was just a kid, and a little kid at that. The look annoyed Lilly so much that she forgot her urgent news about the swans. She rolled her eyes at Jerome. Who cared about him anyway? She did notice how his dark hair fell across his cheekbones and how much taller he was now, nearly as tall as Pa. But who cared about his dark hair and his tallness? She didn't.

"Dad needs your help over at the ranch," Jerome said, catching his breath. "A grizzly cub is wreaking havoc among the swans and tearing up the grounds. He's gotten into the pond and can't get out—probably caught between logs, or maybe tangled up in night-shade. We tried to run him out of there, but no luck. Dad says to hurry." Without looking at her he added, "Lillian can come too if she wants, long as she keeps out of the way of trouble."

Trouble. Lilly's middle name. What did she care about Jerome and trouble?

She didn't.

Pa looked at Lilly and then at Nell. The fire crackled in the stove as Nell put the knitting needles in her lap. She shrugged her shoulders and Lilly grabbed her coat.

Anna shook her head as Lilly flew out the door after them.

"He thinks it could be the bear that's been killing those swans,"

Jerome said as he opened the door of his father's Ford.

Pa leaned across the hood. "What?"

Lilly nodded, suddenly important too. "I saw them today, three of them by the marsh. I pulled them out of the mud. The grizzly bear didn't get to these swans. They'd been shot."

"You were out there by yourself?" Pa leveled a fiery look at her.

"I wanted to surprise you by telling you when they returned."

"I'll deal with you later," he said. To Jerome he said, "You sure that the swans you're finding haven't been shot?"

The cold, wild smell of danger from earlier that day turned in the air and Lilly's shoulders tightened, sending a sharp pain into her chest. The metal handle of the Ford's back door chilled her hand. She stood paralyzed, dreading the dead swans and the fights Pa and Nell were sure to have over Dean Drake.

Jerome shrugged. "Hurry," he said. "My dad and that bear are waiting on us."

---

Amid a cacophony of high-pitched screeches and growls, Jerome led Pa and Lilly past his father's ranch gate and over to the ponds. A wire fence surrounded them. It was meant to be a barricade against wild animals, to protect injured trumpeters and keep them close. Charlie had three full-grown swans in there that he'd rescued, one male and two females. According to Pa he'd repaired that fence a dozen times—each time a bear or a wild cat tore through it.

A large piece of the fence was down, trampled in a fit of fury to the ground and left there. A feral wind raged across the ponds, peaking the water and smashing the muddy shore. Lilly's braids blew into her face and whipped her eyes. That dreadful smell of mold, must, feces and urine mixed into the wind and turned Lilly's stomach weak. That rank, dirty smell announced the intruder before she saw him.

In the pond a young grizzly bear splashed and struggled to get free. His light brown hair stood tall, the silver tips glittering in the sun. He lifted his lips when he saw them, saw her, showing his sharp teeth. When he rose up on his trapped legs, his front claws reached out and tore at the air, swiping at an invisible foe. He wanted out of there, but he was going nowhere soon. He pulled hard against the logs and weeds, growling deep in his throat. It was a fierce, haunting sound that tipped Lilly up on her toes, wanting to flee.

The three trumpeter swans squawked and paced at the far end of the pond, lifting and closing their great wings. The sun shone through the white feathers, surrounding them in a soft halo. They trilled a high-pitched alarm, and then let out deep trumpeting protests, demanding that the bear leave now.

"He's been like that for an hour. Dad can't get him out," Jerome said. He turned his brown eyes on Lilly, looking like he'd made a decision. "We'll go inside, leave this to our folks."

She didn't like Jerome bossing her around and she found the courage she'd lost only moments before. "Let's take cover in those bushes near the shed. We can watch from there," she said.

"My dad won't like it."

"He's not thinking about us right now."

And he wasn't. Jerome's father taunted the bear, evidently hoping to lure him out of the water once Pa freed him. The bear was tangled in the same way as the fledgling they had tried to save last year. With a long knife Charlie had tied to a stick, Pa shoved at the weeds and logs that held the young cub in place. The knife disappeared below the waterline and the young bear became more agitated. The pond turned a dirty red.

"That doesn't look good," Lilly said.

She heard a door open and turned to see Jerome's mother standing on the porch of the house. Lenore West had pulled her brown hair up under a scarf and small tuffs of it had fallen out. She folded her hands over her apron and refolded them every few seconds, shaking her head slowly, worry lining her brow.

Jerome shook his head and opened the door to the shed. "We might need it for safety."

"We can't hide, Jerome, we've got to do something." Lilly hated feeling helpless. The swans on the other side of the pond were going crazy. She could talk to them. She felt something magical growing inside her in the same way that new ideas woke up in her brain. She could talk to the swans and calm them down. Maybe if the swans were quiet, the bear would relax enough for Pa to get a good aim at the nightshade, to push the logs aside and free the bear's leg.

"He can't cut the weeds because that cub won't stay still," Lilly said. "And the swans are about to strangle themselves on the fence." She ducked out of Jerome's grip and walked out toward the swans. "Shhhh," She cooed. "Hush little babies, don't you cry," She sang, "Mama's gonna sing you a lullaby."

The swans paused to look at her. Sunlight landed softly on their downy backs. Jerome might've thought he was above Lilly because he was older, but she had a gift with wild animals. "Hush little babies, don't say a word," she continued, "Mama's gonna buy you a mocking bird."

Out of the corner of her eye, she saw Pa take another swipe at the nightshade wrapped around that cub's foot, levering the stick to move the logs. Somehow, it freed the young bear. At the same time a loud pounding came from the gate and there was the mother bear, galloping past Pa and toward Charlie West. She was after her cub, huge and magnificent, long red fur shimmering with golden tips as she ran, her growls piercing the heavens. She was a creature not of this world, her fury rising out of her chest.

Charlie West grabbed Lilly on his way to the shed and Jerome slammed the door behind them. Through the window she saw her father scoot behind a willow tree, holding the long knife out in the direction of the bears. They didn't give him a second look. The baby tore down another large section of fence and the mother followed.

"You'll have to mend that fence," Sam said to Charlie West when it was all over.

Charlie nodded. "Looks like we've got another visitor. Someone you know?" He pointed to a man sitting on a mule out in the field.

Pa grimaced and shook his head. "Dean Drake," he said with a shrug. "Probably sat there and watched the whole thing."

"I saw him down at the fire hall last fall," Jerome said, trying to sound like he belonged in a grown up conversation, an omen of things to come.

Suddenly she felt small and insignificant. A very dark loneliness sat on her heart. With a wild grizzly bear running after her cub and Dean Drake stalking the grounds, no one noticed that she had just sung to and quieted the trumpeter swans.

# 6

Lilly's father kept his promise, and that changed everything.

On her birthday, the spring wind blew and the red sun came up as they rode their bicycles out to the Cattail Marsh to see the trumpeter swans. Sam hung his camera over his shoulder, pedaling hard with his good leg. Nell's blue skirt billowed behind her, all speed and wind, a delight in the cool spring air, life born anew. Anna had put her hair up in a French twist and it all but failed in the wind.

Lilly pedaled as fast as her skinny legs would go, her nearly white braids flying behind her. A wide basket snuggled the fender of her bicycle and hid her birthday lunch, complete with chocolate cupcakes that Anna had made. She loved chocolate cupcakes. They were her favorite birthday treat. Leaning over the handlebars of her bicycle, she made herself small, as though she had not, just that day, turned eleven.

"I wasn't sure Pa would do it," she said to her sister, "take us to the marsh for my birthday."

"I was sure he wouldn't," Anna said. "That's why I bet against it."

"Yeah. You lost."

"Don't I know it."

Both of them had heard Pa and Nell fighting over things he said he'd do and didn't. The long list of broken promises filled tense hours between Sam and Nell: plow up the garden, repair the fence where a cougar had gone through, attend Anna's choir concert, bring in wood before going on a photo trip. Nell towered over Pa, her strong-boned face and flat forehead made bigger yet by the severe way she pulled her brown hair back into a bun. Her smile hid somewhere behind a stern warning, wanting all good things for their lives, for Sam and her daughters.

Her face said it all. "I told you so" and "I knew this would happen" and "It's not too late to change" and "it's time to change now" all thrown forward with a glance or a sound. Lilly watched her father grimace and pull another drink from his whiskey.

Her mother's face could be a sweet welcome, a firm teacher's look, or a fearsome thing that stopped Lilly in her tracks. Her mother's large head, shaking or nodding, seemed the wrong size for her small-boned body. It was like the head of a bull on a wood duck. Lilly didn't think her mother thought that Pa would keep his promise either. But Sam did keep his promise and, early that morning, Nell put away her battle looks and the blankets that he'd need to sleep in the overstuffed chair.

With that one promise, Lilly and her family rode their bicycles across the flatlands to the marsh into what would be a changed world.

A burst of wind hit her face and lifted the hair on her arms. The air smelled wrong. A pressure—a slow dread—expanded in her chest. She disregarded it, smiling as she watched her mother and father pedal in tandem across the valley. At his best this early in the morning her father sprinted through the fields, yielding slightly, so that Nell could keep up, and then racing to catch up to her when she passed him.

The big birds were there, the rare and beautiful trumpeter swans in the wetlands, and they intended to catch them on film. Lilly figured the photographs for a birthday gift, a baby swan cuddled into a mother's wing, the father walking proudly near the nest, a menace to any danger, a playful line of white powder puffs follow-ing their parents out into the deep waters, memories to keep Lilly company as she grew up and grew old.

Even with his bad knee, her father flew across the land, his good leg strong, making up for the bad, like his good-hearted laughter, and keeping his promise, washing away the sour smell of bad whiskey.

The townspeople called him a short, stocky man. Lilly heard it once outside of the Wild Moon Saloon. Short, stocky. What that meant, really, she didn't know. Short, she understood. Sam was not too tall, and Nell hemmed his trousers. Stocky, though, was an odd description. It made her think of the canned food Nell had put up in the cellar. Stocky meant frugal and careful to always have extra on hand, never knowing when hard times might hit. Never enough.

This morning, with his graying hair, his bad knee, his short height, his eye for a beautiful bird or beaver caught in the middle of a dam, whiskey or not, Sam Connelly was more than enough. Of course he got angry sometimes, Lilly thought, remembering last year in the marsh with the swan killer. As soon as she thought of Dean Drake she wanted to erase him from her mind. It was too late, though. With the storm brewing and the dead swans earlier that season, uncertainty had already crawled into her heart.

"Anna," she said, "I don't know if we should go to the marsh in this storm, even if Pa did keep his promise." Lilly felt the storm as a bad sign. As young as she was, she'd seen flash floods and trails washed out. She'd been caught in the woods with lightning all around, the world suddenly on fire, and then the fires quickly doused by the downpour. The memory made her queasy.

"This is a temporary storm," Anna said, her tone birthday-nice. "You'll see." That was Sam's favorite expression. According to Lilly's father, all storms were temporary. There was nothing that couldn't be fixed.

Nell must have overheard, and she slowed her bicycle to ride beside Lilly. "Rain or no rain, a spring birthday is the best of all," she said, smiling into the wind. "You were born right at the time when the world renews itself, in step with nature, blossoming like the wild roses."

"But we'll all be sopping wet if that storm comes in," Lilly said, worry sitting down on her like a large horse. Her chest tightened, stealing her breath, and made it hard for her to push forward. The wind sounded harsh. The light darkened as the sun crept behind the wall of clouds. She wanted to turn them all around. If her father kept a promise that might put them in danger, she'd be at fault. The harm would be to all of them, but it would belong to Lilly.

"A spring storm is nothing," Nell said.

Lilly looked sideways at her mother, only half-believing her.

----

The ride took no time at all and Lilly couldn't stop thinking about the swan killer. They called her "spider legs" at the one-room school-house in the mission town. Spiders bite. Spiders spew poison, she reminded the ones with unkind words. That's what she would tell the swan killer when she found him. A chill crossed her back.

Please, let us find only live beautiful swans today. May no swans fall from the sky on my birthday or any day, she prayed. Then she pushed the thought from her head, as though thinking it could make it so. Better to think about spider legs than mean men. After today she'd be spider legs no longer. She could already feel the muscles shaping around her bones. Her arms were growing into wings. She could run or ride or fly. Nothing could stop her now that she'd pushed the man out of her mind, nothing could stop her that couldn't be fixed.

A silky mist surrounded the Cattail Marsh that day. The clouds gathered and broke apart, the wind orchestrating a dance on the sky, close and dark, separate and free, blue shining through like a dozen eyes opening and closing. Unlike the hazy heat of summer, a cool vapor rose up to meet the storm.

Lilly squinted, trying to see the wood ducks on the pond. Getting off of her bicycle she stepped carefully so she wouldn't sink too deeply into the mud and dirty her yellow birthday dress. Like a magician, Nell had pulled the dress from the bottom of her leather trunk. The yellow satin hung in stiff folds, nearly standing itself up, ready to twirl and dance or, in Lilly's case, ride to the Cattail Marsh.

Lilly had other reasons for being careful. She didn't want to step on a painted turtle or a garden snake. She didn't want to scare the trumpeters or a wood duck. She flipped her braids back as she turned quickly to see a ghostly muskrat and then a beaver. A blue-winged teal flew overhead. At the edge of the water a sand hill crane squawked, his body seeming too round and big for his long legs.

In another part of the fog, a flock of swans with broods of tiny cygnets floated on the water, beautiful and graceful. Mallard ducks shot around them, skirting the swans' nesting grounds. The drakes drifted through the mist with their beautiful iridescent green heads leading the way.

There was no sign of the swan killer.

Sam, Nell and Anna parked their bikes and rushed to the edge of the marsh, where the swans glided and ducked and tipped their tail feathers into the air to pull weeds from the pond with their flat, black bills. Lilly watched the cygnets swirl around their mothers. She put her bicycle with the others and walked to the edge of the marsh.

"Come on," Anna said. "Be in your birthday pictures."

"Not yet," Lilly said. She wanted to watch, not be watched. Moving away, she carefully lifted her awkward legs to the dry land. Those gangly legs were too long, and her back felt as curved as a swan's neck. Hearing the camera click, she stepped behind a tree and turned away. When it stopped clicking she turned again toward the marsh. Pa had set the tripod in a far corner and covered the camera with canvas. Nell helped him arrange the camera for the best angles, and, Lilly guessed, angles that would least frighten the shy trumpeters.

Anna pulled her rust-colored skirt above her knees and wandered off toward the open field. She cocked her head, flipping her brown hair, and lifted one arm, as though she might be talking to someone. Lilly's sister daydreaming: a girl in love. Lilly knew that normally Anna wouldn't want to leave George James King for an entire day.

On this one thing they all agreed: Nell, Sam, and Anna all

believed in great eleventh birthdays. They knew that an eleven-year-old could create anything from science, God, or nothing. Put a slender blade of grass in an eleven-year-old's hand and she'd paint the clouds yellow, or dust a meadow with stars. She might turn the grass blade into a wand that helped birth a bison calf or send Raven far away from the swan eggs. A palm full of dirt in an eleven-year-old's care turned into a forest of little people, with maybe one inquisitive giant lurking behind a large ponderosa pine.

And that's what Lilly did. She gripped the mud at the swamp's edge and it oozed through her fingers. She sidled up to the large ponderosa, pressed the mud into the ponderosa's trunk, and called forth a giant, reciting words she imagined one might say to request one.

"O wonder of all tall ones, be kind, be generous, be free to know that you are safe to show your face, with swans and clouds, with snow geese and blue-winged teals and green-headed ducks and painted turtles, with photo taking parents and sisters—one who is eleven. One who is eleven, who wishes on the sky and the sun hiding up above, wants you to come out of your own hiding now, and be here with your giant love."

The clouds shifted and the sun shone briefly before it hid again. Before her very eyes the pine tree turned into a handsome, vast giant. Eleven. She, Lillian Grace Connelly of the Mission Mountains, had a whole year to figure out what being eleven meant: A year of giants and cloud paintings, of swan friends and star meadows, of glorious dreams, awake or asleep.

She sat comfortably in the hands of the giant and watched one large trumpeter swan fluff out her feathers and sputter. She watched her spread her wings as if to fly as she walked quickly to the water, but she wouldn't fly, not with young ones on the water.

Lilly watched her parents as they photographed the wild swans. Nell said something and pointed. Sam turned his head and then his camera. Nell bent her knees to dodge the lens, dropping her skirt hem into the water and turning the edge of it a deep, royal blue. How could Lilly have known that this would be her last memory of her parents happy and together? Pa in love with trumpeter swans,

Nell in a rich blue skirt dancing around his camera, in love with Pa.

The light changed as the dark clouds grew, broke apart, and moved aside, letting the light through. The mist parted and lifted, then settled in again, brighter. Lilly counted sixteen adult trumpeters floating in and out of the fog. While the clouds momentarily cleared, moist droplets on the trumpeters' feathers sparkled like tiny distant suns. The cygnets were less than a week old and fluffy white.

As if teasing, the clouds blew back in and thunder sounded. A thousand purple fingers of wild lupine waved in the wind. Pink dots of wild rose petals swirled off their bushes in large gusts. Lilly breathed the seasoned air into her lungs, which carried it to her heart, where a hundred tiny stars were born. Just that morning Nell had told Lilly that the stars in her heart would mature and grow into great ideas one day. She said that all great ideas began in the hearts of eleven-year-olds.

Suddenly Lilly's giant stiffened and disappeared back into the woods at the edge of the marsh. An intruder had entered the marsh. And giants don't like intruders. From her perch on the pine, she saw the man and recognized him. His hair hung to his shoulders and he wore dark pants and a thick leather cape. Under the cape he carried a shotgun. He came and stood on the ground right underneath Lilly, not even gazing up at her. She looked over at her family. Anna, just out of range of the camera, was exploring meadow flowers. Maybe she saw an owl or a hawk's nest, or maybe she saw George James King leaning toward her, on one knee, proposing.

Sam and Nell stood on the shore near the swans, where the cygnets scooted around their parents, tilting their tails to the sky. They dipped their heads into the ponds, surfacing with marsh weed covering their heads. The man near the Ponderosa Pine raised his shotgun and pointed it at the swans. Lilly tried to yell, to tell them to run, run, fly. But she knew the large birds couldn't fly and her voice stuck in her chest as though a large hand had seized her throat.

The swans didn't need her warning. They sensed the danger and trilled loudly, instantly restless, flapping their great wings, going nowhere. In the fall, when the trumpeters fly, they glide with their legs stretched out behind them and their long necks stretched out in front, their wings reaching seven feet across the sky. But in the spring they lose their flying feathers, keeping them close to their young until fall. By the time the feathers grew back and they could fly again, the cygnets would be ready to soar along side them. Together they would go, one large family, to their wintering grounds in Wyoming or California.

Unable to flee, the trumpeters screamed high-pitched notes that hurt her ears.

Something exploded. A large swan dropped his neck to the water, floating and curling on the pond like a white ribbon cast aside from a kid's birthday present, her worst birthday present. Rain started and Lilly wanted to disappear into those drops, and evaporate back up into the sky where she could live in the clouds, far away from there. The wood from the pine branch hurt her legs. She gripped the bark. Nothing was real.

"Stop him!" Pa yelled.

The hunter slid his steel green eyes toward Lilly. It was Dean Drake. Of course it was Dean Drake. She knew all along that he'd be there. She knew and she let them all ride carefree to the water anyway.

He turned his back to her, back toward the marsh and looked down the barrel of his shotgun, sending the sharpest pain through Lilly's chest.

"Stop!" She yelled, but a clap of thunder drowned out her voice as if she hadn't even spoken. Drake swung his gun across the marsh, aiming at everything within the half circle he drew. Everything important to Lilly lay within that half circle.

She didn't know if the giant came to life again and pushed her, or if she jumped. She landed on Drake as the next blast rung in her ears, silencing the entire world. She took him to the ground with the force of her weight, shoving her hands into his beard and pulling hard. He tossed her like a rag doll into the mud. She found her feet and dove at him again, scratching his face with her nails, drawing blood, aiming for his eyes, and managing to knock the rifle from his grip. His large fist slammed into her face. For an instant everything turned black.

She came to with the last gunshot pounding in her ears. Her face burned like trapped fire, waiting to explode. Her hip throbbed where she had landed on something solid and sharp. Lifting herself off of the ground she saw the marsh. Her body froze in motion. Lilly had awakened to a world so wrong she closed her eyes to make it go away.

But, when she opened them again, the new world stayed. The hunter's gun had painted the marsh a deep, dark red. Dead swans and hundreds of pink feathers floated on the water. Her parents lay in those feathers.

Ravens screeched and flitted from tree to tree, as though trying to right this fallen world. One of the ravens landed on the giant's outstretched arm. The giant stood completely still. Soon the ravens' screeching turned high-pitched, and blended with something more familiar, something Lilly knew by heart: her sister's voice.

Anna was running toward Nell and Pa. She sank into the marsh, her skirt wet to her waist, hands covered with mud, wet hair pasted to her cheeks. The rain soaked Anna's blouse. She didn't look at the intruder. Anna wrapped her arms around Nell's waist, pulled her out of the water, and placed her on dry land. She went back into the red marsh for Pa and pulled him out by his arms.

Lilly stared at the shattered masterpiece in front of her.

The steely-eyed killer slimed his eyes toward Lilly and lifted his shotgun.

She shook her fists at him, ready to tear his eyes out. But what could she do with a shotgun pointed at her? Would he paint her red too?

Dean Drake lowered the gun toward the ground and turned back toward the swans that were floating on the water. He slushed through the Cattail Marsh, ignoring Anna, his shotgun tucked into his armpit. Taking a swan neck in each hand, he dragged them out of the water and stuffed them into a green canvas bag. He walked back into the pond, protecting his shotgun, and grabbed two more swans. They filled the bag, pink feathers spilling out the top. This time he was not leaving them to rot.

Rage filled Lilly's belly. She reached the swamp in a second and threw herself into Dean Drake, ramming her head into his stomach. The hit knocked him back a step and she pushed him into the water. She jumped on his head and held it there. Let him drink the blood he'd spilled.

He was stronger than Lilly and pushed her off like a pesky fly. Using the butt of his gun he kept her at bay. She cursed at him and called him names, the worst things she could think of, but it was nothing. He slung the bag over his shoulder, tucked his shotgun into his armpit, and disappeared. Just like that he was gone, like a bad water snake, or a dry land rattler.

The sharp smell of gunpowder lingered in the air, caught in Lilly's throat and turned her mouth bitter. She was eleven. The words echoed through her in a meaningless shudder. The world was supposed to be her place. She stood there dripping wet and stunned, her mind spinning around.

She saw that the muskrat, the beaver, the mallards, the sand hill crane, and the blue winged teal had all ducked away somewhere. Only the purple lupine and the wild rose bushes remained. Anna's face looked oddly like Nell's, the mist and rain sitting on her stiff, wide cheekbones like sweat.

Anna's screams took the form of words. Now, with the rain pounding down on them, Lilly heard the words clearly. Her name. "Lillian? Lilly? Where are you?"

She knew Anna's voice. This was her sister's command voice. Lilly limped over to the red marsh. "Sister?"

"Ride over to Charlie West's," Anna said. "Bring him, and tell him to get the ambulance here quick. Fly, baby, fly!"

Lilly pulled the lunch basket with cupcakes off her bike. She pedaled hard, racing the rain, the pain in her hip pushing her forward, the downpour numbing the fire in her face. The rain pelted her a thousand times a minute.

It tore at her chest, and she flew.

# 7

A swan that could have escaped the hunter's rifle blast might have swept in quickly with powerful wings and Lilly might have followed her, looking for the world to be put back into its natural order. She would have cocked her head and shaken the pondweed out of her ears and stood slack-mouthed, watching.

But as far as Lilly knew, no swans had escaped the slaughter. As far as she knew, only Anna and Lilly had escaped the hunter's shotgun.

"I'll get my dad," Jerome West said in a strangely high-pitched voice when Lilly told him that their parents had been shot. He insisted she wear his coat when he came back from talking to his father. George, who'd been visiting, followed him. He brought a towel and patted it against Lilly's face.

She rode back out to the marsh with them, Jerome's coat hanging loosely on her shoulders. The rain pelted Jerome's father's Ford and Lilly breathed in the worn smell of the leather seats. Windshield wipers flapped at the sky, something dark and stirring, and the tires screamed. They screamed like the ravens, like Anna screaming Lilly's name, like her father screaming "stop him", like Lilly's heart screaming the hunter into oblivion. She had never heard so much screaming. The screams burned through her skin, melted down through her bones and seared the marrow black. That sound lived for years and could be easily ignited on uncertain mornings when a hawk called short and too loudly.

George wore a brown raincoat and a wide-brimmed hat, looking as if he'd been pulled from a river where he'd been fishing. He held Lilly's hand. It felt awkward, since he usually held Anna's hand. She wasn't sure about such kindness from him. Typically, he told her to get lost, that he and Anna had better things to do than to entertain Lilly all day.

It took ten minutes of forever time, time forgotten by God, to get back to Lilly's family. Dripping pines marched by the motorcar windows. A few wet pine needles fell to the ground and the storm grew quiet. When they finally arrived Anna sat next to the still bodies of Pa and Nell. Pa's head was twisted oddly to the side. Anna had pulled Nell up into her lap. Dead swans floated on the dark ponds, half-sunk, or draped across logs. The sun found a hole in the clouds and turned the grassy waters silver.

Anna was stunningly quiet, gripping Nell's skirt in her fist. The French twist in her hair dripped like pitch down her shoulders. She'd been full of dreams one minute, mostly about George James King, Lilly imagined. What was she filled with now? Nothing. A simple emptiness. When she looked up, she began shaking. And then shaking Nell. Lilly thought they must be cold.

"No! You can't stop, Mama! You've got to breathe!" Anna said. "She just stopped breathing!"

The ambulance pulled up. Charlie West, quick out the door, pulled Nell from Anna and over to solid ground. Right after Charlie, and kneeling next to Nell, was Dean Drake.

"I've got it," Drake said, clearly trying to make her breathe again.

Lilly thought she must be imagining things and shook her head. But no, there he was, the man who had just shot her parents, leaning over Nell. She stood by, paralyzed and confused as he pushed on her mother's chest hard enough to break her ribs. Then Nell coughed up swamp water and gasped for air. The sound of air rushing back into her lungs roared in Lilly's ears. Nell didn't open her eyes but her chest rose and fell. It was a simple natural rhythm made ragged by the shotgun pellets lodged near her lung, where the blue material of her dress turned dark red, almost black.

Fury grabbed hold of Lilly. She flew at Drake, pounding his face and chest with her fists. "Leave her alone!" She yelled. "Leave her alone!"

Charlie pulled her off of him and pinned her arms in his hug. "Shhhhh," he said. "It's OK. He's helping. She's breathing again." He turned to Jerome. "Help him get Nell into the ambulance."

Jerome and Drake moved her mother onto a stretcher and carried her to the ambulance. Charlie loosened his grip on Lilly and she turned to him.

"He shot them," she said. She said the words simply, like white butterflies landing on a nearby leaf, something everyone could see.

Charlie shook his head. "You're upset. And no one can blame you. But Dean Drake just saved your mother's life."

"No, look at his face. There's blood where I scratched him." She meant from earlier, when she'd jumped out of the tree on top of him.

"I know," Charlie said. "I just watched you attack him."

The earth shifted under Lilly and fog filled her brain. She tested the ground with her foot, pushing hard at it, making sure she was still standing there at the Cattail Marsh, making sure this was the same world she had stood in an hour before. Drake shooting and saving their mother made no sense at all. But it was him, dark pants, steely green eyes, the rank smell of bear. Some version of reality twisted up inside her, forever changed. Here was Nell, nearly dead one minute and breathing good air the next, and Dean Drake a part of both things. A raven cawed. A winged shadow crossed her face. In less than an hour the world had gone dark and wrong.

No one tried to make her father breathe again. In that darkened world, Lilly couldn't help but wonder if it was because Sam Connelly resented help. He always called himself an independent and said she was too much like him. He even kicked her out of the barn one day when he was putting horseshoes on the brown mare, telling her to go help Nell. She needed Lilly and he didn't. Even then, she knew he was wrong. He needed her like the land needs the rain, like the flowers need the sun. She sat on a stool in the corner of the mare's stall, stubbornly refusing to go.

Lilly watched the men carry Pa's still body to the ambulance. She went to him, the copper smell of blood filling her nostrils.

"Jerome," Charlie West called, "get her into the car."

Lilly didn't want to go to the car. She wanted to help her father breathe again. She grabbed his ice-cold hand and threw herself on him, pushing on his chest the way she'd seen Drake push on her mother's chest moments before. The taste of bile scorched her throat and she swallowed hard. If Nell could breathe, so could Pa.

"Jerome!" Charlie called again, his voice sounding desperate.

Jerome pulled Lilly toward his father's motorcar and put her in the front seat. She was as limp as Pa's icy hand, a rag doll to be tossed and set down to behave.

"Lilly." Jerome said her name like it was an endangered swan egg.

As Jerome started to drive she kept thinking she could make Pa breathe. If Dean Drake could make her mother breathe, why couldn't she make her father breathe? She was much braver, and she was strong, and she knew how to gather love from all good things.

"Turn around," she said. "I gotta help Pa!"

Jerome blew air through his cheeks and shook his head. "They've got your father." His voice was kind and he'd lost that I'm-older-than-you attitude. Lilly knew that if she could get to her father, she could make him right. "Then take me to the hospital with him," she said quietly.

"I'll take you home, and then you can tell my dad what you want," he said.

"No one's at home." Sickness swelled up in her stomach at the thought of the emptiness at their cabin. She was so cold. She was shivering and her teeth chattered. She pulled Jerome's coat tight.

He looked on her with pity, she thought, understanding the thoughts in her head. "I'll take you to the ranch. My mother is waiting for us. She'll have some hot tea."

Pity and tea were too much.

"No, I want to see Pa. I can help him." She opened the door of the moving auto.

Jerome slammed on the brakes. As quick as the wind he was at her door pushing her back on the seat and closing the door behind her. "We'll let my mother decide whether to take you to your father," he said, his eyes wide with fear and his voice high-pitched again. He looked small in the morning light, with the Mission Mountains standing tall behind him.

Lilly glared at him as he walked around the front of the Ford and climbed back into the driver's seat.

Anna climbed into the back seat with George, a blank, confused expression on her face. She looked back and forth between Lilly and Jerome and said nothing, a sad, humming sound coming from her throat. Lilly folded her hands in her lap to keep from covering her ears.

When they finally reached the West place, Jerome sat Lilly at his mother's kitchen table, as if she couldn't put herself on a chair. And maybe she couldn't. By her own guess her legs had lost their ability to move, taken on a stubborn mind of their own that Lilly felt mildly fascinated by. He gave her a cup of hot milk and quietly explained the situation to his mother.

Mrs. West wore dark trousers that might have been Charlie's by the size of them. They fell in balloon folds at her hips, just under a leather belt that gathered them to her waist. She had rolled them up at the bottom. Her gray sweater lay softly against her chest. In a bag nearby Lilly could see remnants of the yarn she had used to make the sweater, something soft and comforting. Her brown hair curled at her neck and her smile faded as she tucked the hair behind her ear. She had hazel eyes, like Nell's, full of kindness and worry.

Mrs. West brought blankets and drew a bath for Anna, saying she'd catch her death. As if death was something a person could catch. Then Lilly thought, yes, that's exactly it; a person can catch a death.

"You're awfully quiet," Jerome said.

She glared at him before she relented, too weak to keep her anger going. In too many ways she was OK—her heart still beat, she could breathe, thoughts were scrambling around her brain, and her eyes still worked. She looked around the room. She smelled the milk scalding and heard the potatoes boiling on the wood stove. Late morning light glistened on the water outside. The day was passing. Jerome's ranch was still a home for injured swans. They swam there and trilled for food like they did every morning. Everything was the same as it had been yesterday and the day before, except that Lilly was eleven.

Jerome looked at her with sympathy.

"Are they dead?" She asked.

The light went out of him. He went limp, as if the giant had gotten a hold of him and turned him into a ragged puppet. In her heart, though, Lilly knew this was foolishness. The giant was gone. He'd turned back into a simple, wet pine tree, never to return, dead at the scene, three bicycles lying near his wooden feet. Chocolate cupcakes were scattered from the dropped basket like fairy tale crumbs left on a trail. Find me.

"Your mother should be OK. The ambulance took her to Missoula. We'll know more when Dad gets back." In the time it took to drive from the marsh to the ranch Jerome's voice had thickened and turned certain, like a man's voice.

"Pa?"

Jerome shook his head. He looked so young as he turned to his mother.

"Lilly, honey," his mother said, tucking her hair behind her ear again and dropping her eyes to look directly into Lilly's, "your father didn't make it."

Lilly looked at her sister. Anna's shoulders heaved under George's grip, as her trembling turned into sobbing. The red marsh had splattered Anna's dress. The sight of it felt like a knife in Lilly's belly.

"Didn't make it?" The words were a hushed hymn in her throat.

Jerome's mother came over and sat beside her, turning partially toward Anna. She held Lilly's hand in her warm palm, and Lilly could feel her holding Anna with her soft eyes. "There was nothing anyone could do for your father. He was already gone by the time

Charlie and the others got there. I'm so sorry."

Lilly sat, dazed and distant, wanting to walk to her sister and wrap her arms around her. She could see that in spite of the blanket Mrs. West had brought her, Anna was wet and cold. Her shivering sobs cut through the air like quilting needles, sewing Lilly into something new and odd, her real life cut away from her just like that. She had to make Anna understand. There was no need for tears. In their family, they saved crying for real tragedies. This was not real. Nell would be OK. The doctors would take care of her. And Pa had to be somewhere. He couldn't be gone. This storm too would pass, and this experience would simply be stitched into the quilt of their lives.

"Annie, Nell will be good as goose feathers again. This is a temporary storm," she said, using Pa's words, words that were now distant and far away, words that she snagged with the unlikely imposter of hope. "Watch and see."

Anna lifted her head from George's chest long enough to look at Lilly. Her red eyes looked like several years had been washed out from behind them, an infant grazing the air for a spoonful of food.

She leaned into George, who was swaying as if the world had also been washed out from under him. Like Anna's eyes, he was empty, with nothing left. Her sister had lost her shoes and Lilly moved to find them. Anna caught her arms around her and pulled her into Mrs. West's blanket.

"Baby," she said.

Like Nell usually said.

After a few minutes Jerome eased Lilly away from Anna, gently working the quilt threads free. She pushed against his hands, reaching for her sister.

"I'll be OK soon," Anna said.

Jerome wrapped Lilly in a blanket, his arms around her. Although she let him hold her, she felt connected to nothing. She pulled the blanket tight, wrapping herself in its loneliness.

---

Jerome had taken Lilly home from the swamp another time, when she was nine. She'd been on a science hunt and had ridden her bicycle to the marsh by herself. Frogs had jumped over tree stumps or across the water and she splashed after them, the water feeling cool and good on her legs. She tried to catch one in a glass jar. Just one, to bring home to Anna. It would take her mind off George James King, who wouldn't give her the time of day that summer.

Her sister sat sullenly day after day. She wouldn't eat, or color, or even roll down a hill with her. Lilly didn't understand it, but she knew the cure: one hopping mad frog. They could release it out back of the house and watch it jump off toward the creek. The frog could easily follow the creek back to the swamp.

Frogs were fast and not so easy to catch. Lilly had spotted a big one sunning on the end of a log, lunged for it, tripped, and fell into the swamp. The splash scared the frog and off he went, scooting across the water. The water plastered her skirt to legs and she spit out duckweed.

Of all the times for Jerome West to show up.

"Here I am, just riding my bike back from fishing," he'd said, "when I see an abandoned bicycle. I go looking for its owner and what do I find? Skinny Lillian dripping with swamp weed. Pretty outfit."

"Better'n those cut-off trousers of yours and anybody's white shirt."

"My Dad's. You need some help?"

"If you can catch a frog."

"A little young to be looking for your prince, aren't you?"

She stared blankly at him.

"Kiss a frog, get your prince charming. Don't you read?"

"Sure I read. The newspaper, science books, and the bible. Is there more?"

"You go to school don't you?"

"School's boring, except for biology. You gonna help me or not?"

"Not. But I will ride back to your house with you. I'll tell your parents that you fell into the creek a mile from home."

"That's a lie."

"One that will serve you well," Jerome said, "unless they gave you permission to ride out here by yourself. You're only nine." Like he was a big man. He was all of eleven then.

"I can't lie," she said, lying.

"Suit yourself. Either way, I'm taking you home."

She had liked Jerome West for that reason. He had made a simple decision and returned Lilly to her parents. Not that she wouldn't have returned herself. It's just that he was kind and she liked his kindness. She also liked his thin voice, which had now vanished with the storm.

Lilly sat in the kitchen with this Jerome, the Jerome with the new voice, and mourned the voice that had disappeared. That voice was gone along with so many other things. What a simple way to say something without saying anything. This she also liked.

She looked out the window at the maimed swans on the pond. White feathers were caught on the fence, sad orphans that had tried to escape their fate and failed. A fenced-in pond is such an unnatural home for a swan, she thought, watching one injured swan lift his healthy wing for a lopsided flight that never left the ground.

Any other time she would've been asking Jerome a salmon-fly-hatch-full of questions, and spewing ideas. What makes lightning, bet you don't know, well, I do. It's the angels. Not angels like people think of them, all fluffy and full of light. These angels are tired of light, throwing it off, saying, here you take it for a while.

Jerome would've laughed and asked what happens to it next.

It bounces right back to the angels, Lilly would've said. Sometimes it starts a fire when they won't accept it back. The fire just reaches up toward the sky, scorching the land as it goes, looking for its angel. If you're an angel, you can't just get rid of your light. An angel has to be an angel in the same way that a bear has to be a bear. It can't be anything else.

But this time, sitting in Jerome's kitchen, it seemed like an angel had thrown his light deep inside Lilly. Burning fists seemed to pound at her chest, something raging to get out and back to its rightful owner.

Lilly tried to ignore it, clamping down tightly on her mind. Here she was, finally eleven, and she couldn't think of a single thing to say that had any meaning. Those poor swans. Poor Pa. Poor Nell. She watched Mrs. West dry Anna off, the bath water cooling unused. Her sister looked frail and sick, like a young swan land-locked and dying. She stared at the floor, George at her side, holding her up. Lilly looked away.

She bargained with God. Take my arm, she said, or my hearing, or my love of frogs, my love of swans. I'll keep my spider legs and You can have eleven. Just make my sister well again and bring Pa and Nell back home, whole and healthy. Make all of this go away and I'll never disobey them again. I will mind, I swear I will. I'll write it down, sign it, and send it up to You. Just make Anna well and let Nell and Pa be home cooking dinner when we get there. Make this day go away and I'll give you my eyes.

"I'll even give you my bicycle," she said out loud.

"I don't need your bicycle," Jerome said, looking at her with too much kindness.

She turned her back to him and put her palms together. He's right. You don't need a bicycle, she said. But I'll be good. I'll never sneak out after Pa again, or go anywhere without permission. I'll be good or You can take my favorite swan pictures, or my tongue. Pa says I talk too much anyway. Please, just take my heart, make Nell and Pa well and make Anna happy again. It's a good exchange.

# 8

"Sheriff," Lilly said to Charlie West, pulling on his suit sleeve. They walked down the overgrown dirt road to the Mission Church. The wide steps of the brick building welcomed her to her father's funeral. The Mission Mountains stood in the background, just behind the bell tower, reaching toward heaven, a place where Lilly thought she might see her father again. A warm wind smelled like evergreens and new grass, a smell Pa loved. Fields of balsamroot and arnica stretched out beyond the road, where wild lupine poked purple heads through the blanket of yellow flowers.

"Yes, Lilly?" Charlie wore a brown suit with his work boots. He held his hat at his chest, his face gray. Where his hat had been, his brown hair stuck up.

"I know who killed my father."

His eyes widened at her, a light sweat filming his creased forehead.

"I saw Dean Drake aim a shotgun at him and Nell. He had a bad look in his eye."

Charlie raised his eyebrows. "But Dean Drake got your mom breathing again. Without him she'd be dead."

The air turned thick and misty. "He shot her first," Lilly said.

"Don't go round making up stories, imagining things. This is serious business, killing people. Be careful when you accuse someone."

"I saw him. I did! He had a grudge against Pa."

"Lilly, listen to me." Charlie leaned down, hands on his knees, like she was a small child. "Sometimes the brain mixes things up, especially when you're a kid and you're scared. It's normal to put the blame somewhere, but this won't do. We don't know who shot your parents. Accidents happen."

"It wasn't an accident." She pressed both hands against her head, holding it perfectly still, like it might float away. Talking about the hunter brought back the gunshots. They were exploding in her brain. "He did it on purpose."

"Whoever it was, you can't be sure it wasn't an accident."

"I tried to stop him." She pointed to her bruised eye where Drake had hit her. "I dug my nails into his face. Find him, you'll see I marked him. He threw me off and kept shooting. He knew they were there and he kept shooting."

A sad smile crossed Charlie's face. "I watched you attack him. I'm sure you scratched him then. Look, accident or not, I'll find the man who killed your father. I won't stop looking until I do," he said, taking her hand and walking her toward the door. "Right now, let's go lay your father to rest."

Lilly's head pounded and her chest filled with gunpowder. She heard her mother cry out, her sister scream, and the swans falling into the water. She pulled her hand free from Charlie's and covered her ears. The sounds grew louder. White feathers clouded her head, calming her mind. When Charlie West reached for her again she pulled away and shook.

"I'm fine," she said.

He nodded and softened his voice. "I'll see you inside."

That was when she first saw the swan so far from the marsh. She sat on a log near the rutted road, preening her massive wings. Her long black bill trumpeted out a sound of beautiful victory, a sound that drowned out the deafening gunshots repeating in Lilly's head as she thought about her parents.

If she had been older when her father died, she might not have seen the swan. It most likely would've just gone by her rational mind like a wisp of dense air. But she was eleven and she still lived in that world—a world where a swan could just appear out of nowhere and preen her wings in front of her. At first she thought one of the marsh swans had somehow escaped the hunter's gun at the Cattail Marsh and followed her. Then she thought it was a figment of her imagination, like everyone had said the giant was, like Charlie West said her accusing Dean Drake was.

The swan swept in close, looking at her through one gentle eye. The sounds stopped and a peaceful quiet reigned. Lilly understood then that the swan was a ghost, one of the trumpeters shot and killed by the hunter. Its sweet spirit had followed her to her father's funeral. She had stepped in like a protector to calm Lilly's nerves just as her chest was about to explode.

Lilly was able to go in to the church, where the sweet smoky air hugged her, and colorful lights danced off the windows. She sat in the front pew next to Anna. Anna's brown hair rested on her neck in a bun. She wore a long black skirt and a gray button sweater that Nell had knit for Pa last winter. The large sweater fell limp on her shoulders, shrinking Anna to a near child.

George sat on the other side of her in a gray suit. His slicked-back hair made him look grown up, not at all like the boy he'd been just last week. Lilly had chosen a simple blue dress and she had braided her hair. The Wests sat in the front pew with them and most of the town sat in the pews behind them.

God had not bargained with her one bit. He'd not taken any of Lilly's offers. Not her hands, her voice, her heart. She didn't understand His reasoning. Anna was still a miserable mess. Lilly had never seen her sister so sad. Nell slept silently in the hospital in Missoula. According to Lenore West, who'd taken a train to see her, she had not uttered a word since the shootings. And Pa, well Pa was nowhere, and somewhere. He rested in the wooden box at the front of the Mission Church, the colorful Baby Jesus shining down on him through the stained-glass windows.

It wasn't like Pa to be so still and so quiet. Lilly could've won any argument with him. His stillness made her legs hurt. She wanted to get up and run fast just for him. She pictured her father's face as he sat with Nell, groomed his horse, and polished his shotgun. She remembered how he had looked tying his shotgun onto the mare and untying it, trying to decide what to do about the hunter.

But Pa only moved in her imagination. Lilly's father never said another word.

Like him, she hardly spoke the rest of that day. They buried Pa at the edge of town and Charlie West drove them home. Now, as they left his Ford, the gunshots rang out again, and the screams. Ravens cawed at her. The swan, her friend, swooped in again and quieted the sounds. It was heavenly.

"Do you hear that?" She asked Anna as she walked toward the house with George.

"Hear what?" Anna asked.

"The silence. It's beautiful."

"It's awful, Lilly, it's the sound of loneliness," Anna said.

"No, the gunshots. They've stopped."

"Not before they killed our father. Pa is dead, don't you get it?" She threw Nell's purse to the ground and ran into the house.

George shook his head. "Don't you have a heart? Can't you see what this has done to your sister? You're like stone. I don't know where you come from. Your mother may not come out of this. We just buried your father. Your parents would expect you to proceed with kindness and manners. Anna and I mean to see that you do."

He shook his fists at his sides, his lips quivered, and he stammered as if to say something more. But he stopped himself and went in after Anna.

Lilly heard the brown mare stomping in the barn. She'd have to know that Pa was gone, that he'd never take her into the mountains again. Lilly filled a bucket with oats and went to her. On the way she picked up her mother's purse, knowing that one day she'd give it back to Nell—one day when Nell would open her eyes and say thank you.

After feeding the mare, Lilly quietly followed Anna and George into the house. The swan had disappeared, knowing that the world had shut down around her. Lilly imagined the swan reappearing one day, the way an angel might return to claim his fire, the way a ghost might slip into her bedroom.

That's what Lilly did that afternoon after they buried her father. She slipped into her bedroom, unnoticed and lifeless, in a house that smelled stale and forlorn. God *had* evidently taken her heart after all. It was probably criteria for stopping Drake, to meet him where he lived, to stand on his ground, to live with no heart.

The whole next day after Pa's funeral, the thick air of the house stifled all sounds. When Lilly walked outside in the late morning she heard hushed voices. A neighbor looked up from her garden as if to ask how Nell was doing. She could hear her unspoken whisper, "A terrible thing, that, what happened to your father, your mother, your family. Someone should be made to pay." The neighbors kept the children inside, out of the fields, away from Lilly, and Lilly was glad. She could bring such bad luck to them. They might lose their fathers too. What she saw in the adults' eyes was her cue to disappear. She fled back into her bedroom and shut the door.

An occasional knock brought food in the arms of a tearful or stoic neighbor. Jerome brought over a box of cleaned strawberries and later in the evening he returned. She heard his new voice, the thick man's voice, through the closed bedroom door. She lay there frozen, stone still, on her bed and heard him ask for her. When he opened the door to the bedroom and the hallway light shined in, Lilly turned toward the wall, curled up like the baby she had once been in her mother's arms, any sense of comfort far gone. He set something on the bed next to her.

"Lillian." Jerome said her name quietly, like a question. "I'm sorry, Lillian. I went out to the marsh and got this for you. You'll probably need it to bring home unsuspecting frogs and other scientific creatures."

A soft, rich smell reached her nose. She curled up even tighter, moved closer to the wall. She smashed her face into the pillow, breathing in the dusty cotton cover. The pillowcase scratched her eyes and she squeezed them tight.

"I'll just leave it," Jerome said. "If you need help with anything, remember, I'm here. And Mom and Dad, too. Dad could teach you about swans, the way he taught…" He sucked in the air, as though trying to pull his words back in. "…The way he taught your father."

She held her breath. Kindness hurt. Didn't Jerome know that? She was beyond the sense of comfort his kindness had initially stirred up in her. That time was gone. Be gone too, please, just go.

She let out her breath slowly so as not to move a muscle. When she heard Jerome shut the door quietly behind him, she allowed herself to breathe at a normal rate and turned to see what he had left. Her bike basket, dried and cleaned up, dented by the fall, pressed into the blanket. Lilly looked at it like it was something foreign. A checkered dishtowel covered something inside the basket. She didn't want to look under it.

But, like it or not, she had just turned eleven. Curiosity got the better of her and she picked up the cloth. Chocolate cupcakes filled the basket. They weren't the ones Anna had baked and Lilly had thrown to the ground. Freshly baked cupcakes filled the basket.

Her head went empty.

Something wet and salty flowed down her face and neck. A sound she'd never heard before caught in her throat and punched its way out her mouth.

# Dark Swan

# 9

A few weeks later Charlie West's eyes told Lilly that the danger had spread far and wide. He still didn't believe Drake had killed her father, but she could see that something concerned him. He knew these things: Drake was the one Pa had argued with at the marsh last fall; he was there at the edge of Charlie's ranch when the mother bear came to collect her cub that day, and Drake had stopped making visits to the fire hall. These things made his brow furrow. Lilly could tell they bothered him. Charlie wouldn't talk to her about it, but sure enough he'd seen Dean Drake and trouble walk into the Mission Valley side by side.

Rain hung in the heavy clouds and crashed to the ground, turning it to mud and spreading a gray blanket over the valley. Then the clouds disappeared and the nights were clear and cold. Fog rose off the steamy earth and daylight came through a sultry mist. The Mission Mountains stood tall and regal, the sad sun shining on them a little longer each day. Their snowy edges crawled up the slopes, ever closer to the craggy peaks. Wide swaths of evergreens rolled down the mountainsides.

Soon the pass would be free of seasonal snow, leaving only the persistent snowfields to cross on the way to Pa's cave. He had hidden something important in that cave. Lilly figured it was something about Dean Drake, and she was hell-bent to retrieve whatever it was and bring it home just as soon as she could.

"I can prove Drake had it out for Pa," she told Jerome as they walked to the fence that surrounded his father's ponds. Lilly pulled her sweater sleeves over her hands to keep the morning chill off.

"You're saying he shot your parents, then hung around till the ambulance showed up so he could come forward and save your mother's life?"

Lilly nodded.

"I don't think you know what you saw that day."

"I know," she replied. Jerome had already made it clear that he didn't believe her when she said that she'd jumped on Drake and tried to stop him from shooting them. It hurt her feelings and made her mad, but she shrugged it off. "You can help me stop him. Help me bring him in."

A trumpeter swan floated on the ranch pond, mystical and beautiful, without a care in the world. Sunlight burned through the mist and glittered off her feathers. Yet the sun brought no warmth and the air felt cool on Lilly's cheeks.

Jerome stopped at the gate and turned. "The two of us go after Drake? First of all you're a pint size. Second, my dad wouldn't like me going vigilante. That's why he's the sheriff. He believes in the law." His face looked thin and anxious. Suddenly Lilly understood that he was worried about her. Jerome West cared about her and wanted to protect her. He just didn't know how.

She took advantage. "The best thing you can do for me is to help me find Drake." She recalled the fight Drake had had with her father, and the tracks in the snow outside of their house, signs that someone had been watching them. Then Lilly told Jerome a thing she had no way of proving, the thing that was now the most important of all. "He was after Nell too. He wants something from her and if he can't get it, he'll kill her."

When Jerome opened the gate to the swans' fence, the hinges

squeaked and the fastening chain rattled. As they walked into the injured birds' haven, tall grasses blew in the breeze. The trumpeters and snow geese had matted down the grasses closer to the ponds, smoothing out a soft layer of greens and browns. Near the first shed a patch of wild lupine turned the ground purple, their sweet scent filling the morning air.

Jerome ignored what Lilly had just said and looked at her with a kindness she didn't trust, a kindness that she thought was meant to shut her up. "Help me clean the swan pens," he said. "It'll help you forget all that for a while."

"Forget," Lilly said, her voice coming out flat. Snow geese scooted across the pond, cackling. Two trumpeters paid no attention to them as they poked their heads underwater and dined on duckweed.

"I can't change it," he said. "Maybe if you help me, it'll rest your mind a little."

"Are you making up stuff just to get me to do your work?"

"Not at all. Helping others is good for a person."

"Especially for the person being helped."

"I'm trying to make it easier for you," he said, looking at his boots, "because your dad can't."

Lilly squished her eyes to keep back the sudden tears. If he wouldn't help her find Drake, he had no right acting like he'd help her with anything. And he had no right talking about her father. "You can't make it easier. You're just a kid too, plus boys grow up slower than girls. That makes us about the same age."

"Now you're just being mean, and pretty immature, I might add."

"Fine." She didn't mean it though. What she meant was, fine, you will pay for ignoring my request for help. Revenge clawed out a home in her head.

Jerome drew in a breath. "Whenever I'm upset," he said, "I try to do a good deed for someone who's worse off than me."

"Really?" Lilly spit the word at him. Pa was dead. Nell wouldn't talk to anyone and according to Lenore looked more ragged every day. No one believed that Drake shot her parents. Anna had dissolved into her own world, and George thought Lilly a selfish child. The giant of the forest was gone. The only one who talked to her was Jerome, and too often that was to boss her around. Others avoided her like they might catch her bad luck. In a few short weeks, she'd lost her mother, her father, her sister, and her heart. "How could anyone be worse off than me?"

Jerome gave her another sympathetic look. She was pretty sure he reserved that look for anyone feeling sorry for themselves. His pity hurt, like a sharp stone tossed at her feet.

"I am telling you, I saw the man who shot my parents," she said again. "And I tried to stop him."

"I know, but I don't understand how you saw him. I mean, he was in the bushes across the swamp from your family. There's no way you could've seen him."

"I wasn't with the others. I was sitting in the arms of a giant." She regretted the words the minute they soared out of her mouth. She could feel the red spots burning in her cheeks.

Jerome raised his eyebrows. "A giant?"

"A large pine I climbed and turned into a giant," she said. That was just a few weeks ago when she was a kid. She was something else now. "The giant disappeared when the hunter showed up." Along with my imagination, she nearly added, wanting to make Jerome understand, giving him every reason to mock her, testing his friendship to the far edge. "But I saw Dean Drake. I watched him aim his big gun at my family and at the swans! I jumped on him and scratched him. I saw the man who…shot Pa."

Jerome shook his head. "You jumped on him when he was saving your mother's life." Now the sympathy oozed out of him in a way that made shame swell hot in her cheeks. He had closed his ears to her, failing the test.

"I'll feed the swans in the far pond," she said, wanting to get away.

"Fine," he sighed. But his wind-chapped cheeks blossomed as he smiled.

When Lilly picked up the ten-pound feedbag, he didn't even offer to help her. She was glad he didn't pelt her with any more sympathy. Out of the corner of her eye she could see him watching as she neared one of the pens they kept for injured birds. It had been empty since early spring, since last year's rescued swans were now able to fend for themselves in the main ponds.

Something fluttered right across the place where her heart should've been when she saw the feathers in the shed. A fragile white swan sat in the straw. It looked just like the ghost swan she'd seen the day of Pa's funeral. It was as if this bird had been calling out to her all along. A soft wind blew across her chest, and she felt the swan's heart beat in her own body.

Jerome stood at Lilly's side. "Dad found her at the Cattail Marsh when he was out there looking for evidence. She must've gotten hit the same day that your parents did."

Lilly's throat closed up and her eyes clouded over. The only thing she could see was the trumpeter, her soft white feathers, her black flat bill, her long graceful neck curled into her body. As Lilly entered the pen, the swan grew agitated. But she didn't try to move away. Her wing feathers had been washed mostly free of blood, but some caked, stubborn particles remained. She had crusted blood on her chest, too. That meant that a pellet from the shotgun shell must have entered and exited close to her lungs—a wound almost identical to Nell's wound—a near miracle that she was alive.

"Will she eat?" Lilly asked.

"A little soft food, and she drank some water, barely enough to stay alive. Dad doesn't think the shotgun pellet went through her lungs, or she wouldn't be here. But it came close and she might have some infection in there."

She did have an infection. Lilly could smell the raw wound, almost taste the metallic pus in her mouth. "Have you dressed her for the infection?"

"We've been putting salve on it. Dad thinks she'd do better if just one person cared for her. She gets nervous each time we come near."

"Have you named her?"

Jerome shot an eyebrow up like she'd asked a ridiculous question.

"Well, have you? She needs a name."

Jerome shrugged and looked at the ground.

"She's so smooth and beautiful, like a pearl," Lilly said. Just then the great white bird lifted her head from her wing where it had been resting and looked at Lilly with a cloudy eye. Spirit shot up through Lilly and straightened her back. "Hello, Pearl," she whispered. She turned to Jerome. "Can you go get me a bucket of warm water and a rag?" The caked blood on her chest and wing was a magnet for dirt and infection.

---

That night Lenore West roasted a chicken, made mashed potatoes, and asked Anna and Lilly to stay for dinner. Nell was still in the hospital and the girls didn't cook much. Since Pa had died, Lilly just hadn't been hungry. That night though in a kitchen full of homey smells—not the least of which was buttermilk pie—she felt starved. The chicken melted on her tongue and the buttery smell of the potatoes welcomed her. The soft textures soothed her. For a moment, she felt like she belonged. She shoveled food in like she'd never eaten.

"My goodness, child," Lenore said. "Slow down. There's plenty to go around."

Lilly could almost hear Pa and Nell telling her to mind her manners. Jerome, Charlie, and Anna were staring at her. Her face burned with heat. All set to apologize, she turned to Lenore. But Lenore's eyes told her that she was good, no need for an apology. She just talked to Lilly like she might have talked to Jerome. What she said next shouldn't have surprised Lilly.

"Anna, I want you and Lilly to move in here until you mother comes home from the hospital. It's not right, you girls over there by yourselves."

Anna's face tightened like she'd just hit an invisible wall. "Thank you, Mrs. West. It's really kind," she said. "But we'll stay put, have the house ready for when Mama comes home."

"I think we have to face reality." Lenore's voice softened. "Nell might not be home for a long time. She's not made much of a recovery yet. We've got room here for both of you, and for Nell when she's released."

The idea of living with Jerome sent a spidery web of uncertainty churning through Lilly, and Lenore talking about Nell like she was done and finished chilled her spine. She lost her appetite. Outside, she heard a weak trill, a swan's poor attempt at trumpeting. She was certain it was Pearl, calling for Lilly to take care of her, maybe even thinking it was a good idea for her to be here with her, with Jerome.

Anna put her fork down. "If we move out of the house, the pack-rats will move in and they'll be the ones waiting on Mama's return."

"Who will take care of Lilly?" Lenore said, as if she wasn't sitting right there in one of her kitchen chairs, Lilly's ankles wrapped around its wooden legs.

"I can take care of myself," Lilly said, staring down at the chicken on her plate. It was as if she hadn't spoken. No one else at the table had a voice in this discussion.

"I'll take care of her. I'm near the woman Mama was when she married Pa."

"Nell was seventeen," Lilly said.

"I'll be sixteen this December. Seventeen's just a step away. Besides, George will help."

That got an eye-raise from Lenore. She patted her lips with her napkin. "You getting married?"

Anna shook her head. "We've had too many changes to make another one. But he'll come over if we need him, you know, to cut wood and make repairs. He'll hunt and help bring home meat. We'll do fine."

The words "bring home" did not slip past Lilly. Charlie evidently noticed it too. He cleared his throat and twisted his beard. His hair was flattened in a ring against his head where his hat had been. Quick as a glint in his eye he made a decision. Spooning more pota-toes on his plate, he paused and looked at Lilly with pity—a look she hated. "It's OK, Lenore," he said. "We'll watch over them too."

"I don't like it," she said. "When Nell does come home, I think she should come here first. These girls have too much on their shoulders, taking care of that house and then taking care of the their ma too."

Anna folded her napkin on the table, her food barely touched, and looked reassuringly at Lenore. It was as if Anna really was a grown woman comforting another. "It'll be OK," she said. "We'll keep the house for Nell and when she comes home we'll take care of her."

"What about school? You have to go to school. And money?"

"I've got a job at the Timberline Café. Lilly will stay in school."

"You're leaving school," Lenore said quietly. "I don't like it." But there was nothing she could do about it. Anna wasn't budging. "Plus," Lenore began and stopped. "Plus…how are you going to keep your sister from going after the man she says killed your father?"

Shocked, Lilly shot a look at Jerome. His face turned completely red and she burst into tears. He'd told his mother! Lilly heard Pearl's soft trill again, excused herself from the table, and ran outside, leaving a perfectly good buttermilk pie untouched on the counter. If she'd had a heart left in her chest, right then it would've been pounding hard.

"I hate Jerome," she told Pearl, putting her face low on the gate and smelling the spring earth under the straw. She went inside and Pearl flapped her huge wings, hopping to the far end of the pen. Lilly cooed at her to calm the injured trumpeter down. It was no use. Pearl wanted Lilly to leave. Lilly didn't leave. She scooted along the fence, keeping a careful distance from her, explaining quietly that she was her friend. She wouldn't abandon her. She would never tell her secrets. She would never betray her like Jerome had just betrayed Lilly.

The sky turned brilliant pink as the sun moved west toward the foothills. A branch snapped and the raw smell of a sweating horse burned her nostrils. Pearl flitted away to another corner of her pen, trapped by wood and wire. Lilly could almost taste her yearning for freedom, even though that freedom would kill her. She was injured and needed help for the same reason that Nell needed help.

The animal snorted and Lilly looked up to see its silhouette cross the sky.

Dean Drake rode in the field on his mule, just outside the fence. He pulled the reins tight and stopped, looking over at her and Pearl, two unlikely sisters devastated by his gun. With a bitter laugh he loped off toward the Missions.

She watched him go, frozen in place and afraid to move, afraid to tell anyone. They'd never believe her. Pearl first smashed herself up against the fence, her feathers spilling over the wire, then raced for the shed.

Lilly crawled in after Pearl and lay down on a pile of straw. The straw bit her legs, the pain a relief compared to that in her non-existent heart, and she cried.

# 10

The spring before her father died, Sam and Lilly watched a flock of full-grown trumpeters glide in from southern lands to summer in the Mission Valley. They built nests for their large eggs. The spring rains soaked them and wind danced with the long grasses. Soon tiny birds swam at their mothers' sides. The ponds at the Cattail Marsh had filled with growing cygnets. The cygnets preened themselves, taking oil from a gland near their tails and spreading it over their feathers. It made them waterproof and kept them warm.

When the cygnets were just five days old, their parents taught them to eat duckweed by nibbling it right off their mothers' feathers. The tiny swans pecked at anything shiny that moved, the duckweed, an insect or fish bubble on the water, tiny bits of water on their mother's wing feathers. Eventually their mothers and fathers taught them to feed themselves by tipping upside down in the water, tail feathers pointed toward the sky, and eating the duckweed off the pond. The tiny cygnets ate well and grew into strong, healthy birds. One fall day, when they were nearly four months old, almost full size, their feathers gray, Pa and Lilly had watched as they ran one hundred feet across the land, stretched their wings and flew.

That day Lilly had stepped quietly in her father's footsteps and crouched at the edge of the pond with him, a girl wanting to stay forever close to her father. Now with Pa gone she put everything she had into taking care of Pearl. Somehow, being close to her kept her close to Pa. She tended to Pearl as carefully and delicately as one might hold a new butterfly. She washed her wound and cooed to her and she watched her heal. Pearl couldn't fly, and she was slow to gain back her strength. But the infection was mostly gone. She'd already begun to incorporate the wound into the new bird she'd become. Lilly hoped that somehow she'd find a way to follow in her footsteps.

She cooked grain for Pearl in Lenore's kitchen, making it easy for the swan to digest, and she kept her water fresh. Eventually, when she approached with food, the great white bird walked out of the shed enclosed in her pen and looked up at Lilly, a child to her mother. A leftover fragment of Lilly's heart pulsed and grew when she saw Pearl take that step toward her.

She forgave Jerome, knowing that even with his I-know-more-than-you adult attitude he was still just a kid like her. He'd meant to help keep Lilly safe by telling his mother that she planned to go after Dean Drake. But the way he really helped Lilly was by giving her Pearl. When Pearl took that first willing step toward her, Lilly knew that there was hope, that life could mend itself, that the hole in her chest where her father lived would close and scar over, and she would feel strong again, that Nell would come home.

———

And Nell did come home. She came home a full month after Lenore said she wouldn't. The Wests took the train to Missoula to collect her. They delivered her early in the day, when the warm sun made the land smell like lilacs. Anna had made pancakes and had just washed the last dish from the breakfast table.

Nell looked ragged and frail in the borrowed dress Lenore had taken and dressed her in before bringing her home from the hospital. She wore a brown sweater over the dress. Her hair had been put into a bun that looked unnatural and tight compared with the slack skin on her face. Her eyes looked nowhere and somewhere far away at the same time. Nell didn't seem to recognize Anna and Lilly. But then she might not have recognized anything, Lilly thought, not the cook stove, not the railing of the stairs, not a rock wall she had built in the garden. She lived in some other world and not there, in her own home in the Mission Valley.

"There's nothing more they can do for her at the hospital," Charlie said. His face had deep lines at the corners of his mouth where his smile froze. His hair fell into another set of lines on his forehead. "She's more likely to heal at home, with her family."

"Coffee?" Anna asked.

"I'll fix it," Lilly said. But she couldn't take her eyes off Nell. Charlie and Lenore held her between them, her arms flung over their shoulders, the brown sweater over Lenore's dress scrunched up at her waist, that vacant stare in her eyes. Anna quickly took Lenore's place, gently holding Nell's fluid hand at her neck. Lilly's mother looked like something not quite alive. But she was alive. Lilly kept this knowing close in her mind, and tears of gratitude spilled out her eyes.

Charlie helped Anna get Nell to bed.

Lilly put the coffee grounds into the clean pot with water, and set it on the hottest part of the cook stove.

Lenore looked tired and sad. Wisps of brown hair fell across her cheekbones. Her green eyes flipped to Nell's room and back to Lilly at the stove. "The doctors don't know if she'll heal," she said.

"They only know so much," Charlie said, leaving Anna with Nell to change her into a sleeping gown and tuck her under the bed covers. "They don't even know why she won't communicate. It's like a sleeping sickness, they say, or maybe she's catatonic, or maybe something happened to her brain. They really don't know. They can't possibly know what will make her well again if they don't know what ails her."

"She got shot close to the lung, but now I think the wound in her mind is the bigger problem. She looks terrified, stuck in that awful day," Lenore said.

"The wound is free of infection. So that's good news," Charlie said.

"Well, I just wouldn't get my hopes up too much," Lenore said. "Take it slow, talk to her, fill the room with flowers and good home-cooked smells, give her water and simple foods."

Much like Lilly had done with Pearl, she thought, watching Lenore palm an empty coffee cup, enjoying its imaginary heat.

Charlie turned slowly to Lilly. "You still gonna stop the swan killer?"

Suddenly Lilly was seething inside. She stared at him. "What have you done to stop him? Have you even tried? Dean Drake."

Sheriff West shook his head. "Maybe and maybe not. Either way it is not a young girl's job to solve a crime."

"At least now you admit it was a crime."

"Lilly! Mind your manners," Lenore said.

Her horrified look shook Lilly, but Lilly held her glare. "You could measure the boot-prints dried in the mud near Nell's window."

Charlie shook his head. "Let's have a look."

Lilly felt bad for being rude, but more than that she felt smug.

Just then Nell screamed. It was a blood-curdling scream that mixed with the sound of the coffee boiling over. They ran to her room. Her room smelled damp and dusty. Spider webs decorated the upper corners. Nell was stone white, a fallen statue.

"She saw a face in the window," Anna said.

"Did you see it?" Charlie asked, all detective-like.

Anna nodded. "A man."

Lilly charged out the door and up the trail toward the pass before anyone could stop her. She'd seen his tracks two times and she knew which way he traveled. Her lungs hurt and her legs burned. She thought of Pa. She thought of Pearl. She thought of Nell in her bed, not able to talk, but able to scream. Up ahead a green coat brushed through the pines. With mountain lion stealth Lilly moved toward it. The green cloth disappeared and the sound of a slow-moving mule took its place.

---

Lilly stood in the doorway of Nell's room and stared at her. Her face was plaster white and docile. The doctor said she wasn't quite catatonic; she was more lost in thought, locked up in her mind somewhere, afraid to move or talk. The doctor thought she saw something terrible that the rest of them couldn't see. But he was wrong about that part. Lilly could still see the shotgun shells and the pellets fly—as if in slow motion—into her parents, into the swans.

She wondered what Nell thought of Dean Drake now, the way he would suddenly appear and disappear without much to trace him. She wondered if her mother would still defend him to Pa, if Pa had still been here to take up his end of the fight. Maybe if Lilly stood there long enough Nell would tell her. Finally she gave up, dusted the dresser, and swept the spider webs from the corners. She dragged a chair over and sat next to Nell.

"I'm going to get you to the bathroom, but you're going to have to help me," Lilly said. She had watched Anna struggle with their mother to help her walk. Nell was weak and heavy in her weakened state.

Lilly pulled back the covers and took hold of Nell's legs. She moved them to the side of the bed so that her feet dangled just above the floor. From under the bed Lilly took out her work boots and put them on her. Her legs looked thin and weak when she attempted to stand on them. They had lost muscle in the weeks she'd been idle in the hospital.

Pulling her arm around her shoulder Lilly pulled her mother up off of the mattress. As if in slow motion, her legs collapsed and she fell back into bed. It was a bad sign. Nell not being able to stand on her own two legs, her arms loose and yielding, her hands without grip, her eyes staring at some unknown world. They were all bad signs. Lilly took her boots off, put her legs back on the bed, and pulled the covers up.

She went out to the barn and found the chamber pot that Pa had found and saved for a rainy day. Just in case there was a need for it. Lilly was certain he hadn't imagined this would be the rainy day. She took it to Nell's room and helped her use it. In that short distance, her legs didn't have the time to fall out from under her.

Lilly steadied her mother with her palms, her own legs shaking, her mind going empty.

It embarrassed her to be there with her mother like that, helping her with the most basic thing that a body could do. At that moment she was grateful that Nell seemed so distant and unfeeling. After she got her mother back into bed she sat there thinking. They'd have to find a way to strengthen their mother's legs or she'd never get up and walk again. Lilly knew that she had to find a way to get her moving.

"I know who shot you," she said, trying to jolt her into action. "Dean Drake. I remember you and Pa fighting over him." Guilt ran through Lilly, mentioning Pa's name like that. She wondered if Nell knew that Pa was dead. In her best dreams she imagined that Nell met Pa's spirit in that in-between world where she lived. Maybe he visited her there and Nell wanted to stay with Sam in that otherworld.

At her worst times she feared that Nell might not know that Pa was gone.

Gone.

"I saw Drake outside the house this week." She put the emphasis on the name Drake. Sure enough, a tiny jolt of energy started to run through Nell. It was a fine vibration rumbling across her skin. "He escaped into the pines."

"Who you talking to?" Jerome stood in the doorway. He wore an over-sized coat unbuttoned and pulled back with a hand on his hip, like a gunslinger.

Lilly blushed and didn't answer.

"Yourself?"

"I'm going to stop him," she finally said, "whether you help me or not."

"You mean Dean Drake? We've talked about this. I'm not helping you without my dad's permission. I think you should do the same. It's dangerous."

"Stop being a child." Lilly was already fuming. She wasn't calm, but she knew she'd get further in convincing Jerome to help her if her voice was calm, so she kept the rest of her insults to herself. "Your dad will let you help capture a bona fide criminal."

"We got no proof that he is a criminal." His eyes brightened. "Maybe there's a way to get some proof."

"That's what I'm saying! You and me go get the proof." Nell seemed to be vibrating at high speed now. It was nothing normal vision could see, but Lilly could see it with her swan vision. This conversation was agitating her. She didn't want to agitate her mother, but she did want her to get up and walk. Sometimes Lilly was best at getting moving when she was mad. Maybe Nell was too. "You owe me for telling your mom that I was going after Drake."

"I was trying to keep you safe."

She burned her eyes into him, letting him know that she didn't like it, but letting it stand nonetheless. She looked back at her mother. Her face was soft and pleasant now, as if she lived in a pretty dream. It was not at all the face of someone who had had a shotgun pellet tear into her chest, nearly puncturing her lung. "My mother says that a beautiful white swan full of grace and beauty lives inside of every young person. A swan told Pa that the young ones know the truth.'"

"Swans don't talk." Jerome said. Lilly could hardly stand his pragmatism.

"Swans talked to my parents." They did. Her parents had told her as much. "Pa said the land is named for the swans. Swan Valley. Swan Crossing. Swan Pond. Some call heaven 'The Place of the Swans.' That's where Pa lives."

From the look on Nell's face, her words seemed to catch in her ears. She opened her eyes wide and, for the first time, looked right at Lilly. Lilly's breath caught in her throat.

"Mama," she said, her chest beating hard, her legs going weak.

Through the window the sun shone on her mother's face as the panic passed and her expression softened again. Hers was the face of a woman who floated on clouds. Her eyes closed.

Lilly knew it then. Nell had left on her eleventh birthday for a really good reason. Who wouldn't want to be somewhere in a lighted forest with angels all around, when shotgun pellets were flying?

"Now don't go crazy but, when you first started the swan story, I think your mother smiled."

"Did you see her open her eyes and look right at me?"

He shook his head.

"Help me find Dean Drake, and bring him to your father."

"Have you been back out to the swamp since, since...?"

"Since my father was killed? No."

"Maybe there is something there. What about your father's camera?"

Lilly stood up straight. Pa might have caught Drake on film. "You're a genius, Jerome West! But don't tell anyone I said so."

He smiled, and a small piece of her heart came home.

"Let's go tell your dad that Nell looked at me with recognition, like she understood what was going on," Lilly said. "She might wake up soon and she could tell us something. And we have to tell him about the camera."

"I didn't see Nell look at you. But I did see her smile. Let's wait for Dad to come in from the woods." He looked across the bed, toward the window where a crow sat in a tree and cawed. "On second thought, we should let my dad go look for the camera. He'll be able to find the person who did this. Me and you, we'll just do our chores and go to school, maybe just give a few suggestions to my dad."

"I'm not going to school," Lilly said, instantly wishing she hadn't. "But don't go telling on me."

"No one to tell. Teacher will know and your mother is indisposed."

"Where'd you get a word like that, indisposed?"

"You'd learn big words too if you attend class."

"Can't. I've got to redispose my parents."

"That isn't a word." He looked smug about that. "Besides, you don't have the competencies to redispose your parents." His smug face turned instantly sad.

"I got plenty of competencies."

"You don't even know what competencies are."

"So."

"They are things you can do really good."

"Last chance. You going with me or not?"

"Not."

"Fine. I'll go alone then." She kissed Nell on the forehead, went downstairs and fed Pa's brown mare, dragged her bike out of the barn, and left Jerome standing slack-mouthed on the porch.

---

Partway up the pass Lilly spotted smoke coming off a cooking fire in an open clearing. She hesitated behind a boulder where she hid her bicycle. Deer tracks led to a rumbling creek. The sound covered her footsteps. Inching along the boulders, she slid toward the camp, fear pounding in her chest. Carefully, slowly, she poked her head around the rocks.

There was Charlie West, staring into the fire. He wore a light canvas coat, unbuttoned and revealing a leather vest underneath, a sharp corner of his badge peeking out. His horse, tied to a near-by tree, side-stepped and tossed his head away from the puffs of smoke. Clearly annoyed, he flared his nostrils.

"You shouldn't be out here by yourself," Charlie said without lifting his head to look at Lilly.

"I've got no one to be out here with me," she said, at the edge of tears with the truth of it. Her family had just gotten smaller and her only friend kept abandoning her. It left her wildly lonely. She bit her lip.

"Because other kids are in school or tending to their work." He motioned for Lilly to sit across the fire from him. "It's way too dangerous for you to be out here alone."

"Pa said that Drake had it out for him because he married Nell, and because Nell loved Pa."

"I have asked you to leave it to me." He lifted his head, tilting his wide-brimmed hat into the wind.

"You don't understand. If Nell's love had been reversed, and she loved Drake instead of Pa, Pa never would have taken it out on Nell.

Pa would have protected Nell and put her happiness above his own."

"If it was Drake who shot your parents, and I'm not saying it was, then we've got real trouble. No offense, but you are just a kid. If he really shot your parents and you really tried to stop him like you said, then he knows that you're dangerous to him. You're a target, Lilly."

"They were targets! He took aim and pulled the trigger." As she ran that day over and over in her mind, she saw the man point the gun in her father's direction. "He'd have to be blind to have missed Pa and Nell standing there." She kept the pain she felt at bay. If she gave it room, it would swallow her whole. She missed her father and she wanted him home. She wanted him to ride the brown mare again and put the goat out to pasture. She wanted him to feed the stove and let the house swell with heat. She wanted him to talk to her about swans, to tell her about their flight patterns, their babies, their dangers.

Maybe jailing the swan killer would put everything back to normal, would get Nell up to cook potatoes for dinner, would make Pa stand up and walk back into their house. But she knew it wasn't so. Pa wasn't coming back. He'd already crossed some invisible line that Lilly hadn't known existed. Even so she hoped for him to return and didn't want to let go of the idea that somehow she could make this right.

She looked up and saw an old mine tunnel in the hillside behind Charlie, the mouth of the tunnel inviting her to enter. It was like the tunnel she'd seen when she followed her father up the pass, when he carried her over the snowfield. She looked out across the gully where the stream flowed, and wiped the hurt from her eyes. Too much had changed since that day of Lilly and Pa and the snowfield.

"Did you see my father's camera in the marsh?" she asked. "It didn't make it home. It's got to still be out there. It probably has pictures on it. Maybe pictures of Drake."

"You're too young to know this, so I'm going to tell you. These mountains are huge and Dean Drake could be on the other side of them already, beyond the Swans, maybe up toward Glacier or over to the Blackfoot or way down near Butte, Dillon, as far as Idaho or Utah. The country's too vast, and Drake, as you love to point out, is not a nice man. Men like him cross boundaries where even the wilderness grows thick. One lone rider is not going to find him. 'Specially not one lone rider on a bicycle, who is a kid."

The wind blew in and Lilly lifted her face to it. Leaves from a mountain maple danced to its rhythm and a wild cherry tree blossomed just over Charlie's shoulder. For just a moment the sweet scent squashed the foul smell of mistrust growing inside of her. But it didn't last. If others wouldn't believe her, how could she count on them? She pushed the dirt into the fire with her foot.

"My mother opened her eyes and looked directly at me today. She recognized me. I'm certain she knew exactly where she was," she said. "She'll be waking up soon and talking. She'll tell you the same thing I'm telling you."

"Just so we understand each other, you go vigilante on me and I will arrest you, even if you are a kid."

She looked at the ground where she had made a tiny valley with the toe of her shoe. When she raised her eyes, Charlie was looking at her with sympathy and Lilly understood where Jerome had gotten that look. The one that said, poor you, I'll take care of things now, you just go rest your pretty little head. She narrowed her eyes and glared at Charlie. "The camera?"

He shook his head and doused the fire. "Haven't seen it."

"I'm going with you."

"Only place you're going is home," he said. "Go get your bike. I'll take that thing away from you if you follow me again."

"You can't. You don't have authority over me."

"I'm sure I can find a law that gives it to me."

She pulled her bike out and dragged her feet as she traced Charlie and his horse back to town.

———————

Three days after Nell looked directly at Lilly, three days after Charlie chewed her out for finding him in the mountains, she packed one of

Pa's old fishing nets on her bike. Jerome relented and went out to the Cattail Marsh with her to find Pa's camera. The cottonwoods were bright green with new leaves that perfumed the air. The sun skirted around white clouds, heating the long grasses and trees. A warm wind caught the wisps of blond hair that had escaped Lilly's braids and blew them against her cheeks. It pressed her blue skirt against her knees, turning the soft cotton into trousers. Her legs were strong from weeks of riding in the mountains and she thought about the strength in her legs compared to the weakness in her mother's legs.

It wasn't fair or right that Lilly should be healthy and her mother unable to manage even the simple task of feeding herself or drinking from a clay cup and Lilly felt bad for it. Somehow, Nell had to get strong again.

It took no time at all for Lilly and Jerome to cross through the forest and fields to the Cattail Marsh. Four big trumpeters and several yearlings swam away from them as they approached. On a nest of twigs and leaves, on the far side of the marsh, a plump swan sat quietly with tiny white heads at her wings. She was maybe four years old, nesting her first brood in spite of the early season carnage.

A large male stood nearby, his bill tilted, his neck strong and full of purpose. He lifted his head, alert to sounds and trumpeted out a warning. He walked back and forth in front of the nest. He stretched his long neck and spread his wings. The marsh was no longer red, the blood washed off by God or rain or both, the leftover dead swans most likely carried off by bear or coyote.

Lilly scanned the edges of the water for her father's camera. She didn't see it, but that didn't mean it wasn't there. It could've fallen into the long grasses or the bushes. For all she knew, the trumpeters had pulled it into their nest and continued to build around it. The notion made her smile.

"Imagine life inside a swan egg," she whispered.

"Why would I do that, Lilly?"

"To be hidden and sheltered, with two huge guardians, a father pacing protectively and a mother that never leaves the nest, that would be divine. It would be safe in there." Suddenly her chest ached. Her knees went weak with the words. Comfort and safety had vanished from the world, from her world.

Jerome's canvas coat flapped in the wind as he smiled at her. "I've got my slingshot with me," he said. "I'll protect you."

"I know where a gun is."

He raised his eyebrows at that. "In the barn, your father's shotgun."

"No. A pistol. I was with Pa last fall when he hid it in the mountains."

"We shouldn't be thinking about using guns."

"Why not? Other people do."

"It's dangerous. We should leave that stuff to my father." He dropped his eyes. "You should come live with us, Lilly—you, Anna, and Nell. My mother would love it."

She shook her head. "Anna's made up her mind." Anna said no, but Lilly didn't want anyone watching over her, because, in this case, she was certain that watching over her meant telling her what to do. And she didn't want anyone telling her what to do.

"You could convince her to change it."

"Think what it must have been like inside of your mother's belly," she said, ignoring the idea of living with Jerome, dragging the subject back to swans. "I wonder if unborn babies talk to unhatched cygnets. Do you think they live together in some lighted place before entering this world? Maybe the same place that the dead go?"

"Unhatched? I'm not sure that's a word. Swans and babies? Mostly, I don't think about it." He pushed his hair back off his forehead. Like he does when I'm making a fool of myself, Lilly thought.

"Where is your imagination, Jerome West?"

"I like to read real facts at school, instead of making things up."

She twisted on the ball of her foot in the grass. School was the last thing on her mind. Her father's death, her mother's frailty, Anna's determination to support them, the swan killer, these were the things she thought about.

"You going back in the fall?" Jerome asked.

She shook her head. "I've got Nell to take care of."

"Anna can do that. You scared?"

"For Nell?" She shook her head again. It was true, she wasn't afraid. She had a plan to get Nell strong again, to make her well, to put things right. "I keep telling you. I've got to stop the man who killed Pa. When that's done, and Nell is OK, I'll go to school." Once she stopped Dean Drake, she could think of other important things.

Jerome sighed and pursed his lips, but said nothing.

They walked over to the place where her parents had been shot. The ground betrayed nothing of the deaths that had occurred there many weeks ago, but the air grew thick with the ghosts of slaughtered swans, a mist lifting up off of the water. She looked around for her father and struggled to breathe. Her legs turned to logs, stiffly bound to the land. She couldn't move them.

Jerome took her hand. "Do you see your father's camera anywhere?"

She shook her head. A soft pink haze covered the swamp and blurred her vision. She couldn't see anything. When it cleared, the resting swan stood up from her nest. The cygnets splashed into the water. They had all survived the slaughter. The swan killer had not ruined everything.

Lilly wondered if, before they were born, the sun had brightened the inside of the cygnets' shells. This brightening might have been the very thing that their tiny bills picked at to find their way into the world. She wanted to be there, held safely inside of her mother's heart, where she was just a thought or a possibility, and her mother was strong still and her father lived. She wanted to be there where the cygnets' tiny heads popped out from under the thin white skinned shells and poked under their mother's wing for the first time. She wanted to be there and not here, where her father had been killed.

"It's got to be here somewhere," Jerome said after a few minutes.

"If it's not here, it's not here."

Jerome peered sideways at her, the sun shining off his face. He tightened his fingers around Lilly's.

She let go of his hand, went back to her bicycle and untied her father's large fishing net. The rope felt thick and stiff in her fingers. It smelled like wood smoke from the barn.

Jerome stood staring over her shoulder. "What on earth are

you doing with that? You'll get in a world of trouble if you start capturing swans."

"Not swans. I'm setting a trap for the killer. No one believes me, so I'm going to catch him in this."

"Have you lost your mind?"

"Help me set it up. I'm putting it exactly where he stood to kill… the swans." She didn't want to say, "to kill Pa." She was convinced that if she said those words in the presence of the swans her father would really be gone for good. If she said those words, capturing the swan killer would lose the magic to return Pa to them and make her mother's legs strong again.

If she didn't already know it she never could have told that Jerome was two years older than her, especially not by his knowledge of setting a trap. He stepped right in the middle of the net, accidentally hooking the edge on a bush.

"Stay off it. The net has to surround him. If one edge is caught on the bushes, he'll be able to walk out of it." Lilly didn't know what she'd do if she caught him.

"This is way worse than catching frogs, Lilly," Jerome said as he backed away, toward his bike.

"Don't leave me alone out here," she yelled after him. "Your Pa won't like it."

He disappeared and returned with a pair of binoculars.

"Those are Pa's! Was his camera there, too?" If they found the camera, and the film wasn't ruined, she might not need the net. The clouds broke open and patches of blue sky appeared, the sun shining off of the eyepieces.

"No camera." Jerome rubbed the lenses on his shirt and they sat, waiting for Drake to appear. Through the binoculars, the mother swan's feathers were ragged and splashed gray with mud. The father ruffled his feathers and pulled his wings up high. The clouds closed again and a storm moved in. The wind picked up and blew a light rain into their faces. They hid under a tree and watched the female stay near her nest with the cygnets. The father paced back and forth. When the rain stopped, a misty steam rose off the pond.

"Look," Jerome said. Two giant ravens sat in the ponderosa pine tree that had once been her giant. That time was gone, but the danger stayed, especially for the trumpeters. If there had been any more eggs, the ravens would sink their dark beaks through the shells and suck the tiny cygnets right out.

"Too many natural dangers," Lilly said.

"Life inside a swan egg isn't exactly safe after all," Jerome muttered.

An eerie feeling crept over Lilly. They weren't the only ones in the swamp's haze. She heard a stick break. She heard someone breathing. A rough, dark smell made the hair on her arms stand tall. The smell curled her stomach and made her want to run. It was the same one she'd smelled the day the swans were slaughtered, the day her mother was shot, the day Pa was…the day Pa was indisposed.

A nearby deer raised her head, looked around with darting eyes, and bound off toward the hills. Lilly's knees went slack. Darkness came over her. She turned in time to see some green cloth move behind the bushes.

"Jerome," she whispered, "someone's here."

He nodded and put a finger to his lips.

Her stomach was ice cold.

On the other side of the marsh, Dean Drake stepped out of the bushes, walked close to the nest, and bent down to the water. The female scooted off with her babies across the pond. The male flapped his wings in fury, lifting them over his back and raising his chest out of the water. He jutted his bill out and hissed at the foe.

Having found what he was looking for, Drake turned his back on the swan, swaggered to the bushes, and disappeared. The male moved close to the female and their babies, trumpeting out loud noises, bellowing a counter menace, warning the threat gone. The ravens took flight, cawing and scratching at the air. The leaves shifted in the wind and another stick cracked. Then nothing. Just dark, frightening silence. Lilly's stomach hit her throat.

"Let's go," Jerome said.

She nodded and looked up. Sitting on a rock in the bushes, Dean Drake stared straight at them, holding her father's camera.

# 11

They rode as fast as they could to Jerome's ranch, the rain kicking up again and soaking their skin. Bursting through the door of Charlie's shop, they found him with his feet up on the wooden desk, reading one of Jerome's mechanic's magazines. A half-mended chair sat on a workbench along the back wall of the shop. A fire smoldered in the corner stove where a tiny wisp of smoke escaped the vent.

Charlie looked up from the magazine. "Where have you kids been?"

"At the Cattail Marsh," Lilly said.

He lifted one eyebrow at Jerome. "You following her ways now? I expect you to teach her right from wrong, even if her parents already taught her and she is old enough to figure it out for herself."

"Sorry Dad." Jerome hung his head.

"Don't 'sorry' me. You've got a head on your shoulders, use it."

"Not him. Me. *I* was at the pond," Lilly blurted. "Dean Drake was there, watching me. I told Jerome and he said we should tell you." She twisted her hands together and looked at Mr. West to see if he believed her.

He sat up in his chair and leaned forward. "First, it's no good you wandering around out there. Second, I talked to Drake, found him near the pass. He admits he was out to the marsh early that day your Pa was killed. That's how he got there so fast when your mom stopped breathing. He heard the commotion, and followed the ambulance. You might have seen him out there because he was out there. He saw a group of hunters, no one he recognized. He thinks one of them must have accidentally shot your parents."

"You talked to him?" A black cloud filled Lilly's head. "Why didn't you tell me? And why wouldn't the person who shot them just come forward then and say 'I shot a man, it was an accident?'"

"That person is probably scared. Or maybe doesn't know he hit someone. I'll keep looking for him, but there is no guarantee that I'll find him, especially if he's not from the valley."

"No. It was Drake." She balled her fists at her side, beads of sweat forming on her forehead. The heat in Charlie's shop reminded Lilly of Running Bear's lodge; only here it was penned up in a smaller space, without an ounce of kindness in it. "I don't know why you won't believe me. There's more."

He cocked his head at Lilly.

"I saw him pick up Pa's camera today."

"You're sure it was the camera?"

"There will be pictures. Drake could be in the background."

"Could be. Like I said, he admits to being out there."

"There might be a picture of him pointing his shotgun at Pa."

"I'll find him and ask him about the camera. No reason he wouldn't just hand it over if he has it. Now you run along home and do some extra chores. Make your ma proud."

"My ma would want the man who shot them to pay for what he did." Sadness welled up in her throat. The truth was she wasn't sure if Nell would want Drake to pay, or if she'd believe that Drake shot them. For all Lilly knew, her mother would come back to herself, start talking and still think Drake was basically a good guy who was confused.

Charlie nodded thoughtfully. "I suppose she would."

His face softened and when Lilly saw it, she wanted so badly to cry. "I want him gone," she finally managed to say. "I want him to never have existed."

Then Charlie West smiled that terrible smile again, the one that made her feel small and insignificant. He still didn't believe her. "We all want the person who did this brought to justice."

His tone was empty and left Lilly's chest feeling hollow and bitter. She narrowed her eyes. "I smelled him today, that same sour smell from the day of the shooting." She twisted her hands again and they turned red and raw, like hands that had just gutted a deer. "He knows I saw him shoot my parents," she said. "You're right. He's after me."

"Lilly, of course you'd be scared witless at the marsh by yourself." He raised his eyebrows at Jerome. "If you were out there by yourself, which I don't quite believe. You lost your father at that marsh. You heard his accusations about Dean Drake. You're putting those two things together in the same box where they don't necessarily belong. If it was Drake, and it was an accident, I'm not sure what kind of time he'll serve. There's no way to make sense of accidents. If you ask me, not even God gets why things go awry."

"It wasn't an accident." Outside she heard Pearl trumpeting a danger alarm. A wisp of smoke looking like a ghostly Pearl joined her in that sweltering room. Her chest wound was no longer swollen and the blood on her feathers had faded to pink. Although she knew Pearl was in her pen and not next to her, Lilly felt certain that part of the big bird had crossed through the wall to comfort her. "This is the one thing I can do for Pa and Nell. Drake is going to suffer, one way or another."

Charlie shook his head. "Don't test me on this."

"He's acting innocent and he's not!"

"I'll take care of it."

Lilly turned and stomped out. Jerome followed. "You're not going back out there," he said.

"Got to get my net up," she said.

"Can't capture anything without someone to pull the other end."

"You're so smart."

"You're so stubborn! You can't stop him by yourself."

"I got to. There's no one to help me." Her body suddenly ached, like the flu had set in. She wanted Dean Drake to hurt the way that she hurt. She wanted him to know pain right at the center of his being, right where his heart should've been.

"But Dad said he'd talk to him about the camera. He can get it back." Jerome took her hand. She didn't want to admit it but the warmth of it calmed her.

"Jerome, go back out there with me."

"You heard my dad. I'll never be allowed to leave home again. How about we go get the net on Saturday, after things quiet down?"

"He's out there now, and I'm going."

Jerome leaned his bike against the shed near Pearl's pen and folded his arms. Pearl lay in the grass and her long neck stretched on the ground. Her feathers looked matted and rough, graying at the edges. She barely lifted her head at the sound of them approaching.

"She's sick," Lilly said, opening the gate. "You didn't tell me."

"I didn't know," Jerome said. "She was fine this morning."

Moisture pasted the downy feathers to her head and her eyes were glassy, milky. Lilly sat beside her and felt the slow beat of her heart. "She's dying."

"That can't be. She was fine earlier." He looked panicked.

But Lilly knew she was right. She could feel Pearl's soul hovering above her body, barely attached, too weak to rally and sing her last song. Jerome ran off and came back with his father.

Charlie knelt in the pen next to the sick trumpeter. Moments before, they had argued. Now they were on the same side to help this precious, frail trumpeter, and Lilly felt glad for the help. Charlie lifted Pearl's head, searching her eyes, and gently laid it back in the grass. He picked up her feet and spread her webbed toes. He pulled the feathers away from her healed wound.

"She's eaten something bad," he said, one of his eyes twitching, looking at her food dish. Lilly followed his gaze. A greasy film covered a small circle of the feed.

"Do you think she's been poisoned?" Lilly pointed to the dish.

Charlie looked closer, shrugged his shoulders and took the dish out of the pen. He returned with fresh water. Cupping the water and holding it at her bill, he attempted to pour it into her throat. It spilled uselessly to the ground.

"Hold her head up so I can pour the water down her throat," he said.

Lilly shook her head. "She'll drown."

"We've got to wash the poison out of her system. Water will help. If she's got an ounce of life left in her, her natural survival instincts will kick in." He looked at Lilly. She saw a softness there that she didn't recognize. "Go on now, hold her head for me."

Lilly held Pearl's fragile neck straight. As soon as Charlie poured water into her throat, her muscles tightened and she sat up tall, fiercely pecking at him with her flat black bill. She lifted her wings looking like a royal bird, ready to fly.

# 12

Anna left for work when Lilly got home from Jerome's ranch. Nell was sleeping and Lilly sat on the edge of her bed. She wrapped her arms around her mother's shoulders, wanting to tell her mother about how sick Pearl had been, that she'd eaten something poisonous, had probably been poisoned, something Lilly suspected Drake had thrown on her feed.

Lilly wanted Nell to get up, to hold her, and reassure her that everything she loved would not die. She wanted Nell to tell her that Pearl would be fine and so would she. Lilly wanted her mother back. She wanted her to talk and to laugh again, to scold Lilly and tell her what to do and what not to do. She wanted Nell, alive and well, baking bread and tilling the garden, riding the brown mare to gather her up from her misbehaviors.

But Nell did none of these things. She didn't open her eyes when Lilly's tears soaked her chest. She didn't move a hand to wipe the tears away or move her mouth to tell her it would be OK, or walk her into the kitchen to help with dinner. Nell lay peacefully in her bed in the Mission Valley, but clearly she was somewhere else.

She awoke only briefly in the late afternoon to use the chamber pot and to eat some hot grains. Lilly spoon-fed the cereal to her mother like Nell must have done with Lilly when she was a baby. She stayed by her mother's side until she fell fast asleep again. The sun came out, and it shone through the flowered curtains Nell had made, lighting her cheeks. Lilly touched them gently. "I'm not going to let him get to you too," she whispered to her mother.

She thought about the strength she'd felt in her legs while riding her bicycle. She wanted to give that strength to Nell. She wanted to ride with her mother again, but Nell could barely get to the chamber pot, even with Lilly helping. Moving the blanket away from Nell's body she picked up her legs and pushed them in a motion as if she rode a bicycle. Nell opened her eyes and looked at something above her. She did not resist Lilly, or the pressure she put on her legs. They were noodle loose and Lilly kept going, counting the repetitions, first one leg and then the other, trying to get her muscles to take hold and work.

After twenty repetitions on each leg, she pulled the blanket up close to Nell's chin. Her mother closed her eyes and rested peacefully. At a loss of what to do next, Lilly rummaged around the room, looking for something useful, although she didn't really know what she wanted other than for Nell to be fully in control again, other than to hear her father's voice in the barn where his brown mare waited for his return.

She found one of Pa's brown work shirts and his brown coveralls. They were way too big so she rolled up the pant legs so they wouldn't trip her. Outside, in the barn she fed the mare. The horse stared at her and neighed before she ate her oats, as if saying that she missed him too.

While the mare ate, Lilly took Pa's shotgun down off the wall. Eleven-year-olds had no business with a shotgun. But then eleven was a time of courage. Good or bad. Trying to remember what Pa had told her about using the shotgun, she loaded it. She'd only pull the trigger if she needed to, if she was in grave danger, if it was her or him. And she'd aim high. To scare him.

No. She had no business with a shotgun and she knew it.

She put extra shells in her pocket and strapped the shotgun to her bike. When the mare finished eating, she brushed her out. "I won't let Pa's killer go free," she promised as she brushed. The mare rubbed her nose against Lilly's shoulder, and she felt the soft invitation, inviting her to ride. But Lilly was scared of horses. And the mare was huge. Plus, it didn't seem right, riding on Pa's horse without him.

Instead, she rode her bike back to the marsh. Like a hunter, she sat quietly by a tree with the shotgun across her lap. The net was right where she'd left it. The late afternoon sun was hot, and it dried the land.

Lilly missed her parents. Sadness crept up and surged through her veins. Tears caressed her face like the old friends they'd become, leaving her limp and ragged as an old doll. She closed her eyes. Maybe it wouldn't hurt so badly if she didn't look at the world going on as if nothing horrible had happened. The trumpeter sitting near her babies, muskrats swimming, baby mallards paddling after their mother, the long grasses and tree branches bending in the wind all went on unchanged by her father's death.

Closing her eyes felt good. It might be OK to sleep, just for a minute.

In that sleep she dreamed of a brilliant white trumpeter, spreading her velvet wings over her, holding Lilly quietly in the milk-light cave of her feathers. She woke to the trumpeter's trilling. In the nest, a downy white head popped out from under the mother's wing, and then another.

One by one she saw all six cygnets cuddling with their mother. She leaned the shotgun against the tree and crawled on her stomach to get closer, scooting across the grasslands like a water snake. The twigs and branches of the nest backed up to a half circle of bushes, guarding them from intruders. A friendly frog splashed at the edge of the water and the fuzzy cygnet heads perked up at the sound, eyes wide as they looked at the world. They scooted across the water toward her, and raced back to the safety of their mother. They ventured out again, splashing the water, dipping their heads and coming up with pondweed. The sun glittered off their backs as they settled back down. A tall maple rustled in the wind above them. Ripples from their tiny bodies spread across the water.

This is love, Lilly thought. Nell? Pa? She imagined her mother could see anything from where she slept, and Pa could see everything from wherever he was. Know this, she said to her parents, your Lillian has been blessed by swans.

Thank you. Thank you.

Keeping low, her belly close to the ground, she backed away from the pond. Her purpose for being at the marsh evaporated like misty rays on water. She leaned against the tree and remembered what Nell had said: never ever shun a blessing. The sun had sunk near the western hills and sent a blast of brilliant pink across the sky. Something close to forgiveness settled over Lilly. She could go home. Maybe she could go back to school in the fall. Maybe things would somehow be OK.

But then she couldn't find Pa's shotgun. She had leaned it and her bicycle against the large ponderosa pine. She went from tree to tree looking for the shotgun. She plodded through the long grasses, waded though the cattails.

The trumpeters trilled. The male lifted his wings, charged at the water, and ran back to the nest. He paced back and forth, throwing his black bill into the air, protecting his young. Lilly hated herself for upsetting him, but she couldn't go home without that shotgun. It had been Pa's prize possession, a gift from Horse Child.

When he was young, he hunted with that shotgun. She had watched him clean it a dozen times. She had to find it. She couldn't lose another part of her father.

Over the male's trumpeting, she heard leaves rustling. Overhead a flurry of crows cawed. A hawk flew. She caught a whiff of that rank odor and saw a flash of green jacket in the long grass on the other side of the swamp. She heard the blast as if in a dream, not believing this could be happening again. She ran hard through the water, toward the babies. The water pushed her back toward the bank and the bushes scratched her legs. She tripped and fell into the mud.

Drake captured the yearling trumpeter he had just shot. He caught it in the net Lilly had hidden, and pulled it out of the water. He looked at her with his frosty green eyes. "Thank you, ma'am," he said, lifting the net in a salute. Then he was gone.

Lilly ran, pond water spilling out of the rolled-up legs of Pa's coveralls. She had to stop him. But she couldn't do it by herself. She had to tell someone. The thought hit her gut like the shot that Drake had just fired: there wasn't anyone to tell. Anna was working, Nell couldn't stay awake, and Pa, well, Pa was nowhere. Even if it was possible, she couldn't tell Pa that Drake probably took his shotgun. She couldn't tell Pa that Drake had just killed another swan and took it away in his net.

When she reached her bicycle, she saw the shotgun leaning against the back tire. Her hands shook as she tied it to the fender. The hunter had had Pa's shotgun in his hands, and he had killed another swan. Had he killed it with her father's shotgun? She didn't know. But yes, of course he had.

Lilly rode so hard her legs ached and her lungs burned. The wind blew the rank smell right past her. As dusk settled, the sound of hooves on rocks followed the low screech of an owl. Dark shapes flew and something scrambled through the forest. She pedaled even faster, her legs stronger than her missing heart had ever been, the dust of courage flying in the wind.

---

That night she dreamed about her father. He wore the same coveralls she had hung on a chair to dry, water stains still creeping up the pant legs. He chastised her for going to the marsh alone, said if she was going to go out there, she was to go with someone. He sat down and told her this story:

"There was once a fragile young girl who had been struck with a sickness of the blood. The illness made her weepy and tender. One night she crawled into her mother's arms and asked her mother how long she would live. Her mother, a wise woman, told the girl that she would live a long time, longer than all the tulips in the garden, longer than the blooming lilac, long enough to see the trumpeter swans through many seasons. She would live to see her children born, and their children born. The girl settled down and slept. She woke to find bandits in her home and her mother gone.

"The girl wept and wept. Because the summer heat had begun and her tears dried before they reached her cheeks, the townspeople thought she was happy and that she had worked a spell to make her mother disappear. The girl sat lonely and alone through the days, wondering where her mother had gone. Finally, the minister came and told the girl that they had found her mother in the woods. The bandits had murdered her mother. The minister was sorry.

"The girl's sickness rose up in her blood and she fell very ill. On the night that she was sure she'd die, a large ghostly swan flew into her room and held the girl in her wings and sang a soft song. The girl became stronger. Her voice started to sound like her mother's. Each night the swan held her and sang to her. Soon the girl sang with the swan.

"The swan rocked the girl to sleep every night until the girl's eighteenth birthday, a birthday that no one in the town thought the girl would see. The girl celebrated by climbing a mountain, enjoying the new strength in her legs. She returned that night to tell the swan what she had done. In place of the swan stood the girl's mother. The girl fell to her knees and cried at her mother's feet. Her mother touched her hair with a white hand and floated away.

"The girl's blood turned richly pure and she lived to have many children and many more grandchildren."

Pa finished telling his story and looked at Lilly. "Your mother will be fine. She'll come through this," he said, looking back toward the mountains as if searching for something that would help Nell talk again.

———

Lilly woke up sweating, the room sweltering hot. The bed swam under her and the wind blew in through an open window. The quilt pressed down, trapping her just this side of the dream where her father had lived. Downstairs she could hear Anna in a cleaning frenzy. She pulled herself out of bed and went downstairs, her nightgown hanging to her knees.

"What are you doing?" Lilly asked.

"Getting rid of Pa's things," Anna said.

"You're throwing out his pictures!"

"They mean nothing to him now."

"Stop! That's all we have left of him."

Anna wore a brown calf-length skirt and a striped sweater. Her hair hung to her shoulders and she hadn't yet combed it. "I'm tired of feeling bad. He's not here and it's time to move on." She had a box in her hands, and moved toward the fireplace with it. The fire was huge, giant-sized for such a summer morning. The box held the entire collection of Pa's photos.

"Stop it!" Lilly said. "It's only been two months."

"Two months of forever." Anna lifted the box to throw it.

"No!" Lilly dove at her, grabbing the box with both hands, pressing her palms and fingers into it with the grip of a wolverine. She spun around, putting her back to the fire.

"Stop that," Anna said, her voice high-pitched and strange. "Move."

Lilly backed toward the fire. Her braids had grown long over the year since Pa and Lilly had climbed over the pass, since Pa first made his fatal promise to take her out to see the swans for her eleventh birthday. They reached down to the middle of her back. During the night they had come loose and she felt the heat on her hair as if it might ignite at any minute. She raised her elbows like the great wings of a wild swan and she puffed her chest. "If they go into the flames, I'm going with them," she said.

"Get away from there now."

Anna pulled on the box and Lilly tightened her grip. Her fingers ached. Anna yanked her forward so that her elbows straightened and her body spun sideways to the fire, but she didn't let go. A sound came from their mother's room. Nell coughing.

Or trying to move.

"Nell would never approve of this," Lilly said. "He was my father too!"

Anna yanked the box hard and, as if in slow motion, it slipped out of Lilly's fingers into the air above. It floated there, suspended in time, time slowing down. The box landed a fair distance from the fire, pictures spilling everywhere, Pa and Nell looking up at them, wondering what the girls fought over. Lilly rescued handfuls of them, as many as she could, gathering them frantically in her nightgown and covering them like precious gold, then stuffing them into the box.

Anna grabbed the ones Lilly couldn't reach in time and threw them into the flames. A wild demon had crawled into her sister, and Lilly didn't recognize her. Dumbfounded, her mouth hanging open, she watched the pictures blacken and disintegrate, the memories fluttering piece by piece in the smoke.

───────────

When Anna went to work, Lilly put the box of rescued photos under their bed. She'd find a safe place for them later. First, she went to her mother, who lay quietly under her quilt, eyes closed, lost in her silent world, unaware of her daughters' fight. Lilly was glad that Nell missed the fight. She imagined Nell on her bicycle. She moved her legs in the circular motion as if she were riding around town or up the hill to the pass. She had increased the repetitions to thirty per leg, two or three times a day, hoping Nell's muscles would grow strong again.

When Lilly finished she rubbed her mother's legs with a lotion that she had made from goose fat. Nell opened her eyes for the event and stared at the ceiling, noticing something there, something completely invisible to Lilly. Lilly was certain that if she could just find her swan vision, she could see it too, and maybe even join her mother there in that other world. Maybe even see Pa there. But her swan vision fell flat and ignored her calls.

After she made sure Nell was settled, she rode over to Jerome's. She cooed softly to let Pearl know that she was there, and walked into her pen with the box of Pa's rescued pictures. Pearl lifted her head, looking sad and mournful, as if she too had just lost her father. She hadn't touched her food and the water dish was still full. A sour smell filled the shed and Lilly knew something was still wrong.

Continuing to coo softly, she moved closer. The box was a bright gold color and the swan pulled her head away from it. Exerting great effort Pearl got up off the straw and shied away from Lilly toward the far wall, turning her chest into the small beam of sunlight that came through the shed door. A small lump swelled up and out, just under her wing feathers. She had gotten an infection in the wound again, probably because one of the pellets was still lodged under her skin. Maybe because the poison she'd eaten had weakened her system.

Lenore knocked on the gate. She wore a tan dress that gathered at the waist, flared out and hung to the middle of her tall boots. Her hair was piled on her head in curls and she had the look of a city woman, oddly out of place on a Montana ranch. Lilly quickly buried the box of photos in the straw. Lenore came through the gate with a wet rag and some cleaning solution for Lilly.

"I thought she didn't seem right," Lenore said. "But she won't let anyone near her, even weak as she is she put up quite a fuss."

"I'll clean it out good today and tomorrow."

"I'm not sure if she'll let even you close."

"Doesn't look like she's got much strength to refuse it. I don't think she'll be able to fight off that infection unless that pellet surfaces and I can get it out of there."

"Can I do anything?"

Lilly shook her head. Pearl would be easier to manage if it was just the two of them. She didn't like people, and Lilly guessed no one told her that she was a person. "Are you going somewhere?" Lilly asked.

"Over to visit Nell. She might like to see an old friend. Plus I don't like her to be alone so much. While you're here with Pearl, I'll be at the house with Nell."

Lilly thought about telling Lenore about how weak Nell was

when it came time for her stand, that she'd been bicycling her legs to make her strong. She thought about asking Lenore for help. She thought about it and then thought that she'd probably just think she was crazy to worry about Nell riding a bicycle when she could barely stand.

"She won't know you're there," Lilly said.

Lenore tilted her smile. "She'll know. I'll be leaving shortly. Let me know if you need anything."

"Where's Jerome?"

"He's here. I'll send him out to help."

"I don't really need help, but thanks."

Lenore nodded and Lilly watched her leave, a sad feeling in her stomach, glad she was going to be with Nell. The morning clouds cleared and the sun shone bright on the ponds. A light wind ruffled the young trumpeter's feathers.

Setting the bucket of water and the rag aside, she took out a folding knife and moved closer to Pearl. She had to cut that wound open to clean out the infection. Pearl lifted her wings, drooping the left one, and pulled away, but she had nowhere to go. She had cornered herself in the shed. Her eyes looked glassy and far away, much like Nell's eyes.

When Lilly moved closer to Pearl, she pecked at her with her black bill and caught her shoulder. It hurt like someone had just nailed her with a rock. She sat just out of her range and sang to her. Pearl went quiet. After about ten minutes she settled and Lilly moved closer again. This time Pearl pressed herself up against the wall but didn't strike out. Lilly waited and moved close enough to pet her warm feathers. They were too warm. She looked up, her rheumy eyes sleepy and dull.

"It's gonna be OK," Lilly said as she moved the feathers away from the injury. The big bird didn't like that and hit Lilly again with her bill.

"Ouch," Jerome said. "Looks like that hurt. I thought I'd watch, unless, of course, I can help." He stood in the doorway of the shed in a cotton sweater and brown shorts. She hadn't heard him come in but she was glad he was there. Pearl was not going to let her close enough to drain that wound. It hurt to admit it, but she did need help.

"Can you get behind her and hold her?" Lilly asked, just like Pa had asked her to do when they cut the young trumpeter free last fall.

"Not with that chest wound," he said, his eyes wide. "She'll never stand for it."

"You'll have to hold her low on her belly."

"She'll clip us both with her wings."

"She's weak." Lilly smiled. "And you are strong."

"I must be crazy." He moved around behind Pearl and talked softly to her. She was worn out with nowhere to go. Once Jerome captured her wings, Lilly cut into and pressed the wound. Pearl winced and pulled back into Jerome, then went limp. Playing dead was the one thing she probably thought could save her.

Pus spilled out onto her feathers. A shiny silver pellet sat in the middle of the puss. After washing the area really well Lilly put the salve on it. The more of the infection she could kill from the outside, the sooner the wound would heal.

When they finished Lilly put the bucket aside and they sat with Pearl. The majestic swan slept in fits and starts, lifting her head quickly and then dropping it slowly back to the straw. Lilly wondered how long it would take her to have a somewhat normal life again. She could see Jerome watching her from his seat in the straw, probably wondering the same thing about her.

---

The next day she retrieved the box of photos from Pearl's shed and tied it, a towel and a box of matches to her bicycle and rode to the mountain camp where she'd found Charlie West earlier that year. The fire ring was still there in the middle of the pine trees. From the clearing she gazed at the valley below, identifying the dotted ponds of the marsh. She found the old mine tunnel that she saw that day and climbed inside. The tunnel smelled damp and musty and she waited for her eyes to adjust. A pile of dead branches, dry and brittle, had been stacked along an edge of the tunnel. They had likely been there a long time. The walls were rough, ragged edged dirt, dirt that could crumble quickly and close off the opening.

A tight twinge flipped over in her stomach as she found a perfect hiding spot for the photos. Near the dark passage two boulders leaned into each other like sweethearts. She wrapped the photos and the matches in the towel and tucked them between the rocks.

When she came out of the tunnel, a smoky haze hung in the trees from a forest fire burning in the distance. Before she got off the trail, near her home, smoke poured in, covering the mountains like the misty dead. She looked for her father in the silky haze. But he was nowhere. He was gone, like the fledgling they'd cut free from the nightshade last fall was gone, which was just a way of saying he was dead without saying he was dead.

# 13

Late into that summer smoke from the distant forest fires continued to cover the valley. Lilly wandered back and forth in that smoke, from the Mission Mountains to the Cattail Marsh to the mountains again, fearing that the killer would show up somewhere and she'd miss him. She didn't take Pa's shotgun again. She made a sling shot like Jerome's, as if that could help her in any real trouble, and she carried a large stick to go after Drake if he got too close to the swans or tried to shoot more people.

She was only eleven, just a fledgling herself, but the weight of adulthood pressed against her. She imagined her webbed feet and her feathers flat. As she rode her bicycle the wind blew her sun-whitened hair away from her face. She pedaled harder than she had strength, but the strength came. She wanted to take some of it home and offer it up to her mother like a bouquet of wild flowers.

Her legs had grown so strong she could climb a tree or a mountain. Wild animals didn't scare her, feeling half wild herself. If she ran into a moose or a bear, she'd test her speed along with her strength. And if the animal was faster than Lilly, maybe she would have a visit with God and ask Him, just what are the rules now? Why did Pa die?

At times she'd sense something just over her shoulder, a noise creeping through the woods—a bear, maybe, or a ghost. The killer ran renegade through her thoughts. In her mind, she clearly saw his steely green eyes, as cold as winter tunnels.

By fall the cygnets in the Cattail Marsh had grown into awkward gray birds almost as big as the adults. They flapped their gangly wings hard, trying to fly. They ran, jumped and landed a few feet away. In September the adult male waddled out of the water and fluttered his wings, then tucked his nose under first one wing, then the other, and across his back. He preened himself in this way for a few minutes while the sun dried his white feathers. Then he stretched his long neck out and raised his wings. He ran, lifting and lowering them, making a great swooshing sound, and again, until, in a great moment of glory, he took to the air.

He flew out past the marsh and back toward his family. He circled the fledglings while his mate swam the edges of the pond. He landed next to her. They floated in unison to one end of the pond, turned and ran back across the water, lifted their great wide wings against the wind and, together, they took flight, a great white expanse against the blue sky. The adult pair glided back down to the marsh and landed with grace. They had regained their flying feathers.

Lilly longed to go with them, to soar freely above the land, to sleep with her mother, to be gone with her father, to leave this world behind, to return in the spring when the marsh came out of its dim winter light into brightness and new growth. If she could fly, she could find Pa sitting on a rock somewhere or maybe in a cloud. He'd be there waiting for her, smoking his pipe, his camera in hand, shined up, all problems fixed.

Each day the adults flew and the fledglings tried to follow. The young swans swam back and forth flapping their wings and trumpeting desperately to their parents, afraid of being left behind. Near the end of September, one particularly large and stubborn fledgling ran, made a real leap of faith. He landed a good twenty feet away from where he'd started. He swam restlessly back and forth across the water, then waddled onto the muddy shoreline and out toward the Ponderosa Pine that had once been Lilly's giant. He ran on his spider-thin legs in the same way that Lilly had pedaled her bicycle, quick and sharp, then in great long strides, his wings flapping fiercely. His black webbed feet barely splashed the water. His gray chest puffed with swan breath, he lifted his wings. The wind came up under them and he flew.

He circled the marsh three times and landed with a clumsy splash. Lilly laughed quietly and put her hands together in a prayer of thanks, grateful to see a four-month-old trumpeter take his first flight. Something good had happened. Maybe this bad time in their lives was over. Maybe, just maybe, more good could follow.

The other cygnets surrounded the first flyer as he settled. They squawked and trumpeted, splashing the water with their wings and swimming in circles until another brave swan took a run at the wild air above him. In turn, every one of them ran and jumped for the sky. They persevered until, one day in early October, Lilly rode her bike out to the marsh and they were gone.

———————

The swans were not all that had vanished from the valley that fall. Lilly still carried her slingshot, her father's folding knife, and her stick with her, but she hadn't seen Drake since late summer. She began to doubt herself. Maybe he had shot her parents by accident. She wondered if she'd really seen him that day where she thought she'd seen him. Had she really attacked him? Had it really been his blood she'd washed out from under her fingernails in Lenore West's kitchen sink the day her father died? Maybe it was a different errant hunter she'd watched make that terrible mistake.

In early November, before the snow fell in earnest, she biked out to the marsh for one last chance to catch a glimpse of Drake. If he'd be anywhere in the valley, he'd be where the swans made their summer home. Maybe doing the same thing Lilly was doing. Maybe he, too, was looking for that jagged white line in the sky where a flock of swans headed south for the winter. The day was dark, the gray clouds hanging low in the sky. A swan had come in over the night and she found him in the marsh, the marsh icing up in the wind. The trumpeter was water-locked and swimming a small circle inside of the encroaching ice.

In the fall, Pa had told her, swans take their time going south. They fly casually and stop often, visiting several different feeding spots along the way. One swan will lead the flock for a while, then drop back and allow another swan to lead. They fly in loose lines near the tops of the mountains. Some trumpeters fly higher than the others, or off to one side, never forming the migration V of some flocks. If the sky is clear and you try, Pa had said, you'll see them. If the clouds are too low just open your ears and you'll hear their trumpeting.

When he was a young man, just before Anna and Lilly were born, Pa had rescued a lone swan trapped by thick winter ice. He said he always took more chances than he should have. "Don't you be like me," he had told her. The swan had swum in circles, trying to keep the encroaching ice at bay. The frigid wind blew through the pines and, no matter how hard the swan worked, the circle of clear water got smaller and smaller. Without help, the ice would eventually surround her and she'd die there, frozen in the pond.

Pa stepped gingerly out on the slick surface. It held. He took another step, which also held, each step a testament to courage. Or stupidity, he'd said. About ten steps out he heard the ice crack. He got down on his belly and scooted across the frozen pond toward the trapped trumpeter. The ice broke and Pa fell through. The natural tendency of most people would be to struggle to get out, but Pa had been to hunters' safety classes at the fire hall. He did what the firemen had taught him. He didn't struggle, he simply put his bare hands on the ice and they held him there.

The swan trumpeted loudly, making quite a racket. She flapped her good wing, swam up next to Pa and away, trying to keep the water clear for him too. With his hands stuck to the ice and nearly frozen, he tried to pull himself out of the water. Each time he put weight on the ice, it broke. Each time he was slightly closer to the shoreline. Frozen to the bone, he knew he would not last long in that water. Pa started yelling, just in case someone was around. He had always been lucky, he'd said, a funny look in his eye. That day luck was his friend, Charlie West, who happened to be riding his horse into town.

Charlie came over to see what the noise was about and found Pa shivering and blue in the Cattail Marsh. He got off his horse and threw a rope to Pa, who grabbed hold of it and continued to break his way through the ice. Meanwhile Charlie hit the ice with the butt of his rifle and broke large chunks away from the shore. Once Pa got close enough, Charlie looped the rope around his saddle horn and directed his horse to pull him out of the water.

Once Lilly's father was back at the ranch safe and warm, Charlie gathered a group of men and they rescued the swan. They set up a shelter for it in an old chicken coop near a pond on Charlie's ranch where it lived until it died many years later.

A thought rushed into Lilly's head, reckless and forlorn: If she could free this swan perhaps her father would come back to her. She was his daughter and the swan needed Lilly like she needed her father. And she was still eleven, the magical age when she could make anything happen. She looked around and found a big rock to throw onto the ice. It popped right through creating a perfect hole, which was a beginning. She dragged a fallen pine branch over and heaved it toward the edge of the frozen water.

The swan spooked and flapped his wings, trying to fly, still going in circles and never getting off the pond. Another rock did the trick. A clear path of water opened up, creating a nice little runway for the bird to escape the invading ice. Lilly backed up, sat by the pine tree, and waited. Before long he took the pathway out of the water, running his black leathery feet across dry land and flapping his wings. He took the second chance Lilly had given him and, without returning Lilly's father, he flew away.

---

Winter approached, more dark clouds moved in, snow fell and Lilly had plenty of time to think, to consider, to go over and over the day in the Cattail Marsh when her father died. She tried, but couldn't get it out of her mind. The day itself pulled at her, begging, no, demanding her attention, until Lilly realized her doubts had stirred up and strengthened her obsession with Dean Drake.

She put her doubts aside and the memory grew softer. She knew what she knew. Regardless of what Charlie West or anyone else said, she knew that she had seen Dean Drake shoot her father. She saw it with her own eyes, if not from the arms of a giant, then from the branches of a Ponderosa Pine. She had hidden in the tree and she had watched him approach. She jumped on him just as the shots rang out, too late to save her father, too late to keep Nell from being hurt. She jumped on him and he shot them anyway.

Lilly saw his steely green eyes, his black greasy hair, his stiff dirty pants, his shotgun tucked to his shoulder, his green bag spilling over with feathers. Dean Drake took aim and pulled the trigger. No accident about it. And just like that she was back to knowing that if Charlie West didn't stop Dean Drake she would.

As she walked down Mission's snow covered street to the hardware store she promised her father, wherever he was, that she would stop Drake from hurting anyone else. Pa had kept his promise to take Lilly out to the Cattail Marsh to see the trumpeter swans on her birthday and it had killed him.

"Where do you think Drake is?" she asked the air, as if her father really was somewhere nearby and he could hear her, as if he'd give a sign that he knew the answer. "I've got swan eyes," she said. "I can see you looking down from the sky and I know that you're trying to protect me."

*Lilly, you have got to stop lying*, Pa said, appearing beside her. His shoulders drooped and his eyes were glazed and vacant. He looked so sad.

Shocked that she had summoned her father, she didn't want him to be any sadder, so she told another lie. "I will, Pa. I'll stop lying."

*Remember this,* he said. *Nothing good comes from revenge. Bring him to justice and we all get into heaven.*

"I'll remember," she said, telling yet another lie. She felt bad, summoning her father and lying to him like that, but it didn't stop her from deceiving Pa's ghostly self.

The wind changed, the clouds pulled close and claustrophobic, gray hills of fluff hiding the mountains. She thought she saw her father nod to her. She saw him disappear. Such power, swan power, the power of eleven, the true and remarkable power of love. Lilly smiled at the dark and gloomy sky, a little frightened by such powers.

———————

A long time ago Nell had told her that Lillian really meant Elizabeth. She didn't understand that at all. Why didn't they just name her Elizabeth then? Elizabeth meant God has sworn. She completely understood why they didn't name her God Has Sworn. She could never imagine teachers calling to her: "God Has Sworn Connelly, please come to the front of the room." They'd have to shorten it to something like GHS. And that, put together with her last name, made her sound like a tractor.

When she was young she was stunned to learn that God swore. Her mother cleared that up right away. She said it meant that God has promised something. She held Lilly and told her that God kept his promise to her when the swans delivered Lilly, a sweet feathery package.

Nell and Pa were so happy with her tiny feet, her little pug nose and her shiny white hair. They thanked God every day for Anna and Lilly. Nell said this mostly when Pa came home with whiskey and went to bed early. She said this through tears at first. Later, she said it after she stopped clenching her fists. Pa was a good man. She said that too.

God had kept his promise. On Lilly's eleventh birthday, Pa had kept his. Now she would keep hers. She would find Dean Drake and she would stop him from hurting others.

She walked into the hardware store, where George waited on her. He wore a flannel shirt and green wool pants, and he'd combed his hair up and back so that it rose forward like a tiny loaf of bread. His family owned the store. She'd heard him tell Anna that he wanted to buy it one day. He stood behind a horseshoe-shaped counter with a bronze cash register at one end of it and a display of ropes at the other end. Trays of candy filled one whole side of the horseshoe.

"Aren't you supposed to be in school?" he asked.

"Do you have any small link chain?" she asked, countering a question with a question, something Nell was against. She put a handful of change on the counter.

"First, let's talk about school, why aren't you there?"

"We got out early."

"Where'd you get the money for this chain?"

"Nell and Pa."

George leaned over the counter and whispered, "Lilly, liars don't get much farther than the county jail."

She squished her face. "I earned it."

"That's better. How?"

"Doing chores for Nell and Pa. Do you have the chain?"

George sighed. "When?"

"Before," she said and stopped, a word stuck in her throat. It was like a frog, wanting to hop right off of her Lilly-pad tongue. A logjam held the frog tight. That's the problem with lying. When you tell the truth, no one believes you. "Before that man shot my parents."

"Still convinced he did it on purpose?"

She looked aside. Canning jars stood on a shelf near the far wall. A bin of leftover seeds from spring overflowed under spices hung to dry on a piece of twine strung between two beams. She could smell the thyme, sage, and lemon grass, all herbs Nell used to grow in her garden. Off to the left, heavy wool coats hung in a row. Beyond them, feed bins lined the wall along with trays of hammers, wrenches, and screwdrivers.

Drake appeared in a doorway that led to the back room.

Her legs stiffened as her throat flipped backwards and closed shut. It was the first time she'd seen him since late summer. She pried her throat free.

"He's here," she whispered.

George looked toward the back. "Yeah, he comes in when he has hides to trade or sell."

"Swan hides?"

"Naw. They're illegal. We can't take them. Bear, fox, coyote. We take those."

"He shouldn't be hunting swans."

"Don't know that he does. But hungry people figure the law doesn't apply."

"He killed Pa and you do business with him."

George shook his head. "Kiddo, we don't know who shot Sam. It was a hunting accident. Sheriff says so. The investigation says so. No one hurt your parents on purpose. Just some stupid guy not paying attention. Accidents, they just happen."

This was the first she'd heard of the results of the Sheriff's investigation. None of it made sense and she asked George the same question she had asked Charlie West.

"Why doesn't the man come forward then, if it was an accident, and say he's sorry? Why doesn't he say, I'm so stupid, swans, people, they all look alike to me." She started to cry and stopped in an instant. "I can't talk to you or anyone. This was no accident. I saw the whole thing. You tell me I'm crazy. Jerome's father accuses me of lying. Well, maybe I do lie sometimes and I do feel crazy with everyone telling me I'm wrong, but I saw the whole thing!" She clenched her fists to keep them from trembling. When she could keep her hands steady, she swept the money into her palm. She stared at the back room. "Even if it was an accident, he shouldn't get away with it," she said nice and loud. "He should be thrown in the county jail until he can be more careful!"

George put his hand over Lilly's. "We all agree whoever did this should be more careful, and be held accountable. Here's the problem: You're only eleven and memory is a funny thing. Even I know that, and I didn't finish school. You have a chance here if you go to school. Your mom and dad wanted to give you a chance. Anna and me, we want you to have that chance. Go to school."

Him pairing himself with Anna like that sent an iron rod down

Lilly's back. "How much is the chain?" she asked, her voice taken over by a feeble stranger that strangled her.

"Fifteen cents."

She placed the change on the counter. George left and came back with several lengths of small link chain that he put in a bag and pushed across to her. She pulled it out and let the icy metal slide though her fingers.

"Go to school," he repeated.

She put the chain back in its bag. "See you at the house."

---

Lilly did go directly to the school, but it had already been let out for the day. So she rode over to Jerome's and found him in his dad's shop, reading a book on mechanics.

Perfect.

"Will you help me make chains for my bike tires?" She held out the sack. He'd been hunting with his father over the weekend, and she could smell the ripe deer meat hanging in the nearby barn.

"It's not that far of a walk to school and back. If winter gets really bad I'll borrow Dad's Ford and give you a ride, or we'll all stay home. Otherwise you can walk. Walking, it's good for building strong legs, good as bike riding."

"Will you help me?" She asked again. She heard the firewood cracking in the stove. Heat waves wafted off the iron like tiny ghosts.

Jerome closed the book. "Do you think you should go out to the marsh so often? You should be at school, making friends, joining the choir, being in the school play, things like that."

"You're the one who suggested I go back out there."

"I didn't mean every day."

"I go because I want to."

"You should go to school."

"You should stop trying to act so mature."

He smiled at that. "Well, I am older than you," he said. "You are my best friend and I have certain responsibilities to you."

"Like what?"

He stood up and leaned toward her, his face stopping just inches away from Lilly's. She could barely breathe. "Like keeping you out of trouble. Which is why I don't know if I should help you. I think you should leave the marsh alone."

"Sometimes I go into the mountains."

"You shouldn't be doing that either!" He took a step back.

He'd cut his own hair and it hung crooked at the top of his forehead, making him look awkward and shy. His eyes softened, his large pupils holding Lilly in their warmth. Wind sang though the shop walls. Snow had begun to fall and already embraced the windowsills. Jerome tilted his head at her with a crooked smile. For the first time in months she felt safe.

"Dean Drake was at the hardware store today," she said.

"So, he's shown up again."

She nodded.

"My dad still thinks the evidence against him is sketchy at best."

"I have to get Pa's camera back."

"The film is likely ruined by now." He reached out and took her hand in his. Warmth went up her arm and through her body, a kind warmth that she'd never felt before, something new in eleven edging toward twelve.

A sinister light from the sun behind the dark clouds poured through the shop window and the warmth evaporated.

"Please help me," she said, something breaking in her voice. She started shivering. She heard the gunshots again, and Anna's screams. She crossed her fingers behind her back with her free hand. She counted backwards from ten to make the sounds go away.

A ghostly Pearl fluttered into her peripheral vision, stretching her neck long, intent and hungry. Her white chest feathers rose and fell slowly, and she saw that the swelling had gone away completely. She watched Pearl breathe and the sound of guns and voices faded to a murmur. Lilly realized that Jerome could not see her. She'd come to help, to make the sounds go away, and she had somehow hidden herself from Jerome.

Lilly also realized that if Jerome would do this one thing for her,

her eleventh year—though more than half over—would get back to normal. Normal, that is, in how Nell defined the age of eleven: a year of wonder and awe.

Jerome let go of her hand and shook his head like something was amiss.

"Will you help me?" Lilly held her breath again and the swan breathed for her. She swallowed her fear and, strangely, Lilly felt a little a bit of magic in that. Just a little. She had some control, and oh that felt good.

"Give me the chain and come back tomorrow."

"Thank you. You are my hero," she said, hopping backwards out the door, nearly tripping over the doorstep. "I knew you'd do it."

"Tomorrow, here, after I've seen you in class."

She stopped and thought. "Class. Sure." And she was out the door.

# 14

The snow fell in large flakes now on her head and face as she left Jerome's ranch. She skipped happily through the snow toward home, leaving footprints behind her. She had an ally in Jerome. He would make the bike chains and she would cherish them.

Anna caught up to Lilly, fresh out of breath, sucking on her lower lip. She had tucked her hair under a knit hat. Under her wool coat Lilly could see the hem of Anna's apron. She must've just gotten off work at the Timberline.

"George tells me you haven't been going to school," she said. "He's very worried about you."

"He's not my dad." The words rolled off of a tongue of rust and fire, and Lilly didn't recognize her own voice.

"He cares, Lilly, and he's doing the best he can to help us. We are all doing the best we can, except you. You have to go to school." Her voice was too loud and lines formed in her forehead. She bit down so hard on her lower lip that it swelled, making her look much older than fifteen. Lilly reminded herself that Anna would be sixteen in December. "Teacher also says you haven't been to school. Pa would want you in school."

"Pa's not here to care." She saw the hurt flash in Anna's eyes, but she didn't regret her words. Neither Anna nor George had any right to tell Lilly what to do. "Besides, I have been going sometimes."

But she hadn't gone to classes in weeks. This was crazy lying, like saying the table got up and walked around the room and stole the hidden chocolate. The table ate the chocolate, not me. She didn't care. Why should she go to school when no one showed interest in the fact that she could identify the man who shot their parents? She knew who killed their father and she hated him.

*Oh, little girl, I'm not worried about the truth in this case. I'm worried about the strong emotion. If you don't turn it, it'll turn you.*

Lilly started. "Did you hear that, Anna? It sounded like Nell."

Anna looked at her with pity, the very other thing she hated.

*Not hate.*

"Nell isn't talking," her sister said. "We hope she will, but she hasn't uttered a word so far."

Anna was right. The voice was Lilly remembering.

"That yellow skirt I had?" She asked.

Anna nodded. Snow fell in light, full flakes, and it haloed her face. Behind her the clouds parted and the tips of the Mission Range had already turned perfectly white. Their jagged peaks crossed the sky. The moon had slivered over the weeks and disappeared. Even with the snow a black night would follow.

"I told Nell I hated the color yellow," Lilly said. "She called that a pretty powerful reaction to a color. She said that I could change my feelings by changing my mind. She said I could change my feelings in the same way that I changed my dress. She would tell me to go to school."

"Nell was a wise person."

"Nell *is* a wise person. I wore that yellow skirt the day she was shot. No wonder I hated yellow." The edge of town smelled like winter pines. The wind picked up. It blew snow across the fields, and into Lilly's face, pelting her with tiny bits of snow. It's sharp teeth bit her cheeks, reminding her how quickly, in less than a moment, life could change.

"You couldn't have hated the color yellow ahead of time for something that hadn't happen yet."

Lilly shrugged. "I did."

Off in the distance the Mission Church bells rang for evening mass. The wind sang a harsh harmony. The sun behind the clouds brightened as the wind once again moved the clouds across the sky, turning the powdery fluffs into strange traveling faces. She thought she saw their father's face as the wind changed and the clouds darkened again.

Anna turned away from the wind and leaned toward Lilly, a protective hand to her face. "Go to school," she said.

"Have *you* gone to school?" The blowing snow swirled into flocks of swans that flew in unreal patterns before her.

"This isn't about me. I'm working, in case you haven't noticed."

"Jerome is making chains for my bike so I can ride it to school this winter." Trusting Anna with this information might help mend the rift between them.

"Other kids walk."

"I like my bicycle."

"More than us, apparently."

"You're happy with George."

"I promised Nell I would take care of you."

Lilly knew the look on her face was a blank stupid one. Maybe even an angry one. She tried to suck the angry part back in. Minutes ago she'd wanted to get along. Anna was finally talking freely to her and she didn't want to stop her. Still, the bitter edge of her voice charged toward her sister. "Nell can take care of me herself when she gets better."

"She asked me to take care of you."

"She talks to you?"

"Baby, she doesn't talk to me now. Before she went mute, before she went into the hospital. At the marsh I promised her I would take care of you." Tears rolled down Anna's face now. They froze on her cheeks. "Before you came back with Charlie West and the others."

"What do you mean?"

"I made a promise to Nell the day she got shot."

"Are you saying that Nell was still talking when I went to town?"

Anna nodded.

"But you never told me that!"

"I thought it would hurt you, that you'd be mad at me because I sent you for help and you didn't get to be there when she spoke her last words. I thought I could tell you once she started talking again. But that's not happened. That day at the marsh she asked me to keep an eye on you. Even then, even in her pain, she was worried."

"She should be worried, but not about me. About Dean Drake. He was in the hardware store today," she said, since they were telling the truth. "He killed Pa."

"Don't start that silly stuff again. Everyone loves Mama and Pa. Sheriff says it was an accident. Says they'll find the person, hold him to task. But no one did this out of vengeance."

A dark spot grew in Lilly, darker than the passing clouds, darker than the midnight forest, darker than the moonless mountains. She bit her cheek. The copper taste of blood filled her mouth. Looking out through slits in her eyes, the world before her narrowed. "I saw what I saw."

"Why would anyone want to hurt our parents?"

"You know something I didn't know, and I know something you don't know. I'm trying to tell you. I tried telling Charlie West. No wonder I like my bike. No one will listen to me. I'm just a kid. I'm just eleven. 'Memory's a funny thing.' No wonder I don't talk to anyone. They all tell me I'm lying or I'm crazy," she said, feeling crazy. "You shoulda told me that Nell talked to you that day."

She scooped up some snow, packed a snowball and threw it as hard as she could in the opposite direction of home. Then she chased after it like a rabid dog.

———————

She ran up the pass toward the old mine tunnel where she had hidden Pa's pictures. The storm kicked up pine needles and snow spun in fast circles. The forest darkened and leaned over her like a hovering father. Memories beat so fast in her chest it made her whole body hurt. Drake coming into the marsh, the loud blast of the shotgun, swans falling, the marsh turning red and bloody, her father collapsing, the dark water splashing around Nell, Anna calling her name and sending her out for Charlie West.

She'd never been truly mad at Anna before. Anna should've told her months ago that she talked to Nell while she went for help. Anna had talked to Nell while Lilly pedaled like a wild coyote to get Charlie West. Anna got to see Nell's eyes while she talked, got to watch her lips move, got to hear her good voice as Nell told her to watch over Lilly. This knowledge carved a gully into her brain. She must never trust Anna again. And if she didn't have her sister, who did she have?

The trail steepened and the light evaporated, leaving a dull sheen on the land. Her lungs hurt. Her legs wobbled. She squinted to see. A branch dropped snow into her face. Her foot slipped on some ice and she fell, catching her arm on a jagged rock. Blood leaked out of it. She hadn't gone very far when she heard a sound coming from the hillside, a sound that sent her stomach tumbling. She picked up her pace and fell again, this time jarring her belly against a stick.

The sound got louder and filled the forest, blanketing the mountain in gray. It hid behind rocks and rumbled under the frozen creek. The sound of hooves clattered off rocks. Horses rode through the woods. No, just one horse, and not a horse, a mule. The rider rose up from the narrow valley below, so close Lilly saw the sweat beading down the brown fur of the mule. That rancid smell of dead bear settled in her lungs. Drake pulled the mule to a halt, leaned toward her, and leered, half petting his shotgun.

"OK, little Miss, you couldn't even keep some swans safe, how you going to keep a girl like yourself safe?" he asked.

She ran and stumbled over her own trembling legs, hating him and hating what he implied, that she couldn't take care of herself, that she couldn't save the swans, that she could not reach back in time and keep her father alive. But, of course, she couldn't.

"You leave me alone." Her breath ragged, her voice sounded as deep as a man's.

"Only if you leave me alone." He turned the dull-eyed mule right at her. Breath from the mule's nostrils circled up and poured over her. She ran behind a set of twin boulders, but he came around fast. She climbed and jumped off the boulders, landing hip first on the rocks below. Then she ran hard, hard as she'd ever run, ignoring the pain in her hip and looking for a place where the mule couldn't follow.

She knew that the abandoned mine tunnel where she had hidden her father's photos was somewhere nearby. But it wasn't. It was too far and Drake was too fast. He chased after Lilly, laughing like the devil. She slipped and fell face first in the snow, then got up and ran again.

"Here you go, one just for you," he said, cornering her against a cluster of rocks. He swung a dead swan at Lilly, hitting her in the arms and body with it. She closed her eyes as it hit her in the head and knocked her down. When she opened her eyes, the dead swan stared at her with thick, black eyes.

"Stop telling people I killed your dad. I don't want to hurt a kid. I'm not that kind. It would hurt Nell and I don't want to hurt Nell. I don't want to hurt you, but I will."

"You think you haven't already hurt Nell?"

"Couldn't be helped."

"She trusted you. She can't even talk now."

"She just needs to know that I'll be the one taking care of her. Then she'll talk."

"She hates you. She doesn't want you around. You killed my father!"

"Listen here. You are wrong about Nell and me. And if you make her hate me, things will not go well for you, or for your sister, or even for Nell."

"You shot him on purpose."

"For the record, I only meant to warn him. I will not go to jail. You've got a lot of power in your hands, little girl. Choose well what you will to do with it."

The ghostly Pearl, the one Lilly saw at Pa's funeral, the one she saw in Jerome's shop, flew to her side, giving her courage. She felt the strength in those great wings. Her chest boiled and Lilly wanted to fly at Dean Drake, knock him off his mule, and claw his eyes out.

"You won't get away with it," Lilly said.

"Oh, I'll get away with it. But you, if you keep talking, I'll be putting some pretty little swan feathers down your throat." He sat back in his saddle. "Do we understand each other?"

She glared at him.

"I guess we do then." He turned the mule back toward the valley.

———

Lilly knew the dead swan was there, somewhere near the rocks where Drake had pinned her and she looked for it. She had to give it some kind of burial, had to find a way of laying it to rest. With the ground frozen she couldn't possibly dig a grave. Listening again for the sound of hooves, but hearing nothing, Lilly searched for the trumpeter and a good resting place for it.

A nook in the boulders covered with pine needles sat huddled under a rock ledge. That would work. But she couldn't find the swan. Dusk deepened and the temperature dropped. Soon it would be completely dark. Barely ten feet away she saw the mound of snow and went to it. A black bill peeked up from the snowdrift.

Biting her lip, she reached down, wrapped her cold fingers around its neck and pulled it out of its early grave. The soft cotton neck was limp in her palm. It's black button eyes looked up at her. Someone had sewn on a flat black bill. Feathers of silk and wool, moth eaten and flattened by time, lined his back in a stiff icy blanket. The dead swan was a homemade stuffed animal, a gift made for some child a long time ago.

Gathering the cotton swan in her arms she ran for the mine tunnel, racing the night and her own fear. Snow froze in her braids. They swung against her cheeks, two icicles rubbing the skin raw. The ghostly Pearl kept pace beside Lilly and the toy swan. Snow piled on Pearl's feathers like a winter coat. She blended into the storm, and stayed with Lilly until she reached the mouth of the tunnel.

Inside, Lilly sat down too quickly on the hard dirt. The freezing cold bit her legs and she listened for the sound of hooves. But Drake had vanished down the mountainside and all was quiet. She felt her way to the back of the tunnel, following the frozen dirt wall to the space between the boulders where she had put the box of photos. Feeling around, she found it there, a precious treasure kept safe. She took it to the mouth of the tunnel.

When she stopped shaking, she was alone with the stuffed swan and the box of photos. Pearl had gone back to her pen at Jerome's ranch. Drake had gone down the mountain. Even the wind and snow calmed down and deserted her. Loneliness crept into her belly and crawled up her throat. Her muscles ached. She felt weak with fear. Maybe she would freeze to death and no one would find her until the spring thaw. She needed a fire.

Someone had built a fire pit at the tunnel's face. Looking around in the half-light, she found the box of matches that she'd hidden with the photos, and went to gather tree branches, keeping one ear tuned for the hunter. When she got back to the tunnel only a sliver of light remained on the western hills. Without the fire she'd be left in a pitch-black, freezing cold night. In that last light she separated photos she couldn't identify, photos of trees or mountains or grasslands, and set them on the damp ground near the fire pit. She carefully placed the other photos back in the box.

Toward the back of the cave, with her hands flat against the dirt, Lilly retraced her path and restored the box to its hidden home. The stuffed swan she left near the fire ring to keep her company. She crumpled the pictures she didn't want, placed branches over them in the shape of a tiny mountain, and lit the fire. The pictures caught the flame immediately.

With each piece of wood she added the flames grew and her bones ached. Something piqued her ears. A sound slithered toward her. Something vile and familiar scented the air, something not of the forest. She thought about the killer. She thought about the sad stuffed swan, a swan someone had made with love. She thought about all the dead swans the day he shot Pa and Nell, the gunshots, Anna screaming, Nell down but still talking. Her muscles went limp and she couldn't move.

The wind blew in on cue, a friend to the fire, and she was warm again. Her whole body ached. Months of bike riding and her legs could still go out from under her. Nell talked to Anna before she went quiet. Lilly curled herself into a ball around the stuffed swan. "Now I lay me down to sleep, I pray the Lord my soul to keep, if I die before I wake I pray the Lord my soul to take." Nell had always said that prayer with her when putting her to bed.

On the hard dirt floor of the old mine tunnel Lilly thought and thought of Nell, her proud asparagus, her cloth-wrapped Christmas presents, her canned beets, her nighttime stories, her fights with Pa, her just one glass of wine. She imagined her mother's arms around her, and, with her arms curled around someone's toy swan, Lilly cried herself to sleep.

———

The slithering sound crashed into her dreams. She tried to pull herself awake but the sound covered her mouth and held her down. It hurt. The sound attacked her face and arms. It pierced deep into her belly, a boot kicking her, a rifle butt slamming her chest. Lilly tried to wake up but a deep, dark dangerous sleep had pinned her to the ground.

Just before sunrise she heard voices and sticks snapping. The hunter had come for her at last. She dreamed it and she knew it was true. It didn't matter. Her body ached so badly from the hard cold dirt, she couldn't feel any worse. The fire had gone out. Stiff and cramped, the weakness in her legs remained, useless things, limp and fragile. Her eyes were frozen shut. The fight gone out of her.

Let him take me, she thought. Let him do with me like he did with the swans and my parents: paint the snow with my blood. Her head hurt and she couldn't move it. Maybe she had frozen into a final shape too, like the Ponderosa Pine that was her giant, like her mother asleep at home.

Maybe that's what happens just before death. Maybe Nell and Lilly would die together, the final ultimate union of mother and daughter, proving that Nell would probably talk to her too. She just hoped the killer would be quick about it. It would hurt. When it was all over and she was no longer a girl, but a spirit, she'd go to Nell and Pa and they would make it better.

Sticks exploded in the forest.

"Over here." Charlie West's voice.

"I'm coming." Jerome.

Lilly forced open her eyes. Charlie, George, Jerome and several neighbor men surrounded the mouth of the tunnel. The red sun rose somewhere above them. She looked at her arms. Fresh bruises snaked across them.

Jerome put down his rifle, took off his coat, and wrapped it around her. It felt so good, the warmth and his arms. "Crazy, crazy Lilly. We were worried sick. Come on. We've got to get you home."

Charlie picked her up, leaving the toy swan on the tunnel floor by the fire ring. No one stooped to retrieve it.

Jerome put his cheek against her forehead. "She's burning with fever," he said. "She's all beat up."

Charlie nodded, his breath a thick stifled moan.

"She must've taken a nasty fall," George said. "Or run into a wild animal." He took Charlie's rifle from him and slung it over his shoulder.

Pa arrived, took Lilly from Charlie, and carried her forever, over hills and valleys. He took her to the top of McDonald Peak, out to the Cattail Marsh, up north to the big lake. He carried her way out over the eastern plains to the Missouri River and they rode a gentle raft down the Mississippi to the Gulf of Mexico. And when he finished traveling with her, he took Lilly back home to the Mission Mountains where she fell asleep in his arms.

She woke in the back of Charlie West's car, in front of their cabin, the leather seats frozen against her legs. A pink sky crowned the mountains. The cabin stood quietly in a field of white. The air smelled pure, innocent, and fresh, like pine trees in a new winter.

Anna opened the door and seemed to run toward her in slow motion.

Charlie carried Lilly into the house and Anna tucked her into bed, under the very warm yellow quilt, a soft yellow that Lilly didn't mind, in fact cherished. The heavy blanket felt good on her shoulders. A dim light filled the room. Outside, wind pressed against the house and the logs groaned. She dropped into a deep sleep where neither the hunter, nor the swans, nor Nell or Pa lived. No sound of guns. No Anna screaming. No Nell talking to Anna while Lilly was gone for help.

――――――――

She woke aching, with hot tea and Anna at her side. "Doctor says you've got pneumonia. You're all bruised up. Probably took a fall. Do you remember?"

Lilly shook her head no and it hurt. The room spun.

"Doctor says you'll be all right, but you got to rest. No bike riding. Doctor's orders. No more mine tunnels. From now on we are going to be careful about what we discuss. The past is off limits. And when you recover, you are going to school."

Anna used that command voice when she was scared. She hadn't thought that she would scare Anna. She'd been taking care of herself all summer and most of the fall, thinking what the heck, I'll go live in the woods, be a mole. Or something like that. She never thought about Anna's fear.

And she was smarter than she'd been two nights ago and she was smarter than the doctor. Lilly had fallen, not once, but several times, with the hunter chasing her. She remembered him beating her with the stuffed swan. Her skin crawled. An enemy wind raced up her spine and chilled her, even though the room steamed with heat. No, Anna was right. The past was off limits. Hearing Anna's voice, in charge or not, made her happy, and this was what she focused on.

"Remember that game we used to play?" she asked her sister. "The one where you make a shape with your hands, and I close my eyes and try to guess it?"

Anna nodded. "Invisible sight."

"Will you play it with me?"

"I don't know. I have work to do."

"Please, just for a few minutes." Lilly closed her eyes. She didn't want to be left alone. She imagined Anna nodding and holding her hands over her heart.

"Love?" Without opening her eyes she guessed again right away. "Me?"

Anna cried. Lilly could hear that and she felt her sister hold her fists very tight.

Nell said, *Yes, she loves you very much.*

With the sound of Nell's voice ringing in her head, she sank into the bed's holy comfort like prayer, wanting to stay for a long time.

# 15

Sometimes when the light was just right and the day late enough, Anna looked a lot like Nell. Her face was wide and open and her head so big for her feather-boned body, a body which, like Nell's, seemed to get lighter each day, a body that could just float up and out of there at any time.

When Lilly looked at Anna she could almost remember her mother as she had been. It felt strange watching Anna in Nell's kitchen while Nell lay motionless in her room. Anna took charge of the kitchen, making biscuits, browning stew meat for dinner, and putting the bread dough to rise on the cook stove.

Food smelled like duckweed to Lilly and she could only think of how Pa would never eat again, his mouth forever still. Things were very different now. No one told her to stay away from the swamp; no one scolded her for telling lies; they didn't tell her she was crazy for seeing Pa or for seeing his killer from the arms of a giant.

Instead, they treated her as tenderly as they'd treat a tiny cygnet. They waited on her, put warm water in the tub for her, and sent her to bed early. Even Lilly wondered if life hadn't been growing and stirring protectively inside of its fragile shell all along and she had just now hatched, stepped out, and begun to live her life. But it was not the life she would have wished for a baby swan.

———————

One morning she wanted to tell Anna about how she'd been cycling their mother's legs, hoping to strengthen them so that Nell could get up and walk again. Lilly wanted to tell Anna so that Anna could take over, moving Nell's thighs and calves close together and then drawing them long and apart. Yet Anna looked so frail and worn, taking care of Nell, and now Lilly, that she couldn't get the words out. She couldn't bear to ask Anna to do more. The words hung in her throat until finally they folded up and packed themselves away.

Silently, she pushed her breakfast away and went back to bed.

Another morning Lilly woke up thrashing. She threw off the covers, opened her eyes, gasping, and caught her breath.

Anna burst through the door. "What's wrong?"

Lilly shook her head. Sweat covered her forehead. She didn't know what was wrong, but something *was* wrong. "I dreamed Pa was under water, trying to tell me something. I couldn't understand them." She started crying.

"Them?" A shadow crossed Anna's face.

"Spirit people. They kept insisting that I go outside. I tried to follow them. Look." The window had iced up overnight and Lilly's handprints were melted into that ice.

Anna shrugged and shook her head, disdain in her weary eyes. Lilly tried to imagine how Anna felt. She'd also lost her father. She worked to support them on top of taking care of the house and Nell. Now Lilly had become a burden too. No wonder she was tired. Lilly scooted down in her bed and turned away from her sister.

She thought about Pearl preening her injured chest. A trumpeter swan has to survive a thousand dangers to make it through a season. Bear, coyote, hunters. She considered the cygnets dashing about and diving under the water. All of them were fragile. Droughts, bad winters, illness, and human-caused poison could do them in. But when things were good, they were sociable, happy birds.

Happy. That was something Lilly couldn't imagine. She closed her eyes, held her breath, clenched her fists, and summoned her mother. But she knew, even before she tried, that she'd fail. Even though Lilly was eleven, she had lost her powers. The stars of eleven had failed her. She could make nothing magical happen.

Anna moved around the bed and knelt in front of her.

"When was that last time you bathed?" Anna asked. "You're scaring all of us to death." She lowered her voice. "Come on. Let's get you cleaned up and back to school."

Out of bed, Lilly shivered and sent Anna a low-lidded don't-know-if-I-can look. Her teeth chattered as she pulled a skirt on over her long johns. She looked out the window, where clouds loomed pensively. A written message hung in the air and she tried to decipher it. That's when she saw the unmistakable jagged lines of the trumpeters in flight. But it was too late for open water. Any potential feed lay frozen in ice. That flock would die.

"You poor things," Lilly said. "What kept you so long at your breeding grounds?" In her heart she knew the answer. The hunter and his gun had stopped them. Maybe Drake could shoot nets that covered a flock and kept it captive in dangerously cold weather. Maybe he let them go just in time to die.

"Baby, there's nothing there," Anna said. "Come on, let's get you some food. You've hardly eaten since you've been sick. Look at you. You're so skinny. You've got to eat. And sleep. Did you sleep last night?"

"Not well," Lilly said, feeling other-worldly, not there, but nowhere else, held in some gray limbo, grown up, but a kid still. "The birds at the marsh are getting better. They are healing, like me and Mama."

"You're confused. You are mixing your dreams up with reality."

"What?" She found the word at the edge of her bill, and she liked the feeling, that of being part of the flock. But Anna was right. She was talking crazy. She had to straighten up and fly right. No. She just had to straighten up.

"You've been dreaming and sleepwalking. Poor sleep and not

eating, it's making you frail. It's all part of your condition."

"Condition?" The word was awkward in her throat. It floated out like a big white swan feather. Her mind had gone into nonsense. She could not get her bearings.

"Never mind," Anna said with a sad and distant note to her voice.

———————

Anna walked Lilly to school. Lilly knew that Anna thought rejoining her normal routine would help her recover, but the pneumonia still swelled in Lilly's lungs and the fever dug at her brain. In the winter clouds she saw raven faces asking for something. The ravens pecked at Lilly's hair and she swatted them away. Anna grabbed her wrists and held them tight.

"Stop it, now," she said. "Go in there and act normal."

Anna seemed far away, as if there was a light veil between them. That veil wrapped itself around Lilly's mind and eyes, working hard to keep the rest of the world at bay.

As Anna left, the black raven wings flapped toward Lilly. They were dark and angry, fresh out of the dream, condemning her for her failures. She didn't save Pa. Nell was sick. And Lilly couldn't find her right mind. She couldn't straighten up and fly right and the black ravens went after her for it.

In school she avoided the sharp beaks by darting her head from side to side. But the beaks were fast and pierced her skull. She felt blood dripping from the holes in her head.

"Go outside," the teacher said. "You're distracting the whole class. This attention seeking is not acceptable. Go on. I'll talk to you after school."

The cold weather needled the skin under Lilly's clothes and made her bones hurt. She was still sick and she knew it. She should be home, in the warmth of their cabin, with warm brandy or oats cooking. She didn't wait for the teacher. Instead she pulled her jacket tight and walked slowly toward home, her legs as heavy as waterlogged wood. She looked to the clouds for a sign. The pure blue sky poured crisp ice down on her back.

One large raven lady came after her. Lilly made a fist and punched the black wings as hard as she could. Soon a whole swarm of crows replaced the raven. They clawed at her and pierced her face. She fought them, with all the strength left in her skinny arms. They pinned her to the ground and yanked her arms behind her, gripping her bony wrists in their talons.

She gave up and played dead.

Anna stood off in the shadows, watching, no, warning the crows.

———————

Lilly woke in a mess of sweat-soaked blankets, the sun coming through her window. She knew she'd been to another world and returned. She hadn't seen her father there, but she knew he lived on the other side of that veil. She missed him so much even her ankles hurt. It turned out he really was gone, like the swan they had tried to save when Lilly was ten. A million years ago.

Even the sun on her face offered no comfort. Nell sleeping downstairs, in her room only made things worse. What would she say if she could join Lilly in conversation? Your father was a good man. He would want you to go to school. He would not want you to put yourself in jeopardy for his sake. Forgive and move on.

*Nothing good comes from revenge*, Pa had said. *Bring him to justice and we all get into heaven.*

But Lilly remembered the sound of Pa's boots stomping in Charlie West's shed the day they brought the dead cygnet to him. Vengeance had boiled in him. He had wanted to hurt Drake.

She knew that he had already hated Dean Drake, long before they found that fledgling trapped in the marsh. She could only imagine what Pa would've said if he knew Drake went after Lilly. The killer had been trying to scare her into keeping quiet. She was so sick it nearly worked. Her head cleared though, and with clarity came a whole new courage.

She tiptoed downstairs and into Nell's room.

It was clean with the scent of sweet grass. Her mother lay under the crazy quilt she made during the long winter that Lilly was

142

five. Her head rested on a pillow, silent and waiting. Her brown hair fanned out and pale skin surrounded her lips. A bit of spittle had bubbled out from her mouth and Lilly wiped it away with her bed coat. She pulled Nell's hands out from under the blankets. Wrapping their fingers together, she held her hand.

"Today I put on the power of heaven," she said, reciting a prayer that Nell had taught her, St. Patrick's Breastplate. "The light of the sun, the radiance of the moon, the splendor of the fire, the fierceness of the lightning, the swiftness of the wind." Then she added her own line. "Today I put on the grace of the swan."

Nell opened her eyes and looked at the space in front of her. "Today I put on God's strength to steer me," Lilly continued with the prayer. "God's power to uphold me, God's wisdom to guide me." And again she added her own lines, "God's feathers for my shelter, God's swans for my flight, God's trumpet for my speech."

She wondered what Nell saw in her world, a world just outside of Lilly's reach. Was it something she had lost or recently misplaced? Lilly searched under the bed, on the nightstand, behind the dresser where dust balls lodged. She pulled the covers off the foot of her bed, thinking she might find it there, balled up like a cast-off sweater. She looked in the corners where spiders left their sinewy webs, and on the windowsills lined with frost. Did Nell think Pa would come home again?

It was far too late for that.

Pa was gone.

He was buried in the frozen ground. He'd already been there for many months.

"You know what would be a really good Christmas present?" Lilly asked.

Nell's quiet steadiness said she didn't know.

"For you to get up and walk into the kitchen on your strong legs," Lilly said. "For you to find your voice and wish us Merry Christmas."

Nell's expression didn't change.

Lilly squeezed her mother's hand. She felt the warmth there. "I'm better now," she said. "I'm going to help you walk again. I'm going to help your legs get strong and your arms build muscle solid enough to lift hay for the brown mare. I'm going to help you like Anna helps you."

Anna came in with a glass of water and a bowl of applesauce. "How is she?"

"Quiet," Lilly said.

"Here is some water, Mama." Anna held Nell's head up to make sure she drank. Nell's lips formed around the edge of the glass, sucking like a baby's mouth. Anna picked up the applesauce and began spoon-feeding her. The natural reflex in Nell set her mouth to working again. It wasn't so much, but it was something.

Lilly let go of her hand and, on a hunch, walked over to the window. Man-sized footsteps were embedded in the snow. "Anna, someone's been out there," she said.

"Probably just Dean when he brought the meat by."

"Dean?" Lilly rose her eyebrows.

"I see no reason to deny his help. We need it." She wiped the bottom of the spoon on the bowl, capturing a drip of the applesauce before it could fall into Nell's hair.

"Anna. He killed Pa!"

Anna stopped, the spoon raised over Nell's lips, and turned to Lilly. Nell's lips reached away from her face, toward the spoon, like they had a mind of their own, sucking empty air like the lips of a displaced fish. "He got Mama's heart going again. Why would he shoot her only to bring her back to life? No. You heard Pa talking bad about him. Sheriff thinks you just mixed up Pa's bad talk with the shooting. So far nothing implicates him."

"I told you; I saw him."

"Lilly, you're wrong on this one. He's kinder than Pa ever gave him credit for. He brought medicine when you were so sick."

Lilly's stomach turned in on itself. Her fingernails dug into her palms. She didn't want medicine Dean Drake had brought to her. Anna didn't know what she had done, joining league with the devil. Lilly's eyes rolled back under her eyelids.

"I saw him," she said again.

"I know, baby. It's been a bad time. But he helped get you home that day you lay in the road screaming about the ravens. I know you don't believe it, but he's a gentleman. Give him a chance. Nell loves him. She must've seen something good there. We need all the kindness we can get right now."

Anna looked down at Nell like she'd suddenly remembered to finish feeding her. She swooped the spoon into Nell's mouth and Nell swallowed, both of them dismissing Lilly with the motion.

"It's wrong," Lilly said. "Letting him in here is all wrong."

Anna ignored Lilly. She cooed to Nell like the child she'd become.

The room filled with thick murky air that Lilly couldn't breathe. If she ever wanted to breathe again she needed to leave right then. In between bites of applesauce Lilly kissed Nell's eyes. When she got close to her, Nell's mouth made that sucking gesture, small and childlike, searching for something that wasn't there.

# 16

Unlike the cygnets, Lilly had no parents to protect her. Pa was gone and Nell didn't wake up for Christmas. It came and went. One night her dream spirit searched for the hunter. She found him, gutting a deer. When he finished he turned to a dead bear and gutted it. Later he cut open a trumpeter swan.

That swan stepped out of the dream, whole and healed. She walked toward Lilly. As she got close, Lilly saw the likeness to Pearl. She trilled her beautiful, sad song. Lilly knew from the sound of the song that trouble was trailing a fool's nest of nightshade.

She woke in the middle of the night and sketched the swans on a clean white page of an art book Anna had given to her for Christmas. She pulled in the nesting swans from the background. Grass, twigs, and bits of old coveralls sat under their peaceful white bellies in the nests. The dried blood on the coveralls had turned black. A male stretched his long neck, perked his head, and listened for the sounds of predators. At the far edge of the pond a two-year-old trumpeter sat with his full adult plumage, black eyes, black legs and feet, and a black flat bill accented with a thin red streak.

Having trouble telling the dream world from the real world of her daily life, Lilly drew a picture of Pearl sitting at her side. Pearl lifted her wing and Lilly stepped under it and hid. She stayed there for what felt like days, safely under her wing, where no one could touch her.

At the bottom of the page, she wrote, "Home at Last," and signed it "The Swan Keeper."

---

The next morning, she dragged herself downstairs to Nell's room and stood in the doorway, nearly out of sight. The sun shone through the window and brightened the logs near the head of Nell's bed where Anna sat. Heavy body smells covered the natural fresh scent of pine logs. Nell's eyes shuttered frantically from side to side, looking first at Anna and then in the direction of Lilly's room, trying to tell Anna something.

Lilly's sister drew in a breath, got out of her chair, walked to the wall and looked behind the dresser. She opened drawers and let her gaze drift toward the stairwell. "What is it you want?" Her voice was like a string of crowded beads tied at her throat. She wore a pale pink dress with a frayed hem.

On the nightstand a water glass dulled at the edges by lip smears stood half full.

As though still dreaming Lilly watched Nell's rhythmic eyes and Anna's pink dress as she slowly covered the room.

"Water?" Anna asked, lifting the smudged glass.

Nell moved her eyes back and forth.

"Hungry?"

Nell tried to form words. Lilly sensed her mother's lost and trapped feeling. If she could speak for her mother, she'd say that a girl needs her mother. Even sick as she was, Nell worried about Lilly and Anna, and it hurt her eleven-year-old soul in a way that Lilly hadn't expected.

"She wants to know that I'm OK," she said, stepping into the room.

"Well, are you OK?" Anna raised her eyebrows—a mother's look, kind but suspicious.

"I'm good. How long has she been like this?"

"Since this morning. She's been moving her eyes frantically, trying to tell me something. This is the first time she's settled down, since you walked in." Anna's eyes softened as she pulled at the frayed edge of her hem, freeing the tiny threads one by one. "You know, Nell lost her own parents early and, after that, she never counted on having many luxuries in her life. I heard her say that to Pa one night. And now, losing Pa. It's not fair."

"Look." Lilly pointed to her mother's hand. Nell moved her little finger, something she hadn't done since she'd been shot. She moved it again. Excitement bolted through Lilly like she had just won the coin-toss, luck throwing her beautiful net over them. Nell's mouth moved, like she wanted to smile. She wanted, Lilly was certain, to tell Anna and Lilly how much she loved them. She wanted to come back to them.

How much of the swan's beauty had she seen in the time she'd been silent? Did she see the angels plant seeds or God water the flowers? Could she see Pa over there in that other world waiting for justice? Or had she seen only terror, the same terror that haunted Lilly when the gunshots sounded in her ears, the screams rang out, and the ghostly swan dove in to protect her?

"Mama, you moved your finger," Lilly said, stating the obvious. Anna sat down on the bed and looked up at Lilly. She never called their mother Mama. Lilly picked up Nell's finger. A smile landed just inside her mother's lips and refused to move beyond, locking her story inside of her own heart.

"Dean Drake shot you," Lilly said, the words simple, clear marbles, expertly flipped, relentless, still hoping to wake her mother out of her immobile state.

"Shhh," Anna said, her eyes wild. "Not here."

"You think Nell doesn't know what happened?" But Lilly knew she shouldn't be talking like this in front of their mother. It would upset her. "I'm going to stop him."

"You are going to mind your manners and think of someone beside yourself," Anna said quietly.

"Imagine putting that man in one of those small jails," Lilly continued. "Remember what Pa said they looked like?"

Anna winced and glared at the same time.

"Like little play cages, like someone could walk away with them. He said a criminal could get his feet through the slats in the bottom and saunter right out of the courthouse, wearing the jail bars like a large metal coat."

"Lilly, I'm warning you. Be quiet."

"The swan killer needs to be brought to justice."

"It won't bring Pa back," Anna said, turning her face away from Nell and Lilly.

"It's the next best thing."

"You've already put yourself in too much danger."

"Did you ever hear them talk about something that brought this on?"

Anna shook her head but Lilly saw a look of recognition and fear cross her face. She opened her mouth and then closed it. "Let it be."

"What is it?" Lilly asked.

"Come into the hallway."

Lilly joined her sister just outside Nell's door, keeping Nell in her line of vision. "What do you remember?"

When Anna told the story, Lilly remembered that she'd heard part of it sometime before. "Drake was a ranch hand on Mama's father's place," Anna said. "She said she could still remember his green eyes shining as he showed her a horse trick, or raced one of the ranch dogs to the corral. An hour later he'd be accusing her of selling him out to her father, or flirting with another ranch hand.

"In her own way she had loved him, but in the end, he betrayed her. When her parents' wagon caught a spoke in the Flathead River, and she flailed in the water trying to save them, he just stood there and watched them go down. He lied and said he tried to help them but the water was too swift. A year went by and he was a help to her. She started to doubt her own experience. Then she doubted her doubts."

"She told you all this?"

Anna nodded.

"It's just like now, Anna. Don't you see it? He shoots them and then he comes around here helping, like he's a good guy."

"He wanted to marry Nell. He was upset when she chose Pa," Anna said. "None of it makes sense. He saved Nell's life. Why would he nearly kill the person he loves?"

Lilly could see Anna's mind working. "Charlie West told me to find something that ties Drake to the swan killings," Lilly said. "And he might be able to do something about Pa and Nell." She thought Nell could hear every word they said. The way Anna kept waving Lilly back away from the door told her that her sister thought so too. Lilly figured agitation was a great motivator, and hoped Nell would get up and get going.

Her plan to engage Nell with her own agitation failed. Lilly's mother closed her eyes, as if she'd never opened them. When Lilly lifted her finger again, it fell back to the quilt like a loose piece of yarn, soft and fluid, waiting for someone to work it into a fine and useful thing.

---

Later that afternoon Lilly swallowed hard and followed her fear out to Running Bear's winter cabin. She walked long through the stiff snow, telling herself a thousand reasons why this was a good idea. Running Bear knew Pa and was loyal to him. He would care about who shot Pa.

Her fear found a bare rock and climbed under it. Anger crawled out. One way or another, Drake was going to pay. The sky darkened, promising a blizzard. It turned unexpectedly, and delivered rain instead, soaking Lilly and turning the snow-crusted fields to ice and mud. She kept walking, tired, shivering and too cold to stay angry, wondering if winter had finally ended.

At the base of the mountains, Running Bear's log cabin peeked through drenched pines. Smoke curled out of the chimney and disappeared into the clouds. As she got closer, dogs surrounded her, barking and howling, their haunches back and tails low. She leaned against a thin fir tree and offered her palms for them to sniff. A small boy dashed to Running Bear's door.

"Daughter of Two Sons," Running Bear said, when Lilly walked in, acknowledging her now like she did exist. He wore a wool tunic tied at his hip by a beaded belt. He sat at a small table that hugged the cabin wall and worked his leather hands around a tin cup.

Water dripped off her braids and soaked her back. A black stove threw off heat, the flames dancing just inside the stove's open door. The warmth settled on her shoulders like a well-needed friend. Steam ghosts rose out of her clothes.

The wind picked up and pelted the walls with rain, whistling through the trees and breaking the branches. Lilly could hear the broken branches tumbling through the yard. A dog howled and somewhere in the near distance others joined him. Running Bear tilted his head to the sound.

"You come as the world changes," he said. "Come, eat, drink coffee, and we will talk about what bothers you."

She wasn't hungry and wanted only the warmth of coffee. Her voice melted like the snow in the rain. Running Bear's eyes cautioned her to be wise, but she was not wise. How could a child like Lilly be wise? She had no business being there with a great leader.

"The dark winds told of your coming, don't leave them to speak for you." Running Bear poured her coffee. "They can't know your mind and you'll go away only to return with the next storm to finish what you came to do now."

Lilly nodded and began to speak, became unbearably cold and stopped.

He must've noticed her shivering because he pushed a plate of dried deer meat across the table. "Meat will make you warm," he said. "It will give you courage."

Again the words froze in her throat. She cast her eyes down, unable to face him. She was not her father. What right did Lilly have to ask Running Bear for anything?

"Granddaughter," he said, the word a kind hand offered to a fallen child.

"Pa is gone," she finally managed to say.

He slowly turned his sad eyes toward the stove. "I know this."

That day with Pa, Running Bear and he had remembered Horse Child, Running Bear's son and Pa's childhood friend who met with an accident in the Butte mines. As Pa and Running Bear had talked about Horse Child their faces had turned to steel, something unsaid burning in them. That same, unsaid thing burned in Running Bear's face again.

"A man shot him and my mother at the swans' crossing. Charlie West says it was an accident, but I saw the mean look in the man's eyes. I tried to stop him from pulling the trigger. It was no accident! Now Pa's gone and Nell won't get up out of bed. We have to help her do the most basic things while her body hangs limp and frail.

"No one believes me when I tell them what I saw." The words spilled out in a tumbling rush. She had to talk quickly, before she lost courage. "I see his footprints in the snow at the edge of our yard. Nell knows he's there. She's agitated and disturbed. I can see it in her eyes. I can smell him in the air after he's gone. Charlie West says he needs proof, that he can't just put men in jail for crimes a girl says they might've committed. This man, Dean Drake, chased me down on his mule and ran me into some boulders. He gave me these." She pushed up her sleeve. The bruises that had looked like the hillside when it was crazy with wild lupine and balsamroot had faded, leaving only tiny yellow and red scars from the cuts. They would also soon disappear.

"You want my help to find him," Running Bear said, pouring more coffee into his cup and palming it like a magic stone, silver and glistening in the burnt orange light of the fire.

She shook her head. "There's no need to find him. I turn around and he's there. He comes around our house in the dark and helps Anna with chores and acts like a friend." Drinking the bitter coffee, she suddenly understood that, with Pa gone, just being the daughter of Two Sons gave her special standing. But she hadn't earned it and she knew it. It came through an action her father hadn't meant to take.

Running Bear waited for Lilly to find the words. "It's Nell. She hasn't uttered a sound since the man shot her. It's like she lives in another world. We help her stand and help her eat. We bathe her and move her legs around to make them strong again, but she's not there. We can't reach her." Earlier that day Nell's eyes had flitted back and forth like wild horses caught in the ropes. With great hope Lilly had watched her mother move a finger. Then she watched her stop and lie there, frozen like the winter ponds.

Running Bear stared into the fire. "It's good that we help with this," he said.

His simple words were all that needed to be said.

The boy who had run to tell him about Lilly sat in the corner nodding his head, his eyes glued to Running Bear. "I'll help Grandpa," he said. He wore a light coat, and mud-streaked brown trousers. He had black hair and dark eyes that held the wisdom of an old man.

"Thank you," Lilly said.

As she started for home, the singing had already begun.

# 17

As spring came and Lilly's birthday neared, she went to visit Jerome. He leaned back in a wooden chair, his feet up on the desk in his father's shop, reading—surprise, surprise—a mechanic's magazine.

He wore a brown wool jacket that seemed too hot for the room. His trousers had been cut off at the knees. When she walked in, he sat up and put his feet on the floor. One of Pa's swan photos hung on the wall above his left shoulder. It was one of a lone swan on the pond, its graceful neck curled into half a heart, the feathers silvery soft in a misty light. Just then the sun shone through the window and bloomed on the swan's tail.

"How are you feeling?" he asked.

"Better," she said, pulling her eyes away from the photo. She actually did feel a lot better, the best she'd felt since they'd found her in the mine tunnel. She was still cold most of the time, a deep cold left over from that night on the mountain. She pulled the sleeves of her sweater down, a sweater that Nell had made for Sam, gray with little specs of color woven into it.

The sleeves scratched her wrists where they were worn. Pa had repeatedly folded them, to keep them out of his work. Still, they got dirty and tattered. Lilly imagined each bit of dirt ground into the sleeves as a tiny piece of her father's life: spring time and Pa mending the fence in the outer field, early summer planting the corn, a fall morning harvesting it, a day with the brown mare hunting for winter meat.

She figured the sweater for an early birthday present from him. The thought reminded her of last year's birthday present and all the harm done. She pushed the memory aside before it could gain power and beat her down. The sweater gave her strength. It was as if she could keep her father close by wearing his clothes. She could be like him, hardworking, brave, and in charge of her life.

"I have a question," she said.

"OK." Jerome sounded cautious.

She pulled the sweater sleeves even further over her fists, holding tight to her father's life. She took in a breath and let it go. Even that little bit of control felt good. "Did you make the bike chains for me?"

Jerome stood up. "Turn around and don't look," he said as he went into another room. She closed her eyes and listened to the squeaking sound that came from the other room. She heard the rustle of a sack, the door closing, and more sack rustling.

"OK, look."

There they were, shiny silver chains in his hands, jingling lightly like Pa's spurs when he rode the brown mare.

"Customized to fit. We can adjust them later, if you end up using a bigger bike, but for now, they should fit perfectly."

Laughing, she ran them through her fingers. "They're beautiful!" she said. And they really were beautiful: tiny silver links, all connecting and belonging, solid and fluid, a family of the perfect size.

"Snow's gone. They won't do you much good this year."

"You are the best friend ever," she said and hopped backwards out the door. "I knew you would do it."

"You're not going to get me into trouble with those, are you?" Jerome called after her.

"Not a lick of it."

---

On the morning before her twelfth birthday, the sun rose pure and bright. It was a golden spray of warmth on the new strawberry flowers that littered the trail. Lilly got up early and rode her bike nowhere in particular. She rode just to ride, for the pure pleasure of feeling the wind on her face and her skirt bellowing at her knees.

Her eleventh year was a scar burned into her bones by the loss of her father, Nell's illness, and the swan slaughter. She rode, challenging destiny, daring fate to hurt her again. She rode to feel the fire of her last day of being eleven. Twelve had its own mysteries and she wanted to know what they were the second the moon turned and she stepped over that line.

She could not wait to put her eleventh year behind her.

Back at the house, she parked the bike at the front porch and walked quietly into Nell's room. She had thought she'd heard her talk last winter, just after Lilly came home from the tunnel, with the fever burning in her brain. Her mother's voice had been weak, but it was her mother's voice telling Lilly that her sister loved her. It was dreamlike, yet it had felt so real. But since the fever had passed there had been nothing from Nell but silence.

Touching the bed gently, she woke Nell. Sleepy eyes looked up at Lilly, blurred and unfocused.

"It's me, Lillian."

Her mother's eyes widened, focused and softened. With her eyes she motioned for water, which Lilly quickly got for her. She opened her mouth as Lilly put the water to her lips and poured in a small drink. "My little girl," Lilly imagined Nell saying when she finished the drink.

With great gentleness, Lilly removed the covers and worked her mother's arms back and forth, lifting invisible boulders for her. As she bicycled Nell's legs she said, "I'll be twelve tomorrow, what is twelve like?"

Her mother's eyes moved to a vase of balsamroot Anna had put in the window. What was it she'd told Lilly about twelve? "Twelve takes all of eleven and weaves it into something precious and pure, something all its own," she remembered her mother saying, "like a velvet coat that you feel right at home in."

Lilly laughed at that thought. "So twelve won't go down the same steep, rocky path that eleven took." Eleven had not been a field full of daisies. "Eleven was a deep crevice I fell into, boulders I crawled over, a cave full of dried bones that buried me."

"So dramatic," she imagined Nell saying. "Twelve is so dramatic." Her mother drank a little more water. She moved her eyes to the vase again, like she was trying to tell Lilly something. Lilly walked over, picked up the vase, and took it back to Nell. She stared right through Lilly, like the ghost she'd become, toward the window where a slight breeze blew in. She put the vase back and closed the window. Outside, underneath the window, she saw man-sized footprints in the spring mud. When she turned back to Nell she had already closed her eyes and fallen back to sleep.

---

In the kitchen Anna sat at the table looking through their mother's cookbook. She lifted her droopy eyes, her cheeks red and wet, when Lilly sat opposite her.

"Will you go out to the Cattail Marsh with me?" Lilly asked. Anna hadn't been out there in the year since their parents were shot.

Horror crossed Anna's face and faded. Did Anna still hear the gunshots too? But no. It was Lilly's question that struck Anna.

"No," she said.

"Why not?"

"Remember what happened the last time we went out there together?"

"Please. Come to the marsh with me. Afterwards we can come home and have lunch with Nell. It's been a year. Tomorrow is the anniversary of..."

"I know. We don't need any more trouble. Things have settled down. Nell is in God's hands. Going out there won't make her or anyone better."

"By 'anyone' do you mean me?" Lilly narrowed her eyes.

"You've not been yourself since the accident."

"And you have?" Lilly's voice climbed into a high pitch and she didn't stop it. "Losing both parents changes a person. I don't have to be much older to know that."

"Don't get hysterical. I'm just saying you're different."

"And I've just been saying that the man who shot our parents did it on purpose. But here you are accepting gifts from him." She pointed to the venison Anna was frying. She thought about the boot prints outside. The thought took hold and she wanted to run out to the woods again. She breathed, grabbed her anger and hid it deep under the rock of her missing heart. "At the marsh we can see if the swans have returned. We can make sure no one is shooting them."

"And wait for another one of us to get shot? Where did you get such a morose streak, child?"

"I'm not a child. I'm almost twelve. Tomorrow. Twelve. It's my one request. I haven't asked for much this year." It was true. Her desires were contrary to others, or worse. Lilly's desires hurt others.

"Listen. You scared me half to death with your little escapade last winter when you didn't come home all night. You were laid up for weeks with pneumonia. You want a repeat performance of that?" Anna got up, filled a pan with water, and set it on the stove next to the venison.

Lilly clenched her fists, anger climbing back out from its hiding place. The gunshots returned. The voices yelled and the shots rang out. She hadn't heard them for a while and they surprised her. They scared her. The ghostly Pearl flitted into view, over the top of her rage and fear, silencing the gunshots. She stood so close to Lilly that Lilly could see her black leather feet claw at the floor. Her feathers glistened in the light from the window. When she lifted her bill, her black eyes soft and misty, Lilly decided to go alone.

It was wrong, not going to see the swans near the anniversary of their deaths. It was wrong, doing nothing to stop Pa's killer. No one else cared about the swan massacre, or that Pa was gone, or that Nell couldn't or wouldn't talk. Lilly cared. She cared a lot. Someday she would stop Dean Drake. Silently, she promised Nell, Pa, the swans and God that she'd keep the swans safe, that she'd protect her mother and bring her back to her nesting place.

"I'll go by myself then," she said quietly.

"No, you will not. Nell will wake up and walk right out of her bed and go looking for you when she finds out. She probably wonders if you ran away last winter and bruised yourself up just for attention."

"Oh, yes, I've had so much attention, it's coming out my ears. I just can't get enough of it."

"What's that supposed to mean?"

"Never mind. I wish Nell would get up from her bed and come looking for me," she said. "That would be worth it."

Anna looked away and went about tending to the stove. "I'll bake a cake and we'll celebrate your birthday right here. Jerome can come if he'd like."

"I don't want a stupid cake!" Lilly ran out the back door and slammed it hard. She sat on the back steps and the gunshots and Anna's screams started again. She closed her eyes. "Pearl, make them stop," she whispered, imagining the great white swan's glowing feathers as a barricade to the sounds. Her black webbed feet locked onto a wet log in front of Lilly as she trumpeted to the wind. Soon Lilly heard only the sound of Pearl's voice mixed with the wind in the poplars.

She grabbed her bike and started riding again, this time at a fast, deliberate pace. The ghostly Pearl flew beside her. Her wide wings flapped like thunder across the heavens and her flat bill stretched out in front of them, leading the way. Yellow balsamroot dotted the forest floor. Fluffy white clouds crossed the sky. A blue-winged teal flew by. Pearl ignored the teal but Lilly knew what it meant. A blue-winged teal this early in the day, this early in the spring, meant that eleven still fluttered in her head. Let Anna think what she wanted. In her mind Lilly could hear their mother, even if no one else could. And that was something good for now.

Before Nell stopped talking, she told Lilly that the world over-flowed with goodness. She said some Indians believe that every person has two souls. The dream soul travels through the spirit world during sleep, where the invisible becomes visible. The dream soul watches swans migrate high above the clouds, watches bears sleep in their dens, and gazes at gold veins sparkling under dirt. In the spirit realm everyone has plenty of food and laughter. Nell had said, remember this, Lilly: there is so much beauty in the world, even your tears water the earth and life grows.

She liked to think of Nell like that, philosophical and kind. She liked to think of Pa with only one glass of whiskey gone, when he stopped drinking soon enough and took Nell out to the porch to look at the stars. On those nights Lilly slept deeply. Her second soul spread its wings and soared, searching for fawns and baby rabbits in long grasses.

Lilly sped toward Jerome's house. When she got close, she stopped and climbed a boulder. The gunshots and Anna's scream-ing had gone but a sound came back and that sound turned into voices, unknown voices that sounded like Dean Drake and his friend from when she was on the mountain with Pa. The voices welled up out of the earth in a corner of Charlie West's ponds, just beyond Pearl's pen, and Lilly feared she was going crazy. The thick whispers curled and grew like smoke from a stove. Lilly shook her head, covered her ears, and hummed quietly until Pearl took the voices away and settled in her pen. Her loud, throaty trumpeting took the voices into the earth where they belonged.

Jerome sat on his front porch reading the same mechanic's mag-azine he'd been reading all winter. He wore brown coveralls and a cowboy hat that sat too close to his ears.

"You're not a cowboy," Lilly said.

"Gift from my father," he said. "You like it?"

She nodded. "Can you get free for the afternoon?" Her hands shook and she clasped them behind her back, hoping to look more innocent than she felt. Eleven had been genuinely innocent, but she was beginning to understand that twelve would have to fake it.

"I've got work to do," he said.

Lilly raised her eyebrows at the magazine.

He raised his eyebrows back at her. "Just taking a break."

"I'm about to step out of line and you might need to call the sheriff."

"Planning on raiding a local garden?"

"I'm going back to the mine tunnel, to get the stuffed swan Drake threw at me."

Jerome waited.

"He was up there for a reason that day. I think his hide out is nearby that mine tunnel. I'm going back to look for signs of it."

"And if you can't find it?"

"Then I'll go to the marsh and wait for him. Sooner or later he'll be out there killing swans. I'm going to follow him to find out where he put my father's camera. He must have a home, and I'll bet that's where the camera is with the film still in it."

"Even if you find it the film might be ruined," Jerome said.

"I'll find out." She took the leather tie off one of her braids and used it to capture them both into one long ponytail. The ponytail reached down past the middle of her back.

Jerome put down the magazine and stood. He seemed tall, much taller than last week. "You are not going into the mountains or to the marsh. I'm done getting you out of trouble."

"I'm afraid to go by myself."

"That's smart."

"Still, I'm going."

"You should not go without me and I just can't go with you."

"You've been riding from the woods to the marsh with me all my life," Lilly said, with a high-pitched twist to her voice. She squished her mouth into the shape of a bill and slit her eyes.

He took off his hat and came toward her. "Shhhh," he said, "don't cry."

"Stay away. Don't touch me." She wasn't crying. It was anger, with a mind of its own, escaping out her eyes.

"I know it's been hard. You miss your pa and Nell's been so sick. Anna's no substitute for your mother. Has Nell talked yet?" Jerome pushed his brown hair out of his eyes and looked off toward the mountains. "You just don't know that Drake did it on purpose. We all want to blame someone."

"Jerome West, go ahead and tell yourself stories." She felt her face darken. "But I'm not going to tell myself lies. I'm going out to the Cattail Marsh to see if the swans have returned. And I'm going to find him."

"If you go, I'll be telling Anna."

"Go ahead and tell her. She'll just send someone after me. If someone comes after me, I won't be alone then, will I?" She gave him her best steely-eyed hunter's stare.

"If you're not back by sundown, I'm coming looking for you."

———————

Her anger turned to fear and back to anger again. She pedaled hard, until the anger grew thick like the woods that twinkled in the sun, keeping her great grief and sadness at bay. Birds sang high in the trees, the incessant, chirping song of a magnificent gathering meant to keep outsiders away. Frogs jumped across the creek running for shelter. Snakes slithered under dead tree leaves, hiding. Three eagles circled above the Mission Valley and Lilly took them for a sign of faith and protection.

The bicycle was no match for the steepness of the mountain and she pushed the pedals hard to climb the game trail up the pass. Drake had likely taken that same trail the night he chased her and warned her to keep quiet about the truth of him killing her father. Looking around for signs of him and his hideout, Lilly found only bear scat and large canine prints in the mud.

Rainbow colors of pink, green, blue, and yellow floated up toward the sun through the pine tops and did nothing to calm her growing uneasiness. When she came upon a meadow where wild lupine grew, she picked a bouquet and tried to enjoy the warm sun on her shoulders. She untied the scarf from her neck, wrapped the flower stems in it and tied the wild beauties to her bike.

She inhaled the fresh air of the spring timber, trying to exhale eleven and breathe in twelve. She really didn't want to be so angry. Anger had led her up the mountain alone, had moved her to go after a killer, had pushed her only friend away. She'd be smarter once she turned twelve. She tried to remember all that Nell and Pa had said about twelve. When she couldn't recall, she made things up: Twelve sprinted along courageously; Twelve took eleven's magic and painted the world real; Twelve told the truth even when no one else would, even when no one would listen. Twelve sought out justice.

Further up the hill, her tires slid in the wet ground and she thought about putting on the bike chains that Jerome had made. No. She didn't want his help. Let Jerome take that. Let him see how she felt. Forlorn. Useless. The bike tires slid sideways in a deep mud hole and she went down in it. Brushing herself off, she got back on and rode.

The mine opening was just ahead. She knew it was just beyond the next turn, the next rise, just past a particularly resilient stretch of trail-flattened snow that glittered in the sun. She gained speed, thinking she could plow through it. Instead, she piled head first, right into it, scraping her palms against the icy crust. The bicycle tipped on top of her and crashed into her head. The pedal sliced into her cheek. A thin bit of blood came away on her fingers. Her back ached and her legs stung.

She flung the bike off and pulled the chains from her pocket. OK, Jerome, she thought, I'll use your chains, just this one time. With bare, red hands, numbed from the snow, she wrapped the shiny metal around the back tire. Sure enough, a perfect fit. The second chain went around the front tire with no problems. She grumbled, annoyed that he had done such a good job on the chains.

She pulled out eight strands of sewing elastic, all the same length, cut precisely for the snow chains. Tying one end of the first piece of elastic to the chain at the top of the back tire, she pulled it snug, and tied the other end at the bottom of the tire. The second piece of elastic crossed over the first, tying the chain sideways and cutting the tire in quarters. She did the same thing to the other side of the tire and then both sides of the front tire. When she was done she tugged at the bike chains. They held tightly.

They worked. Lilly plowed through the stubborn snow to the mine tunnel that she had spent the night in last winter. The old fear that Dean Drake had stirred in her sat handily at the edge of her sight and she imagined it sitting on a hard rock and she told it to stay. She had important things to do.

Inside the tunnel, the cool, damp air made her nose itch. She set the bike aside and stood perfectly still, waiting for her eyes to adjust. Once she could see, she found the stuffed swan right where she had dropped it when Jerome's father pulled her out of the winter cold. She picked it up and hugged it.

Feeling her way down the damp wall to the secret hole where she had stashed her father's box of photos she pulled them out near the sunlight and looked at them. Pa and Anna in the garden, Nell dressed for a Sunday picnic, Anna and Lilly in their work clothes at Nell's side. She looked at the swan photos too. The female on her nest, the cygnets ducking under her belly, the male with his wings lifted to scare a predator, the fledglings trying to fly.

Knowing that the box of pictures was still there and safe made Lilly feel better. She could still see her mother's face before the shooting, when she laughed, full of hope and wonder. When her hopeful face faded, Lilly could simply look at the photos and bring back her glittering eyes.

In a particularly bright photo her father's strong jaw almost moved, his face full of love. She would be happy to share the photos with Anna, someday. She wanted to, but she worried that her sister would say that the past was off limits and go back to tossing the pictures into the fire. Better to wait until Anna had less grief and more sense. Lilly put the photos back in their hiding place and took the stuffed swan.

She tied the cloth creature to the back of her bike, where its bill bounced against her hip as she rode. The spring wind stung her face. Mud caked her skirt. Once she was out of the snow and mud, she stopped long enough to remove the bike chains. She would thank Jerome another time, when she was done being mad at him. After all, she wasn't twelve yet. Eleven could still hold its edge of anger.

She put the stuffed swan on the ground next to the bouquet of wild lupine, imagining the photo she'd have taken if she'd had her father's camera. She clicked the invisible picture. In the dirt she drew another picture, one of a birthday cake with twelve candles. A magic breath in her lungs held briefly until she blew the candles out. Pine needles sailed like smoke and she made the wish for something normal: Pa at home shoeing the brown mare while Nell cooked fry bread. But nothing would ever be normal again. Lilly retied the stuffed swan and wildflowers to the back fender and rode her bicycle down the mountain.

She flew on that bicycle to the Cattail Marsh, stopping near the pine tree that had once been her giant. It groaned in the wind, and silently, like the hunter, she crept through the reeds to the waters and waited for the hunter. From that closeness, she watched the swans. She tried to remember Chaucer's words, words she'd found, of all places, in the school library. The words ran through her mind like a chant, like a wish, like the candles she'd drawn in the dirt.

> *And Lord, the bliss and joy that birds make*
> *When each begins the other in its wings*
> *To take*
> *And each neck about the*
> *Other's neck entwined*
> *Thanking always Venus, noble goddess*
> *Of their kind.*

She'd loved those words and today they spoke of magic. Today, her last day to be eleven, she wanted to make something, one thing, one magical thing happen. If she could do that she could fly into twelve with the entire charm of eleven behind her.

She might even understand Chaucer's words once she was twelve. Twelve was smart. Twelve could sit with the swans all alone with poetry, and memorize the image of the swan, an image to hold for all time, an image to help a girl fly into a good life. She moved closer and said her own prayer: "Now I take me down thy path, where trumpeters fly and cygnets hatch, let their return be grace-filled ether. Wind and love, please come here ever."

Then she heard it. Light, tender, wing-like splashing. She saw the white feather tails and then the long necks leading to the tipped-up black bills. Four bills in all. Four swans had returned. She thanked her missing heart and the ground. She thanked her bicycle and the nearly unused chains. She thanked the Ponderosa pine that had once been her giant. She thanked God. She wasn't certain what He might think about Chaucer, especially the goddess part. But surely God loved swans as Chaucer did. Surely God must have loved Chaucer. Chaucer even started his poem with "Lord."

Finally, she had found someone to ask, not just Chaucer, but books. Books were full of information. She'd learned to consult books and thank God. It was a good system.

In the pond two trumpeters, skeleton light, called to each other. Together they dipped their heads. They lifted and fluttered their wings, and dipped their heads again. Lifting, fluttering, dipping, their breasts touching each other, their black bills meeting, their necks arched together into the perfect shape of a heart. Their wings flapped as they made a big deal of something. Something grand. The female flattened herself in the water. The male, nearly airborne, covered her with his great white wings. Almost silence came across the land. The world stood still. Even the wind halted. Then the wing flapping, the calling, and the ruckus began again. The trumpeters dipped their heads in a celebration. Not a birthday celebration exactly, but the celebration of a birth to come.

As soon as she thought it, she understood what Chaucer meant. She heard the word in her own head and blushed. She knew what they had just done in front of her. Lilly had heard Nell and Pa sometimes, in their bedroom, doing the same thing. With a smile as wide as a trumpeter's wingspan and cheeks as hot as a stormy morning sun, Lilly backed out of the marsh with her bike.

On her last day of being eleven, something magical had happened.

She raced to make it home before dark. Jerome would be glad to know that he wouldn't have to come looking for her. Wait until she told him how the swans mated right in front of her. He'd…well, she didn't know what he'd do. She didn't even know if she *could* tell him. Then she remembered: twelve sprinted along courageously.

When she found Jerome's house empty, Lilly slunk away home with no one to tell. Anna wouldn't want to hear it. She didn't want her to go out there in the first place. And Pa was gone. She didn't give up hope completely. She could always tell Nell, even if Nell was a captive audience.

She hoped to slink into the house unnoticed and write a detailed description of the swans mating. That way, in the years to come, she would remember this day, this moment. Someday, when Lilly was grown, she might match the writing with Pa's photos. One day, in a prayer, she'd tell him about the mating swans. That night she'd tell Nell. Maybe this would be Nell's call to return to them, to talk, to get out of bed and walk again. Maybe this was the one last magical thing that her eleven would ever do.

The dark house gave hope. She could go to the bedroom, write the cherished memory, slip into Nell's room and read it to her. She'd make it as beautiful as possible. Nell could never resist beauty. Afterwards, Lilly would sleep peacefully. She'd wake up twelve and twelve would be a brand new life.

It felt odd, walking into the darkness of her home. If nothing else, Anna was usually cooking or reading in the evenings. Perhaps tonight she was dining with the neighbors or at a town hall meeting.

Lilly gently pushed the door open.

Lights came on. Balloons flew.

"Surprise!" Anna, George, Jerome, Charlie and Lenore all yelled in unison. Anna had baked a cake. Nell sat in the overstuffed chair in the corner with a white quilt pulled over her lap, looking like a porcelain doll.

# 18

That spring, with the lupine blooming and the wild wind moving red clouds across the sky, Nell came back to herself. She flattened her palms into the mattress and sat up in bed. When Lilly bicycled Nell's legs Nell pushed hard against the invisible pedals. Using her own arms and legs to keep her balance she used the chamber pot on her own. As Nell got stronger Lilly and Anna moved it further away from the bed. Finally they put it back out in the barn and, with help, Nell used the bathroom like Anna and Lilly.

Each day Lilly watched as her mother pushed herself a little more and her legs and arms grew stronger. She walked unaided around the kitchen and lifted wood from the pile to feed the stove. She brought water in from the well, stopping occasionally to take a breath and rest and let her strength gather. Lilly's chest swelled with happiness as Nell sat in a chair by the fire, holding a book, reading, a thing she never thought her mother would do again. Anna and Lilly smiled at each other behind Nell's back and nodded their heads at each other.

Their mother had come back to them.

Lilly had heard her father call Nell Flying Girl one night. When she asked why he called her that Pa said it was her name in Running Bear's camp. "Well, why did Running Bear call her that?" Pa didn't answer, but instead looked out toward the pass. Maybe he saw into her future, saw her fly off to the mountains and watch for a long while, waiting, before she came back to the Mission Valley.

Before long Nell moved with confidence. Her legs and torso were her own. Her hands dug dirt in the garden. She smiled often. Only her voice hadn't yet returned. She'd seem to gather thoughts, but no words came out her mouth. She motioned to others to communicate what she wanted. She baked pies, scrubbed floors, repaired the goat's pen, slept hard at night and grew stronger every day.

Lilly wondered what she thought about. When they told her that Pa had been killed, she nodded, her fingers picking at the edge of the table, and stared for a long time at the clouds, her flat forehead tilted upward as if in prayer. Maybe she saw him out there somewhere, waiting for her.

Anna went to work each day at the Timberline Café and left Lilly to school and to watch over Nell. Lilly rallied her courage and told Nell, once again, that Dean Drake shot her. Nell shook her head violently and went to the garden. Lilly followed but her mother ignored her, digging in the dirt until Lilly left her alone and went back inside.

Nell worked all that morning and, as if summoning the devil, Dean Drake showed up in the garden. It was as if she'd dug a hole and he climbed out of the dark hot earth. Lilly watched from the upstairs window. She cringed as he hugged Nell close and pushed the hair away from her forehead.

Lilly flew downstairs to the porch. "You've got no business here!" She found and held a shovel at him.

Nell shook her head and pointed back toward the house.

Drake stared at Lilly with sad, kind eyes. Those eyes confused her. Instead of the steel, there was something soft and malleable in his expression, something like care and concern for another person.

He wore stiff dark pants, with neat hand-stitched seams up the sides, the same pants he'd worn the evening he taunted her with the stuffed swan. His beard was gone and he'd cut his hair shorter. He was a cleaned up version of himself, with a remnant of the rank bear smell on him, lighter now, as if it had been washed off and powdered over.

"He's a dangerous man, Nell." It was the first time Lilly had ever raised her voice to her mother. Nell might have thought it was jealousy. It was not jealousy. It was fear. She had to make her mother know that Dean Drake was no good.

Nell moved closer to him and took his hand. No, she shook her head.

Lilly lifted the shovel and swung it over her shoulder. Nell looked horrified. It was the look of a mother's absolute disapproval.

"I'll get Charlie West if you don't leave," Lilly said.

"It's OK," he told Nell. "She's just scared." He lowered his eyelids toward Nell and spoke in a soft voice. He turned to Lilly—all kindness and light—and reached out a hand to introduce himself. "Dean Drake," he said.

"I know who you are." She met his hand with a glare.

Nell pointed to him and to herself and crossed her arms over her heart, saying that she cared about him, that he was a friend. She put two fingers to her lips and shooed Lilly back into the house.

Lilly didn't budge until her mother stepped forward, her face that of a wild wolf, teeth bared, a Nell she'd rarely seen.

Inside, Lilly washed the breakfast dishes, stopping every few minutes to look out the window. If only Jerome or his father would show up. She was afraid to leave her mother alone with the man. What if she disappeared completely and forever with him? After washing the dishes, Lilly went upstairs and watched them from her bedroom window.

Nell looked happy and young again, pointing to the tiny beet tops, the carrots, and the fence she'd put in for the snow peas. Her hand pointed at the back part of the garden where the dark dirt was dug up and ready to be planted. Her eyes brightened as Dean moved his lips and walked the rich earth with her. As Lilly watched them fear grew inside her like a thick fungus.

The memory came back to her. She had heard Nell tell Anna the story of Dean Drake. It was a night when Pa was gone. Nell had done an unusual thing and drank most of a bottle of wine. She had drunk too much and gotten the kind of loud that would have fought with Pa. Anna steered their mother toward bed in the room just under their own, but Nell hadn't been ready to go to bed.

She wanted to talk. Their mother said she loved a boy once, not their father. She had grown up with Dean Drake, and until she was seventeen years old, he had been her most constant pursuer. She never had any real interest in him as a husband. For a husband she needed a man who would be a good father. Even then, she felt the tiny spirits of Anna and Lilly waiting to be born. Still, all of his attention had been flattering and it spoke to her vanity. In spite of herself, she cared for Dean.

"Later," Nell said, "after he stood aside and let my parents go down in the river, I trembled and my chest felt heavy when I was around him. Just his presence filled my heart with mud.

"But," her mother continued, slurring her words, "I ignored that feeling of dread and thought instead about the way his red bay threw his mane, and how Dean brought me fish for dinner after my parents died. Even after he forced his way into my house one night, insisting he'd take care of me, I just wanted him to stop. After a while," Nell said, "I just wanted him to go away and never come back. He said he was so scared when they went into the river, and he would always regret that he hadn't been able to save them. I forgave him. But as time passed I couldn't face him. He reminded me too much of my folks, of the day they died."

Dean had been distraught when Nell married Pa. At first he'd caused trouble for them, but eventually he went away. After all these years, Nell figured he'd forgotten her.

But she was so wrong. He'd been biding his time. Now she was hurt and not quite herself and she was out there being sweet to him.

Desperate, and feeling helpless, Lilly went downstairs and put a pot of potatoes on the stove to boil without much water. She rubbed soot into the blue skirt she wore, smeared the skirt against her face, and pulled the leather ties from her blond braids. When the potatoes burned, she let smoke fill the house before running out to the garden.

"Mama, help!" She hollered, the wind blowing her smudged skirt against her knees. "I've caught your lunch on fire!"

Drake followed them, something Lilly hadn't counted on. He pushed the pot onto a narrow board, took it outside, and threw dirt on the burned potatoes. He looked back at the house where Lilly stood and walked toward her, his shoulders hunched up, making his neck thick.

While Nell cleaned up the mess Lilly had made, Lilly told Drake to leave. The fire burning in her veins was every bit as hot as the fire in the stove. She told him that she knew exactly where his camp was and she'd be bringing the sheriff up there if he wasn't gone within the minute.

He turned his eyes to the pass and shifted them to Nell and then back to Lilly, acting innocent, like he didn't know what she was talking about. "Go. Now," she said, her voice full of venom. "Or you'll be needing a new camp once I get Charlie up there."

He drew in a breath. "You're upset and you've been through a lot," he said loud enough for Nell to hear. "I mean no harm here. If your mother tells me to leave I will, but right now I think she can use my help."

Lilly didn't budge. "Charlie West will listen to me."

The man raised his eyebrows to that, silently calling her bluff.

"Then there's Joseph Pascal," she said, refusing to utter Running Bear's name in the presence of Dean Drake. "He and his people would like nothing more than to run you out of here. They don't like swan killers. They don't like killers. You come back here and I'll be happy to let them know you've been squatting on their land." She kept her voice down so that Nell couldn't hear. Although she had her back to her mother, she felt her mother's stare. It would be the look she'd seen a hundred times before, the one that said mind your manners or you're going upstairs right this moment to bed until you can learn to behave.

Dean Drake narrowed his eyes and clenched his jaw. "I've got no beef with you," he said, and started toward Nell.

Lilly stepped in front of him. "Go now."

Frowning horribly at her, Nell stepped forward and pushed Lilly to a chair. Brushing Drake's cheek, she kissed him lightly.

He looked, of all things, lovingly at her.

Trapped by her mother's will, Lilly stared at Drake with a drive for vengeance so strong it hurt.

When he left and Nell went back to the garden Lilly went with her, acting like her good daughter. She helped her dig up the ground for potato sprouts and covered them with dark dirt. She mulled over the lie she'd told Drake about knowing where he camped, and the way his eyes had glanced toward the pass. He had gone that way when he left. Lilly could find him, but not nearly so well as Nell could find him, if she'd had the desire. Nell knew him better than anyone, knew his hiding places, knew—only too well—his competencies.

The thought ate at Lilly and she focused on digging a trench for lettuce seeds, pushing the shovel into the soft earth, still moist with the winter run off. The wind kicked up and rattled the new leaves in the cottonwood trees, blowing a familiar smell toward her. She heard shuffling at the edge of the timber and grabbed the shovel firmly, knowing that they could not outrun a bear. The only hope, Pa had schooled Lilly, was to smack him hard on the nose so that he'd turn and flee.

But no bear walked out of the woods. Instead, Dean Drake tied his mule to a tree and stepped back into the garden.

Her brain burned and her legs turned to thunder.

Nell smiled and Lilly could see that she was relieved that he'd come back, that she didn't want him gone. She didn't believe he had shot her. She looked from Drake to Lilly and Lilly saw the loyalty shift in her throat as she moved toward him.

The hair stood up on Lilly's neck, waiting for lightning to strike, her mother falling into Dean Drake's arms like a young girl. He reached down and kissed her mother. Nell's eyes were half-moons by the time she motioned with her hands for him to go away. He paused, positioning a bush between him and Nell so that Nell couldn't see him. Then he turned, put his hand to his lips, and threw Lilly a kiss.

He mounted the mule, leaned down low in his saddle, and motioned for Lilly to come closer.

She did.

"My Nell knows what she wants," he said, his voice joining the wind. "This time around she wants me. I love her. You be a good girl and I'll be good for you all."

He turned the mule and rode toward the pass.

A mighty ache passed through Lilly. She missed her father so much her legs gave out. Only the wind held her up.

# 19

One full turn of the moon after her birthday, Lilly skipped one of the last days of school and went to check on Pearl at Jerome's ranch. The wind blew hard, stinging her face. Grass swirled at her ankles and the blue skirt wrapped around her knees.

Pearl had recovered from her infection and, even with her setbacks, had grown healthy and strong. She still had one good wing and could swim in the pond now with the other swans. She swam right up to Lilly, lifting her graceful neck in an invitation, and swam away, skimming the cool water with her feathers. Her feathers glistened in a sliver of silver sunlight coming through the clouds. Dark clouds gathered and separated. They moved like furred animals across the sky, a storm moving in and out, taking time to brew.

"You've done well caring for her," Jerome said. "She's looking strong." Jerome's hair fell in his eyes. He rested a fishing rod on his shoulder next to the feathered flies hooked into the canvas vest he wore.

"She'll never fly again."

"Not likely, but she's a swimmer and she gets along well with the others. You look upset. She'll be OK."

Lilly turned to him. "That's not it."

Jerome lifted his eyebrows.

"Drake's been coming around," she said, "visiting Nell and she's been letting him in. Like he's something good. She seems to want to replace Pa with him."

"What does Anna say?"

"Anna has been accepting food from him all winter. But lately she's not there when he shows up. He only comes when she's at work. When I try to tell Anna, she says he's not all bad. She says it'll blow over, that Nell is probably hellish lonely without Pa."

Jerome pulled Lilly close, wrapped his arms around her. A warm, silky feeling crawled up her stomach to her chest where her heart should have been, like maybe God hadn't taken her heart after all, like maybe she had a heart and it could love.

"Come on," he said. "I'll walk you home."

By the time they reached the back porch, the storm was on them. Thick torrents of sleet fell and the temperature dropped twenty degrees. The muddy road froze solid.

"My father would have predicted this storm," Lilly said as they stood on the porch. "He was almost always right about storms."

"You miss him," Jerome said, his eyes soft and sad.

"So much it hurts. He'd think this was crazy. Here it is almost summer and it's snowing." The world could twist itself out of control at any minute and there was nothing, not one thing, a person could do about it, not about the weather, not about losing her father, not about Drake in the garden with Nell. Just the memory of Drake's face brought the image of a raven that flew into the sky and back again. Drake was something so wrong. Lilly shook her head to let the image loose.

"A lull in the storm," Jerome said. "Guess I'll make a break for home. Be good."

"OK." She'd be good. She'd be twelve. She leaned off the porch after him. "I just wish Nell would start talking. Then I could understand what she's thinking about Drake."

"She might not share her thoughts with you."

"She could at least tell me to do something, the dishes, clean out the barn, help her in the garden."

"You want her bossing you around?" He raised an eyebrow.

Lilly smiled. "I want her to go out to the marsh with me to see the cygnets."

"Me too," Jerome said, and disappeared in the white bright air.

She stood on the porch watching the snow, thinking about the changes in Pa that began that fall before he died. Something had been bothering him. He made silly mistakes like getting the wrong size screws to fix the gate, or breaking the glass when replacing a window. A neighbor had given him a motorcar and Pa, going against Charlie's mechanical advice, took it on himself to fix the vehicle when it broke down. This resulted in cussing, yelling, tool throwing, and pounding on the auto.

Pa had always been easy and confident, but after that first swan had been shot and killed he seemed to try too hard. He couldn't relax and let things be. When he failed, he took it hard, and then kept trying exactly the same thing, in exactly the same way, as though through sheer force of will he could make things come out differently.

Nell, who hadn't liked his moodiness, tried to console him. She'd brush her hand against his hair, set tea out for him, bake cookies. If this didn't work, they fought. And sometimes, when they fought, things flew. At first Lilly glued things back together, but then they'd fly again. She gave up and simply picked up broken teapots and plates and put them in the garbage. She picked up scissors and pincushions and set them back on the sewing table. She wiped food off the walls, and went to bed hungry. Pa left the house and went riding the brown mare.

Pa had known that Drake was in the area again and it had set him off his normal good mood. If her father was still alive, he wouldn't like it that Drake had come into the house. He wouldn't like it that Drake had held Nell in the garden. That would have put Pa into a dark madness. He wouldn't have set fire to a pan to get rid of the man, like Lilly did. He would have just gotten rid of him.

After Jerome left, Lilly walked into the sweltering house and left the door open. The overstuffed stove threw off an abundance of heat. She wished right then that she had invited Jerome inside to witness Dean Drake sitting in a chair with a book, acting like he belonged. She looked at Anna, who was cooking dinner.

Anna shrugged and mouthed the words, "it's Nell's choice."

"Hello," he said, looking up and smiling at Lilly.

She threw her coat at the chair and went toward the upstairs room. On the way she ducked under the stairs and hid in the stairwell. On another day she'd walked into a too-hot house and climbed under the staircase. In the kitchen Pa and Nell had fought. Pa wore a summer T-shirt and trousers. Sweat dripped off his red face. Squinting his eyes at something unknown, he stoked the already too-hot fire.

Pa had melted the snow right off the roof that day.

"We're not safe here if I can't stop him," Pa had said in a loud voice. "He's killing the swans to get at me. He threatened Lilly. That man is so sneaky. I've got nothing the law could hold him on. He's going around to the fire hall and the men all like him."

"Maybe that should tell you something," Nell had said.

"I just want him to leave us alone. I want peace!"

"Calm down," Nell had said. The sound of her voice in Lilly's mind, from over a year ago, flew in like a brilliant white feather, precious and strong, giving Lilly a courage that started in her feet and slowly filled her chest. She shifted her body into a more comfortable position.

"In Helena I can work for the railroad," Pa had argued. "For a decent wage. It'll be good for all of us to get out of here."

"No," Nell had told him. "This is our home. We're not running."

"He won't stop until he splits us up, no matter what that means," Pa said.

Lilly knew what her father meant. Drake was no idle threat. She couldn't understand Nell. Surely she knew him. Yet, she apparently loved him. She still wasn't quite herself and the doctor said that she might not ever regain her memory about some things. To Lilly it seemed like her mind had come back to her but at the same time belonged to someone else. Otherwise, even if she did love Drake, how could she let him on their property? He had split Nell from her parents. He'd split her from Pa. Now he was working on splitting her from her daughters. Lilly had to make that clear to her mother.

Lilly watched Nell bring him tea. Her face was flushed and youthful, looking so much like Anna had when she first had a crush on George James King.

He took the tea and looked back at his book. As Nell walked away, he grabbed her hand and pulled her into his lap.

Lilly exploded out from under the stairs, knocking over a vase of wild flowers she'd put in front of her parents' picture. She saw the stunned look on her mother's face and ran upstairs. She locked herself in the room and refused to come out for dinner or for evening prayers. She woke early the next morning, went to the schoolhouse, and stood in a snowstorm until the door opened. She stayed until the teacher kicked her out. She had nowhere to go and finally snuck back into the house, unseen by Nell or Drake. Only Anna noticed her ghostly entry. And she had no chance to talk to Lilly once she tucked herself under the yellow quilt.

---

By the next morning Drake was gone. Nell slept late. Anna bustled around the stove and Lilly sat at the kitchen table eating oatmeal and looking out the window. The snow from the spring storm had already begun to melt. The pine smell of sun hitting the trees wafted in from outside. A fox ran by. The ravens yelled after him. In the distance Lilly saw the white feathers of a swan. She shook her head and looked again. Was it clouds? Swans didn't come this close to the mountains. No, those were the white feathers of a swan, she was sure.

Two laughing neighbor boys carried it. As they came closer she realized that it was just a stuffed animal, a polar bear much like the stuffed swan upstairs on her bed, homemade, probably a gift for some kid's birthday party.

"Hurry up, Lilly," Anna said. "You can walk me to work."

Lilly went into her bedroom and came out dressed in a simple skirt and blouse, a book bag hung over her shoulder.

"Now you're studying," Anna laughed. "Now that school's almost out."

That night Anna made a watery potato stew. Nell had gone out for a ride on the brown mare and never showed up for dinner. The water boiled away and the potatoes burned and no one ate, including Anna.

"She probably just rode into town to get supplies and got caught up talking to Lenore West or something," Lilly told Anna.

"She'd be home by now. Stores are all closed."

"She's not really herself." Lilly said it cautiously, not wanting Anna to think she was talking bad about Nell. She just wanted to talk about the real changes in their mother, who was acting like a young girl and not a mother of two.

Anna nodded. "Something is different in her brain. Maybe it was the illness or maybe it's the shock from losing Pa."

Lilly raised her eyebrows at that. "She doesn't seem to miss Pa at all."

"Listen carefully at night," Anna said. "You'll hear her crying."

"I miss him, too."

"I know, baby, me too."

And just like that Lilly was in Anna's arms weeping like the fool she'd spent a whole year trying not to be. When Anna finally led her to bed, it was past Lilly's bedtime, even her summer bedtime, and her tears had dried salty and fine on her cheeks. The late sun had gone down over the western fields. The brilliant last rays had faded hours ago and Nell still had not come home.

Lilly would catch holy hell if she stayed out that late, if there was such a thing as holy hell to catch. She didn't understand how God could put two such things together to be caught by anyone, let alone a twelve-year-old.

"You should give it up," Anna said when she pulled the quilt up over Lilly's shoulders. "This search for some phantom man who doesn't even know we exist."

"He's not a phantom. And I don't have to search, he's right here in our living room half the time."

Anna put up her hand to silence Lilly. "You should give it up and take care of your chores and studies, go have fun with your friends, act like a normal twelve-year-old. Or stay and talk to Nell, so that one day she'll talk back and tell us what she's thinking."

Lilly tilted her head to that and squished her lips together. Anna put a hand on her cheek. "She'll talk again," Anna said. "We just need to be patient." Her sister spoke like a seer about Nell, and funny thing was, Lilly didn't fight her on this. She believed her. Nell would talk again. "Mama seems happy enough with Dean," her sister said. "Let her be happy. We all need to get on with our lives and let the past be."

Lilly heard the front door open and shut. A moment later there was Nell standing in the bedroom doorway, bringing a fistful of Arnica into their room, the yellow flowers wilted on her wrists. Their mother twisted recklessly toward the stairs, shying away from Anna's eyes, as though Anna were the mother about to catch Nell doing something wrong.

"You've been drinking," Anna said.

Nell gave her a dazzling look, a thousand smiles filling her eyes. She bowed and extended her arms, with the yellow blossoms held crosswise, an offering to her girls for being late. Anna quietly took the flowers downstairs. By the time Lilly got out of bed and stood near the railing, the flowers sat prettily on the kitchen table near a bowl of burned potatoes.

"Your dinner," Anna told Nell.

Lilly retreated to the bedroom and watched from the cracked door. She already knew what came next. The thin veneer of happiness in Nell cracked wide open with some secret revelation neither Anna nor Lilly had been allowed witness. Lilly heard the crash before she saw the potatoes splattered against the wall and the broken bowl on the floor.

A fight broke out. But neither Anna nor Lilly had a place in it. It was something private inside of their mother, something churning up and boiling out, something that had finally dawned on Nell. While Anna chose to stay in the kitchen and bear witness to it, Lilly's place was under the yellow quilt. Before Anna cleaned up the mess, Lilly had already tucked herself back into bed.

# 20

Molting swans cast off their flying feathers when their young are born. It's nature's way to keep the swans earthbound for six to seven weeks. The parents have to stay close and protect the babies. To ground a swan, a person only needs to clip four or five feathers. That's not much for a thirty-pound bird.

Something told Lilly that Nell's flying feathers had been clipped and she resented it. She badly wanted her father to be here still to fix things for Nell. She missed her father and his ability to make things right, bring the goat back in, scare off a roaming grizzly, clear snow off the roof from a spring storm. Tend to her cuts and scratches when she fell from a tree she'd climbed. Soothe her long ago heart when other kids called her names.

That night she dreamed of him. He wavered in the distance, his arms and legs fragmented, his head hovering above his body, his blue shirt limp and shabby and torn at his chest. The red splotches on the shirt had faded with time. Beside him, the phantom Pearl preened her wings, her feathers silver in the ghostly light. Pa moved with mechanical motions, like an old farming tool. He moved slowly, like a wounded elk. His mouth quivered like fish lips, oddly, without purpose, as if words could flow out by themselves, could flow like air. In the dream her father did not breathe. He jerked his arms, or tilted his head, but he did not breathe.

When he came closer the swan glided in beside him, lifting her long neck to look over Pa's shoulder. Her soft black eyes set in the milky down of her head beckoned Lilly to pay attention. Something important was about to happen. Pearl shuffled and settled her wings, folding her elbows in close, and Lilly knew that the swan had brought Pa back from the dead to be there with Lilly, and she had a purpose.

Lilly moved close to Pa, trying to figure out what he wanted. Like a frightened child, her father moved away. The night wore on and his shirt changed. The red stains were almost completely gone, washed away by the wind or clouds.

Her father tried to speak. His throat lurched and tightened. His head pushed forward. Her own throat closed up and she found it hard to breathe.

*I need.* The words came out of Pa's mouth rough and raspy. He looked off in the distance. Lilly followed his gaze and saw nothing. He moved toward that nothing in the distance. *I need.*

"What do you need, Pa? Anything to have you back to the way you were before. I'll do it." She watched his movements. She asked the question again, silently, through her mind, willing her father to hear and answer.

When she couldn't get him to respond, she left the yellow quilt and walked along the same space Pa floated through, keeping her eyes on him. Pa was there now, not like he had been, but there, now. With Lilly. He walked outside. She climbed through her window and walked across the roof toward a rock outcropping. Pa beckoned to someone. Anna? Nell? God? Terrified she'd lose him Lilly never took her eyes off his tousled hair or his smeared awkward lips where words tried to form. *I need.*

Pa floated, moving toward the mountains. He followed a man out there, a man standing by the boulders that turned and went into the woods when Pa came near. Lilly followed them, eyes fastened on her father. She recognized the grizzled face of the other man, the green eyes, the dark trousers, but he was of no concern to Lilly when her father was asking for her help. She had to figure out what he needed. She had to get her father to talk. He floated and she followed.

Pearl opened her wings wide and took to the air. Lilly could see the soft down of her belly and her leather black feet as she soared out to the boulders where the man had left large footprints in the mud. She flew back to the window, landing on the wooden ledge, offering a wing for Lilly to step upon. Lilly stepped onto those white feathers, glittering, glowing like the morning sun. She stepped into that space as though she were a ghost rising above the tiny house, rising above the despair and loss. As she took that step, she rose above her father's drunken mood and Nell's childlike ways and she heard their voices out there together, across the land, singing a lullaby, sweet and pure, singing just for Lilly.

---

She woke up to Anna and Nell standing over her. The sky was metallic blue. The whole bright moon crowded the stars. The wind in the nearby aspen hushed the earth.

"She's breathing," Anna said.

Of course I'm breathing, Lilly tried to say, but her lips wouldn't move. They were like Pa's fish lips, trying to talk and failing. She felt dirt in her mouth, the solid earth underneath her. They were one, Lilly and the earth.

"Do you think it's broken?" Anna asked. "We can put a splint on it. Hopefully she has no internal damage."

Hey, I'm right here. No need to talk like I'm the walking dead. I'm fine. Just let me stand up and I'll go inside.

"Her leg's not the only thing hurt. Take a look at this arm, looks like a bad sprain. Better splint it for the night and see how it is come morning. Lucky she lived through the fall.

"More likely a jump. What else would she be doing on the roof in the middle of the night? It's no wonder. Someone in our family was bound to break sooner or later. We're young for taking on this kind of responsibility." Anna kept talking, talking for both herself and Nell.

Hey, look, I'm fine. Just let me get up and walk out of here. Lilly tried to say the words, tried to convey some meaning to Anna. No need for worry.

"One, two, three, lift." Lilly felt herself hovering above the ground, Anna's and Nell's hands gripping her legs and shoulders.

Something solid underneath her supported her back, her leg stiff, like it was encase in a tree trunk. She tried so hard to tell them that she was fine. Finally she understood. While she could see and hear them, they couldn't hear Lilly. Not a word. Like seeing Pa and Pa oblivious to her presence. It hurt a lot more than her leg to think of her father like that, walking alone, aimlessly through space, unable to see his own daughter.

———

When she woke up again Anna was still talking. "You had quite a fall. Lucky to be alive. What were you doing out on the roof?"

"I go where the wind takes me," she said, not really meaning to be smart or mean.

Anna nodded. She had a kind smile, with slightly crooked teeth and full lips. The smile, though, came mostly from her eyes, rich dark browns, a near black that absorbed the pupils. She smiled that smile at Lilly now and this time it was filled with sympathy.

Nell shook her head, a look of disgust crossing her face.

"I can't control my dreams," Lilly said. She wanted to tell them about Pa. But she knew they wouldn't believe her. They would say a dream was just a dream. But Lilly knew that her father had taken a night to visit her in the Mission Valley. He needed something. And Lilly knew what it was: justice.

The wind blew across her face and Lilly saw that they were still outside. Anna and Nell had moved her to the porch bench and tucked a blanket around her. The morning sun had just brought light into the sky, a red tint rising up and spreading across the mountain snow.

Something rushed from her toes through her belly and out her mouth, like an exploding underground spring. She blocked it by shoving a blanket in her mouth.

"You're hurt." Anna thought she was in pain, which she was, but there was more to it. "I think it's a sprain," her sister said. "But look, maybe we should talk about what happened here sometime this afternoon, after you've had a chance to rest."

Nell turned to Anna. "You think that will bring your father back?" Her voice was soft and kind, innocent and hopeful.

Anna and Lilly stared at each other.

"Nell?" Anna said.

But Nell clammed up as if the words had somehow materialized without her permission and she'd gained control of herself again. Pa had been gone a year. She must have finally understood that he wasn't coming back. Lilly turned to Anna, who looked stunned yet satisfied, like she'd just woken a grizzly from her winter hibernation.

---

A few days later Lilly sat at the kitchen table watching Nell, who had gone back to her complete silence. Lilly's leg ached, her arm throbbed, and her head felt like it was full of swamp water. Her foot was swollen but not broken. Apparently she had tried to land on her feet and succeeded. She pulled a white handkerchief, one of Pa's, from her pocket and blew her nose.

"I didn't jump," she said. "I wouldn't do that. I wouldn't kill myself."

Nell nodded, her hair falling around her face. Her dress hung softly off her shoulders, showing the sharp bones that had become more prominent during the past year. The morning light cascaded through the window, turning the kitchen bright and calm, a place where good things happened.

Lilly thought of something that Nell had told her the first time she ever watched a formation of swans cross the sky. "The stars of eleven are here, Lilly, right in your heart," she'd said. "They are waiting for you to grow and they're beautiful. They are yours and they are part of something bigger. The swans, your father and me, we're all flying together. We're all part of the flock. Even you, sweetheart. Even you." Lilly knew then that they'd always be together, that nothing could separate Lilly from her family, that the world was a safe place full of light and soft downy feathers they could cuddle into and sleep easily.

Lilly wished she were a swan. She'd fly out to the marsh. She'd somehow bring last year's dead back to life. She'd find her father in that dream world and bring him home. Instead, she sat at the kitchen table, grounded and full of grief. It was a hard grief that followed her like an old cow where crows landed and cawed.

She couldn't shake the feeling that she had caused this whole mess. She had let her imagination run wild, following Pa up the pass, gleefully accepting that he'd take her to see the swans for her eleventh birthday. At eleven she had killed half a dozen trumpeter swans and her own father just by wanting something.

So far, twelve was no better than eleven. Twelve had followed Pa into a dream and walked right off the sharp end of the roof. Twelve had caused Nell to worry about how to take care of her, when Nell was barely half better herself.

Come here, Nell motioned to Lilly. I've got a surprise for you.

The cabin was warm and Lilly hobbled over to where her mother sat. Nell stood and together they walked to the window. The summer sun shone through, lovely and effervescent. A pair of crutches, painted the same color of pink as Lilly's bicycle leaned against a tree.

"Anna painted them?" Lilly asked.

Nell shook her head.

"Who then?"

She held up her arms, which were covered with patches of pink paint, and smiled.

---

Lilly used those crutches until early August, long after her foot healed. Painting them was the first thing that Nell had done for her since she'd been shot. The world shifted and things had begun to right themselves: her mother was taking care of her again. Her leg was bird-bone light from being babied for a month. It felt hollow and brittle, with dry skin that peeled off in scaly reptilian flakes. It was too much like a spider leg when Lilly finally discarded the crutches. Nevertheless, her clipped feathers had grown back as she walked, ran, and rode her bike. Nell was right: Hatred was too strong of a word. Joy was better. It was time to move on, to let Pa rest, to hope that justice would find its own way.

And Lilly almost did just that. She almost returned to a normal life and let everything go. But then the heat blazed, the sun shining too brightly, and she saw the ghostly Pearl standing by the boulders at the edge of the property. Pearl lifted her wing and preened the matted feathers underneath it. When she finished, she scratched the dirt with her black claws, stretched her neck out long and graceful, and sounded her trumpet, causing Lilly worry.

Later that day Lilly rode to the mine tunnel where she'd stored her father's photos and waited for Jerome. At the bottom of the hill, she stashed her bike in the bushes and climbed to a group of boulders. Steadying herself on one precarious boulder, she took flight and jumped to another. Joy. Much better than hatred. She jumped again. Her weak leg ached, but it held. She'd build the muscles up again in no time. She would never, ever, ever go back to being spider legs.

"I thought you'd learned your lesson about jumping," Jerome said, riding up on a small Morgan, a brave curious horse.

"I'm a Hopi cliff jumper." She jumped to another boulder.

"What?" He got off the horse and tied him to a tree.

"A Hopi cliff jumper. They jump over deep crevices."

"Really."

"Only they don't jump, they fly. It's like you and me walking." Lilly spread her arms and jumped to another boulder. This time her ankle twisted and she went down, catching herself on her arm.

Jerome raced to her side. "You OK?" He looked scared.

"Just a little embarrassed," she smiled.

"It doesn't hurt?"

"Just a little," she said. Pain. It was still better than hatred. The smell of fresh pines settled on the warm rocks. She sat down on a large boulder. From up there she could see everything: the bushes where her bike lay, a path leading into the forest, a train approaching the small town, the new houses on the hill, Running Bear's camp. She looked out over the whole valley and felt the fresh sun in the air.

Suddenly the rank odor of bear rushed in and she heard a horse in the woods. Her stomach hit her throat and she jumped off of the boulder and ran to her bicycle. Her arms hurt. Even her good leg ached. Jerome followed right behind, walking the Morgan.

"Whoever is there surely heard us," he said.

"It's Drake," Lilly hissed, working hard to pull in a deep breath. "I know his smell."

"You sure?"

"Nell disappeared one night early this summer and came home drunk. She had nowhere to go. No one in town saw her that night. She had to have been out here, somewhere with him. She has to know where he goes, where he stays." Every muscle in her body felt tight. "And again there have been boot prints in the mud outside our house. He hasn't been visiting. Not that I know of. He's lurking."

"You don't know it's him outside of the house."

Lilly shook her head. "I know. I smell his danger. He's kind to Nell, but sneaky and secretive toward me."

"You're certain he was the one with the shotgun that day?"

Drake had admitted as much that night last winter when Jerome and his father came to get her from the mine tunnel. Yet that night was such a blur. She was so sick. Dreams mixed with reality and doubt had edged its way in.

So much had happened since then that the whole year was a blur. Memories all clouded together and melted like old snow in a way that she didn't like. She knew she'd been there and he'd come after her. She knew Drake threatened her. She was still certain he had killed her father, but she wasn't as certain as she had been. The doubt bothered her. She shrugged.

Jerome nodded. "Leave your bike here and ride back to town with me."

Lilly thought about how Drake dropped his smile when he turned from Nell to Lilly, like why would he bother to keep up a pretense for a kid, especially for one who was on to him. They knew exactly where they stood with each other. At least that much was clear.

She shook her head. "I can't keep running from him. I've got to put a fear into him, so he'll leave us alone. I just want him to go away. But he won't. There he is, courting Nell, barely widowed, a woman still not come back to her senses. She doesn't know to put him off."

"What do you mean doesn't know to put him off?"

"She's not thinking right. That's the only reason she lets him near."

"Lilly, I don't mean to state the obvious, but maybe she likes him. Besides, you're a girl. What can you do to scare him away? Let's leave now and be safe. Maybe later if it seems right we can make a plan to deal with him. Right now he's got the upper hand. He's in those woods, woods that he knows well, and we don't know where he is. He, on the other hand, probably knows exactly where we are."

Lilly reached up and felt the blood on her head. "I didn't realize I'd cut myself."

Jerome leaned over, like he wanted to look at the cut, and kissed her, soft and full on the lips.

Stunned, fear gave way to a new sudden sweetness and she didn't want him to pull away. An angel had thrown its light right down inside her where it caught fire. She wanted to hold on to it. "Can I trust you?" She asked.

"Yes."

She could feel Drake watching them. Yet every time she turned to look for him, nothing was there. "I know where he stays."

Jerome motioned to the woods and mouthed the word "him?"

She nodded. "He's got to be in another mine tunnel."

"You saw it?"

"No. But I'm certain. Think about it, if there's one mine tunnel in these mountains, there are others."

"Did you tell anyone?"

"No one believes me, they just think I'm crazy. He doesn't like it that I don't want him with Nell. It scares me to think of what might happen if Nell invites him to stay."

"You have to tell my dad."

"He won't listen to me." She couldn't stop thinking of Jerome's kiss, her first kiss, and suddenly she wasn't certain of anything. She shrugged her shoulders, a slow, non-committal gesture that said everything.

Jerome shook his head.

She could tell he was distracted too.

"I shouldn't have kissed you," he said.

She felt her face flush. "Jerome West, I'm not very old, and everybody says it, but something tells me you can't just take back a kiss. Come on."

"Where we going?"

"To the mine tunnel. I want to get Pa's photos that I hid there."

Jerome tied the Morgan to another tree. "Think it's safe?"

Safe as a kiss, Lilly thought.

---

Still feeling Jerome's kiss, Lilly walked into the house that night to the lovely smells of elk meat and gravy cooking. Drake stood at the stove in Nell's apron. Her mother wore a pink dress and a dreamy smile, her hair pinned up in wispy curls, each one an angel's wish. She held her arms open. It had been a long time since she'd called Lilly close to her. She hugged Lilly tightly, then pushed her shoulders gently back, a smile on her lips as she searched for something.

"Mr. Drake is making us dinner," Anna said, as if Lilly couldn't see it for herself. She wore a green dress and had pulled her dark hair back into a tight bun, which tugged at her eyes and narrowed them. "He brought elk and asparagus, and we dug some potatoes. And for dessert he brought these pomegranates and tiny candies."

"Dean," Drake said. "Just call me Dean." He looked over at Lilly, his eyes wide and interested, the green in them now a soft hazel. Lilly couldn't reconcile his clean, shaved face and his slightly balding head with the scraggly man in the marsh. This Drake had become something interesting and kind, something far more dangerous.

Anna smiled too, a wide-eyed carnival smile. "Look what he brought me." She held out her wrist, where she wore a beaded orange and yellow bracelet.

"I have something for you too, Lilly," he said. "Nell had Anna tell me how much you like swans, how upset you are that so many have died over the year." He held out a miniature white trumpeter made of cotton and flannel, with tiny feathers, pearl white beads sewn into the seams, and a black bill painted on. It was a tiny, more elaborate version of the swan he'd thrown at her in the mountains that night, the one she'd retrieved and put in her bedroom. This swan had round, alert eyes and she could feel it watching her, wondering would she take it in and love it?

Maybe if Jerome hadn't just kissed her, if she hadn't just felt the swoon of first love, or if Anna's smile had been more devious, or if Nell had acted more childlike in that moment, she'd have stayed strong in the truth she knew about Dean Drake. In their kitchen, in Nell's apron, he looked innocent. The past and present mixed together like a good stew, dislodging and confusing Lilly's convictions.

"I'm going to chat with Charlie West," he said, stooping down so that he was eye to eye with her. "We're going to find this guy who's killing swans, the man who killed your father, and we're going to stop him."

His words weaseled into her brain right next to the image of him in the marsh pointing a shotgun at her father, right next to the image of him hissing threats at her on the snow-filled mountain that evening. She drew in a breath and let it go very slowly.

"I can see that you are a family that loves trumpeters," he said, motioning to the pictures on the walls. "I'll be honest, I've spent a good deal of time jealous of your father because Nell married him and not me, but he took good care of her and he gave her you girls, God rest his soul. He was a good man and a really good photographer."

"You're saying you'll help stop the swan killer." Lilly almost believed him, almost believed someone else was out there randomly killing trumpeter swans. Someone who looked a lot like Dean Drake, but wasn't Dean Drake. Suddenly she actually wondered if Drake hadn't killed Pa, or if he had and it was an accident. She smiled, feeling half a traitor.

"Yes." And as if reading her mind, he said, "We'll find the man who shot Nell and killed your father and send him to jail. I swear to God."

Lilly bit her lip, and blood dripped into her mouth. He lied. He and Lilly both knew that he lied. With the lie still on his lips, he sat down at their family table and inserted himself into her father's place. Lilly looked at Anna and Nell, both of them nodding and smiling.

Anna set elk stew, asparagus, and potatoes on the table. It had been ages since they'd had good meat and a well-prepared meal. When Nell finally gave the go ahead to eat after saying grace, the others all dug in and piled the food high. The meat looked tender and well seasoned, the potatoes silky. Lilly put a smattering of food on her plate and pushed it around.

"Dean used to work for Nell's parents," Anna said, as if Lilly didn't know. "That's how they met."

Nell smiled at Dean.

Meanness rose and filled Lilly's chest, and nearly came blurting out of her mouth. She held herself in check, not knowing what he'd do if she spoke the truth here at the dinner table, the nearest neighbor at least five minutes away.

To Lilly's surprise, Anna went on the attack for her. "Weren't you there when Nell's parents drowned?" she asked.

Dean stopped in mid-bite and put his fork down. A tear filled the corner of his eye. "Yes," he said quietly. He rubbed a jagged scar at his eyebrow and looked at Anna and then at Lilly. "I've been deeply ashamed and grieved that I didn't save them. I froze with fear, when I should have pulled them out of the water." He looked over at Nell. "I'm so sorry. And now Sam. You've been through too much. I'm hoping you'll let me help you, to make up for the trouble I could have kept from you."

Nell's face went crazy soft, like it swam in tears, but she didn't cry.

"You're a good man, Dean," Anna said, looking like she believed it.

Nell nodded in agreement, happiness spilling out of her.

Anna folded her hands in her lap for a moment, holding them there as if in prayer. She looked from Dean to Nell and back again, a smile curling at her lips. "I'll have more potatoes please," she said, and piled them on her plate. She had let a deep admiration settle in her shoulders and Lilly could tell she thought something good was happening here with the warm food, Nell, and Dean Drake.

Lilly didn't argue it either. She just sat there watching her new family, reality falling down around her like a cracked swan egg the raven pecked too early, and Lilly—barely old enough to breathe—poking her soupy head out.

# 21

Something came over Nell after that meal. She was beside herself with delight, bubbly and cheerful, brought back round to her first love. Lilly understood now, having just kissed Jerome and feeling that strange sensation rise up through her body, her body feeling foreign and unusual, thinking of Jerome all the time. Nell let Lilly talk about school, about swans, about Jerome. She only shut her up when she came around to the topic of the dead swans and that Lilly was certain she could find and capture the hunter. This would be easy, being that he spent nights in their home.

Nell loved Dean Drake. The way she floated around the house, a girl in love, Lilly nearly began to believe that her contact with him did her good. Half the time Lilly felt wrong and crazy. Perhaps Dean—Lilly had taken to calling him that—had a brother, or a look-alike cousin, who shot Nell and Pa. Maybe his look-alike threatened Lilly on the mountain that day. Maybe she'd actually made the whole thing up, made it up that he was threatening to Lilly and kind to Nell.

Dead swans lay on the banks of the marsh where Jerome's father found them from time to time. Pa would have been furious about the senseless kills. If it wasn't Dean, who was it? What had Lilly seen with her own eyes? A true swan keeper would protect the swans and keep them from disappearing completely.

New tracks appeared out behind their house, his presence always palpable. Someone watched Lilly and followed her home from town. She knew it was Drake. Although, he didn't need to stand outside anymore now that Nell let him into the house at any time. Comparing Nell's and Pa's assessments of Drake, Lilly came up with two completely different men.

Even Lilly's own experience—the man swinging a stuffed swan at her, and the man in Nell's apron cooking dinner—came up with a man divided. At times she swore he followed her. She felt someone at her back and stopped, held her breath, imagined the swan's tear shaped neck, and listened. When Lilly listened, really listened, the footsteps stopped. The breathing stopped. She'd let go her breath and walk again.

———————

Just as a snowstorm began that early fall day, Lilly bundled up in several sweaters and a pair of pink mittens that Nell had made. She tied a blue scarf over her head and wrapped the length of it around her neck. Riding her bicycle in a snowstorm proved tough, but she had her bike chains on, and it was worth it to meet Jerome at the soda fountain. Inside, a blond waitress, maybe seventeen, leaned on her elbows across the counter, whispering something in Jerome's ear. Her apron bow turned up toward the ceiling like a swan's tail, flirtation so thick Lilly's head pounded. Jerome turned red. His hands fumbled in his lap.

An empty black stool sat next to him. Lilly took off the scarf, shook it out and slid across the vinyl seat. Her feet barely reached the floor. The scarf felt cold and wet on her thighs and she reveled in the coolness. A malt mixer stood next to the ice cream freezer at the back bar of the tiny café. A pie was baking, apple or huckleberries someone had gathered in late summer.

"I'd swear I'm not a minute late," Lilly said, tugging a napkin from a holder. The waitress stepped back, flipping her eyes from Lilly to Jerome, mute and cautious.

Jerome's hands remained folded in his lap.

A dark worm crawled across Lilly's brain. Nothing in her life was ever safe. "I'll have a glass of water, no ice," she said. "Please." She turned to Jerome. "Young trumpeters have flesh colored bills."

"Like I don't know. Like I haven't been around swans my whole life."

"They're awkward with their bills and it's difficult for them to eat. Before their wings have really taken shape and they've watched and learned from the old swans, they're awkward when they try to fly."

"The girl's a genius about swans."

The older blond girl stood at the sink, her apron bow turned to them, taking an exceptionally long time to pour the glass of water.

"They make short hops across the water, trying to follow their parents' example. The parents run and fly, showing them how to do it."

"Alright already, Lilly, this discourse on swans is getting annoying. I thought you wanted ice cream." Jerome put his hands in his pockets, jingled some coins, and scooted to the back of his stool.

"The older trumpeters," Lilly continued, "have graceful black bills, an elegant red line drawn in thinly at the mandible."

"*At the mandible*," Jerome said, mocking. "Pretty big word for such a young girl. You must finally be tending to your lessons."

"Fledglings learn the grace of flight at about ten to twelve weeks old."

"Yeppers."

"If only man were so lucky." They didn't look at each other. Lilly spread her palms out flat on the counter top, polishing the smooth finish with her fingers.

She smiled sweetly at the blond and thanked her for the water. Not looking at Jerome, she dumped the entire glass of water on his lap, put the glass calmly on the counter, and walked out.

Snow had piled on the seat of her bicycle and a white veil of it continued to fall out of the sky. Lilly pulled her bike away from the wall, wiped off the seat, and rode at top speed to the hardware store, wishing she could just ditch the bike and hop a train. Hobos did it every day. She was no different. She had a house, but it had not been home for a long time, especially not now with Dean Drake stopping by and staying whenever he felt like it.

She had a friend, but he'd apparently just deserted her.

She should've just ridden into the mountains, back to the mine tunnel and stayed there, away from Nell, away from Drake, far, far away from Jerome West. At the hardware store she sat out front on a bench, watched the snowfall, and listened to the door open and close.

As if thinking his name summoned him, Dean Drake stepped out, wearing a long gray coat. "Lilly?" he asked. "You're awfully pale. Are you OK?"

A great cloud settled on her. Dean's coat turned black and he sprouted raven wings. And she knew, in the very dark spot of her missing heart, that nothing good had ever happened.

# In Flight

# 22

Jerome swept in and rescued Lilly from the claws of Dean Drake, promising Drake that he'd see her home safely.

Black wings beat in her head and she didn't want to talk to Jerome. She wanted him to simply go away and leave her alone. The valley was small and she'd crossed it hundreds of times by herself. She didn't need Jerome. She could make it home by herself. This sudden surge of emotions she felt for a boy she'd known her whole life had descended on her like a dark cruel bird. She'd been looking forward to seeing him but now, moments later, she didn't want to be anywhere near him.

They rode their bikes in silence until they reached Lilly's house. By the time they arrived Dean had already tied his mule in the barn and was likely inside making himself quite at home. She climbed the steps of the porch, leaving Jerome at the bottom.

"I'm not going anywhere, Lilly," he said. "Not 'til you apologize to me."

"What?" As if she were the great white swan, she clamped her bill shut to keep from screaming at him. The storm receded and the afternoon sun poked through the clouds to shine on Jerome's dark hair. With that fall sun lighting his face, she could've forgotten her anger and forgiven him. She could have forgotten his bad timing of kissing her and flirting with the soda fountain girl, but she was twelve, her father was dead, Nell loved a murderer, and everything was wrong. "I'm not apologizing."

"What you did was rude and out of line. You embarrassed me."

"Pa told me a story," she said, looking down at him. With the angry blood burning in her veins, she felt as tall as the mountains. "A hunter had shot and injured a trumpeter. It was fall and the other swans had formed their group in the sky. The flock had formed, but they didn't want to leave behind one of their own. The injured swan flew the best she could, but kept falling to earth. She landed in the grassy fields on the way up the pass, home of the grizzly bears."

Jerome shifted on his feet, looked away and sighed.

She was not going to apologize to him. "The hunter chased the swan. The swan slowly made her way to the cliffs. If she could jump from a great height, the wind would catch her wings and she'd fall in line with the rest of her flock. Just as she was about to jump, the hunter popped out from behind a large boulder with his rifle. A grizzly bear saw this and ran between the hunter and the swan. Well, the trumpeter jumped and she flew. In her place the hunter shot the bear. But he only wounded it and the bear charged the hunter, sinking his teeth into his shooting arm. The hunter never took another shot at a swan. In fact, he gave up hunting all together. Many years later, when he died, they found his walls papered with pictures he'd drawn of the grizzly bear and swan, grazing the grass together.

"Pa said the bear represents power, the swan represents the soul." She looked straight down at Jerome. "When it comes to swans we all have a choice: to be the hunter or the bear. Which will you be, Jerome? Will you be someone on my side one day and a traitor the next? Or are you really my friend?"

He put his hands in his pockets, hunched his shoulders up to his ears, and looked toward the mountains, out toward the valley, and then back to her. "I'm not even going to answer that, Lilly, if you don't know by now. You've been in my life forever. Answer your own stupid question." He stormed away.

She let him go. Standing on their porch, she watched Jerome walk across the snow-covered field, toward the deep valley where the land grew wild, and further on where barren dirt gullies edged the river. If he went far enough he'd cross the bones of dead animals and the hidden lair of coyote. Lilly was a young girl, but she had already learned, like a stunted juniper that grows from rocks, to nurture her loneliness and the sweet taste of revenge.

———————

Inside the house, Nell and Dean sat by the fire holding hands and reading. In unison, they looked up.

"Have you recovered from your outburst?" Dean asked.

"Where do you live, Mr. Drake, when you are not here?" she asked.

"Dean. Call me Dean."

Nell looked from Lilly to Drake, a question in her eyes.

Anna hustled around the kitchen stove, ignoring them.

Upstairs, Lilly lay on her bed, and listened to Anna hum while she fixed dinner. The fresh aroma of cornbread and some kind of casserole cooking filled their home. When Anna called Lilly for dinner she refused to go, feigning sickness. She did not want to sit at a table with Drake. Or with Nell. She was furious at her mother for her childlike ways and for bringing a killer into their home, for believing him over her. She wanted her to grow up and be the mother she used to be.

When the sun went down, Lilly lit the lamp, reached under the bed, and pulled out the box of photographs. She had kept the ones of Nell and Pa on top. When she lifted the lid, Pa's gentle eyes stared at her. She touched his forehead. And Nell's beautiful grown-up smile lifted at the corners. The bun at the back of her head tightened her cheeks. She wore the same blue dress in which she'd been shot.

Under the pictures of Nell and Pa were photos of Anna and Lilly when they were young: riding their bikes, sitting under Christmas trees, Anna standing by the brown mare. A photograph of George and Anna walking down a dirt road holding hands surprised Lilly and she wondered if Anna knew that Pa had taken that picture.

Under the family pictures, she found one of some grizzly bears, bears Lilly remembered. They had camped far up the mountainside, although still a long way from the pass. Anna and Nell set up the tent and prepared food for dinner. While Pa and Lilly hunted for firewood, Pa lugged his camera along, just in case he found an interesting shot. Not too far from camp the two stumbled on a large family of bears in a meadow. The silver tips of their humps glistened as they lumbered forward. Their great shoulders rocked as they overturned boulders with their huge paws. They chewed the tall grasses and moved into the huckleberries at the edge of the forest.

Sam assured Lilly that the grizzly bears wanted nothing to do with them. Bears needed to be damned hungry or provoked before they'd approach a human camp, he said. If a grizzly thought that you were after a deer carcass he had, his natural instincts would kick in and you'd be in trouble. Stay away from deer carcasses, cook away from your sleeping area, leave the bears alone, and they'll leave you alone.

Lilly wasn't so sure. Especially since her father stood in front of her, guarding her, to take the pictures, hiding her—worried, but not too worried.

She put the grizzly photo aside and listened. All was quiet downstairs. Even Anna must've been reading. Lilly dug further into the box, where Pa's mining pictures lay dusty and untouched. He took them the year that he worked in Butte, before Anna and Lilly were born. Her hands shook as she flipped through them: a man with his pant leg folded and pinned up to his knee; a man missing three fingers; a man missing his left arm, his face drooping on one side; three men with burned faces; a man face down in the shaft; the graves of several miners; and a group picture of men by the cage that dropped down into the shaft.

She gripped the group photo, peering closely at the steely-eyed man in the background, the man in charge of lowering the cage.

The five men in the front of the picture smiled for the camera. The man in the background slit his eyes to the camera. A ripple crawled across her stomach. The photo was grainy and slightly out of focus, but there was no question. Those cold eyes belonged to Dean Drake.

She heard the thud of a log added to the fire downstairs. A pot scraped across the stove and someone filled it with water. Then the front door opened and closed. Lilly looked out the window and watched Dean walk to his mule, get something out of the saddlebag, and come back to the house. Again the door opened and closed.

"What's that?" Anna asked.

"I need to protect Nell and you girls," Drake said with a laugh. "I can't do that with my bare hands."

A jagged edge ran up Lilly's spine. In the dim lamplight, Pearl floated into the room and touched her cheek with her feathers. She tilted her head and looked at Lilly with her black, dreamy eyes, flattening her black feet against the wooden floor, standing strong. What was she saying? And how could she be in two places at once, here with Lilly and at Jerome's ranch? Lilly did not resist the comfort that the beautiful trumpeter offered. Pearl curled her neck and straightened it, trilling a soft low sound, telling Lilly to calm down. Think clearly.

Lilly looked back at the pictures. The next photo showed Pa clenching his fists, his mouth open, like he might be yelling. Drake stood off to the side, glaring at the camera. His eyes seared into Lilly, like they had that day at the marsh when he shot her parents. The sounds of him downstairs protecting Nell burned Lilly's skin and made her legs go weak.

Pearl cautioned her, resting her rounded, flat bill on her arm. Lilly didn't know what the photos meant. She didn't know whether or not Drake had anything to do with the men's injuries. She couldn't possibly know what kind of time Pa had spent with him in Butte.

A third photo showed Drake alone at the cage, his face contorted, reaching for something. She turned the photo over. Two initials were scribbled across the back in Pa's handwriting: D.D.

Under that photo was a sealed envelop addressed to Dean Drake.

She opened it.

*Dear Mr. Drake,*

*Be advised that if you do not leave the Mission Valley imme-diately, you will be brought to justice for what you did to me in Butte. More than that, you'll be made to pay for what you did to Jimmy Joseph.*

*Signed,*
*Sam Connelly*

Jimmy Joseph, Horse Child, Running Bear's son, died in Butte. The last remnant of doubt that Lilly had about misjudging Dean Drake dissolved. He was guilty, of more than she knew, or might have imagined. Pearl vanished. The room was quiet.

Carefully, Lilly put most of the pictures back in the box in the same order that she had taken them out, with the mining photo-graphs at the bottom. She kept the note and two photos—one of Pa and one of Drake—in the pocket of her brown trousers and hid the box under the bed. She dug around in her sock drawer for her scissors. Opening and shutting them, she listened to the sound of blades. It was nearly a song, like Pearl's soft trill, like the bear's growl, like Nell's pure sweet voiceless voice.

She pulled one of her long braids forward. It was tight, the way she liked it, the way only Nell knew how to braid. The scissors made no sound as they sliced through the hair. The white-blond braid dropped to the floor by her bed and she left it there. The second one was much easier.

When she finished, she picked up the braids and scissors and placed them in a triangle on the dresser. She folded her hands close to her missing heart and whispered the prayer, in the way she remembered it, no longer knowing which parts she'd memo-rized and which parts she'd made up: "Today I put on the power of Heaven, the light of the Sun, the radiance of the Moon, the splendor of Fire, the fierceness of Lightning, the swiftness of Wind, the depth of the Sea, the hardness of Rock, the grace of the Swan."

After Nell had gone to bed and Anna had come upstairs and gotten into bed Lilly quietly folded back the covers. Barely touching the floor, and light as a feather, she got out of bed and snuck downstairs, tiptoeing away from where Drake slept on a mat in the corner. She packed some bread, raisins, and dried meat. Then she went back upstairs and climbed into bed with Anna.

"Wake up," Lilly whispered.

"What?" Anna turned to her.

"He killed Pa."

Anna nodded.

"He's got Nell buffaloed."

"He scares me," Anna said.

"We have to stop him. I'm going to find his hideout. I'm sure he's got an abandoned tunnel or cave in the mountains, where he holds up."

"It's dangerous, and you're too young. Better just to let him hang himself here. Eventually he'll say or do the wrong thing, exposing himself."

Lilly thought about that. It was possible. "What did he get off his mule tonight?"

"A pistol." She turned her head toward the window. "And a rope."

Swamp water filled Lilly's lungs so she could barely breathe. "Tomorrow you keep him here. Tell him I went to Jerome's. I saw him take Pa's camera. The film might still be good and maybe Pa took a picture of him in the marsh that day. Maybe Drake stashed the camera in his hideout."

"I don't like it," her sister said.

After a while Anna wrapped her arms around Lilly and held her tight. "What happened to your hair?"

"I cut it."

"You shoulda let me do it."

Lilly lay next to Anna, feeling her warmth, barely breathing, waiting for morning to come. That night, she put on a terrible strength.

# 23

Early the next morning Lilly dressed in the brown trousers, a brown work shirt and Pa's old sweater. After she'd rolled bedding and a warm coat into a bundle and tied it to her bicycle, she rode to the hardware store and asked George for a small can of green paint and a paintbrush. He delivered them, quizzing her about what she intended to paint.

"My bike," she said, once she gripped the package securely in her hands.

"What happened to your hair?"

"I cut it."

He lifted his head and tilted it. "You shoulda let Anna do it."

Once Lilly painted her bike, she waited an hour, absorbing the autumn sun, waiting for the paint to partially dry. Then retied the bundle onto the back fender, tied Pa's sweater around her waist, got on the now green bicycle, and pedaled hard toward the pass.

The free wind in her hair felt like a friend, and so did the dirt under the tires and the blue, blue sky. They were far better friends than Jerome West had ever been. Riding cleared her head as she followed the game trails. Fresh air filled her lungs and she kept her eyes wide open, watching the trees for anything they might be hiding, like bears, wolves, or a giant bull moose. She watched the mountainside for the dark spots of caves or tunnels, working hard to reach the pass before the sun went down. When the grade became too steep, she left the bike near a tree, hiked for a long time. With the dimming sky, she chose a camp quite a ways below the snowfield that she had climbed with her father.

Across the valley she saw the rolling hills that reached toward the setting sun. The sun left a residue of warm, silky air and the smell of pines. Luck ran in her direction. A thick crib of pine needles nestled between some boulders made a perfect bed. She sat on a boulder and watched the pink light spread across the valley. She ate the food she'd packed. When the bread flaked and fell to pieces in her lap she brushed the crumbs away and pitched the bedding on top of the pine needles. She climbed in, closed her eyes, and snuggled down.

When the sun had completely gone and the moon had barely arrived, the wind blew a dark smell toward the camp. Her eyes popped open, her hearing sharp. Not too far away, heavy footsteps slid across the ground. The thought hit far too late to do anything about it: she hadn't put the food away from her sleeping area. It sat in a pack at the foot of the bedding. She crawled out in the half-moon light and moved the food away.

Back in bed, she squished her eyes closed, curled her toes, and tucked her knees to her chest. She played dead like the swan had when she'd first held him in her lap. If she posed no threat to the bear, the bear would most likely take the food and leave.

"Lilly."

Her eyes bolted open.

"Lilly, it's me."

"Jerome? What are you doing here?"

"Anna said you went looking for Drake's hideout."

She narrowed her eyes at him, although in that light he probably couldn't see it. The partial moon haloed him. He wore a long wool coat and carried a bundle.

"She wasn't supposed to tell anyone," Lilly said.

"She didn't, she just told me. She got worried when you didn't come home. You shouldn't be out here by yourself. I heard a bear crossing the gully only moments ago. He couldn't have passed more than a few yards from where you're camped."

"I'm not talking to you."

"I know."

He rolled his bedding out and lay down next to her. She heard him tossing and turning for a long time before she fell asleep.

---

They woke up to gunfire in the distance, higher up on the pass.

"Someone's hunting," Lilly said.

"Yes, and here you are dressed like a bull elk. How'd you sleep?"

"I had a rock cutting into my side all night. Think that's Drake?"

"There's one way to find out," Jerome said. "Let's head over that way."

"I thought sure Anna would tell you to bring me home."

"She did."

"But?"

"But we've got a killer on our hands."

They stashed their bedrolls and walked toward the gunshots. They passed branches splattered with blood, which led to a trail of crushed bushes. Someone had hunted and chased an animal through the woods. The trail smelled rank, like bear, or elk and as they followed it the smell got stronger. It was a smell Lilly recognized from the marsh, from that winter on the mountain with her father, from home. Where the trail opened up she heard someone whistling. Lilly and Jerome hid behind a tree and looked out on a skinned bear. The silver coat had come off in large tufts and lay scattered across the clearing. It was awful.

Drake was not there.

Suddenly the hair on her neck curled. The rank smell grew stronger, coming from the wrong direction. A hand covered her mouth.

She bit down hard, kicking instinctively into the shin behind her, and ducking out of the man's grip.

Jerome attacked him head on.

Drake picked Jerome up like a rag doll and threw him aside.

Lilly jumped on the hunter's back, digging her nails into his throat. He threw her off and she bounced on the ground. She lunged at him again, going for his eyes. Again he tossed her to the forest floor, but not before she drew blood.

Time slowed down and expanded. Tree leaves settled on the wind.

Jerome ran in slow motion, taking two long strides toward Drake. He lifted a large stick high, swung it down right in front of him, and hit Drake in the head.

Drake pulled a hunting knife out of his belt and stabbed at Jerome, catching his coat with the first slash and his hand with the second.

Blood danced out of Jerome's hand and covered both of them.

For a moment Lilly stood outside of the danger while she floated above the scene and watched the whole thing from the trees.

She shook her head hard, came back to herself, and dove on Drake again. With all her might, like a wild swan enraged, she scratched and clawed, lifting her great wings against him.

Jerome grabbed her. "Run, Lilly! Run!"

She heard Drake laugh as she ran through the woods ahead of Jerome, the same laughter she'd heard at home. Branches broke and that eerie laughter followed.

A distance behind her, running after her, Jerome called her name. Tree branches blocked her path and she pushed them away. When she reached their camp, she grabbed the rolled up bundle and ran hard.

Part way down the hill she turned and looked at Jerome. Blood had splattered his coat and his face. Mud was caked in his hair.

"Are you OK?" She asked in a hushed voice.

"I am," he said, holding his cut hand against his belly. He stepped into a grove of trees and with his free hand pulled her with him. His coat hung in shreds where it had been slashed by the knife. "His hideout has to be nearby."

"He hurt you."

"Hopefully we hurt him too." Jerome smiled.

Behind them bushes moved.

"We have to go." She saw a familiar bicycle, not Jerome's, leaning up against hers. "You rode Pa's bike?"

"I didn't think he'd mind."

Lilly fastened the bundle to the back fender of her bicycle and, with Jerome right behind her, rode down the trail. Guiding the tires carefully, braking, keeping the pace down, she constantly turned to look behind her, waiting for Dean Drake to be on them. They raced past the dried bear grass and through the damp cedar grove. When a dry dirt trail stretched out into the pine forest below, she let go of the brake and flew down the trail.

Somewhere near the bottom, she heard a gunshot and looked back toward the sound. In doing so she hit a slippery patch of dead pine needles. In a slow, dreamlike motion, the bike tires slid out from under her and she went face first down the trail and crashed into a boulder. Everything went black and her second soul floated back up the mountain toward the hunter and his hideout. Pearl flew at her side, her black flat bill turned into the wind, following a smell. It was funny, how fast Lilly's second soul could walk without touching the ground and she thought maybe she was flying on the wings of a swan, that Pearl carried her, that she wanted Lilly to see some dangerous thing.

From that safe distance Lilly watched Drake command the clearing where he'd skinned the bear. His wide brimmed hat threw a shadow over the scratches she had left on his face, and the stubble that covered his chin. From the look in his green eyes, he was determined to take care of his kill.

He cut the heart out of the large creature, and blood splattered over him. From the edge of the clearing came a chirping sound. A squirrel stood there on his back legs. Drake looked at the squirrel. His hand moved like swift water and the knife soared through the air. It caught the squirrel right in the soft flesh of his belly and pinned him to the ground.

With Pearl's help, Lilly flew back to her body and opened her eyes. Something liquid ran down her face into her mouth, leaving a metallic copper taste.

"You knocked yourself out and cut yourself on that boulder. You're bleeding," Jerome said.

But Lilly knew he was wrong. She'd been shot. She lifted her head to look for the bullet hole. Pain crept in like a slow river and she closed her eyes again.

Jerome sat at her side, saying something she couldn't hear.

Unable to move, she felt the cold ground. If this was God's plan, she'd give in to it. She'd just die right there on the mountain, not from being shot, because it turned out she hadn't been shot, but from a gunshot wound, like the hunters' lead pellets that killed a dozen swans years later. Lilly would die from the same shotgun that killed her father and shattered her heart, leaving nothing but an empty hole in her chest. If Pa was alive, he would have stopped Lilly from riding to the pass, or he would have gone with her, or taken care of the danger himself as Lilly went to school.

Jerome tugged her arms. "Get up. We have to get home."

They arrived at Lilly's house moments before Drake came through the door.

Nell soaked a rag in warm water to wash his scratched face.

Anna, Jerome and Lilly stood by, dumbfounded, and watched her. When she finished, she wrapped Jerome's hand in a clean cloth. She soaked another rag in clean water, and like a real Florence Nightingale, she tended to Lilly's wounds.

# 24

Sitting in the Mission Church Lilly checked to make sure she still had Pa's letter to Drake and the two photos in her pocket. They sat next to her father's folding knife. She knelt to pray. Pearl swooped down beside her, and Lilly felt her head clear. Lillian. Elizabeth. God Has Sworn. She had no fear, and grief had left her on that mountainside. All she had left was young rage.

"Lord," she prayed, "guard me today from poison, from burning and drowning, from hurt. Guard the swans, and Anna and George, and Nell and Pa. And Jerome. Make all things right. Guide my hand in this. Amen."

Pearl spread her great wings through the church, and they brightened the room with white light. For an hour Lilly sat quietly, her mind going everywhere and nowhere. She still didn't understand how Pearl could be there with her and at Jerome's ranch at the same time. Maybe her wound had given her exceptional powers—the power to divide herself in two and then come back together again.

The church was so quiet. The peacefulness comforted Lilly. It was as if she could feel all of the prayers, worship and pain that had passed the altar through the years. Those prayers had gathered like a beautiful soft light to fill the stone building and bring love to the valley.

A motorcar passed outside. Inside, a mouse scurried across the floor. Someone played the organ. Amazing Grace. It was beautiful and sad. Her head bowed in prayer and uncertainty about the task ahead of her, Lilly counted on God, grace, and the stretched and uplifted wings of the swan.

Jerome met her outside the church. They'd go together to look for Drake's hideout and when they found it, they'd get his father to go back up there with them. If they found Pa's camera there, that would be even better.

Jerome tilted his head toward her and nodded slowly. "Nice hair," he said.

She squinted at him and squished her lips into the shape of a bill. "Don't."

"I'm just saying."

---

Jerome spotted the tunnel first. They'd been hiking for most of the afternoon and talking. Mostly, Lilly was talking, a real chatterbox.

"This is a secret story," she said, trying to sound like her father, "told by the swan keepers of long ago. The Mission Valley was a breeding ground for a large flock of trumpeter swans, back when the trumpeter roamed freely, guarding a hundred acres at a time from predators. They built their nests in the swampy areas and flew out on the lakes. They ruled the sky, the earth, and the water. They kept their eggs from the cougar and warded off the raven.

"Man saw the bird in all his royalty. Jealous Man watched the bird fly, swim, and walk the earth. Man could only walk and swim. He wanted so badly to fly that he climbed on the back of the swan. The bird crumpled to the ground under Man's weight. When Man got off him, Swan took to the sky and flew far away, returning many days later. Man couldn't bear to have the swan go where he could not go, and caught the bird. He stripped his plumage and pinned the swan to the earth. For a whole season he watched the trumpeter forage in the swamp and walk the wetlands. With his feathers cut, he could no longer fly and the skies became dark.

"The next year the feathers grew back and Swan took to the air never to be seen for many, many years. Man looked everywhere. He sank to his knees and cried. He begged Swan to forgive him, to return. He vowed that he'd let Swan alone, that he'd curb his jealousy, and stop trying to control him. He promised to appreciate the grace of the swan in flight, the wind in swan feathers, the fact that Swan could fly, even though Man himself could not.

"The trumpeters had sympathy for Man and returned to the Mission Valley to build their nests and raise their young. Man watched. For a very long time, Man did not interfere with the grace of the swan.

"But now they do," Lilly continued as they climbed. The way was steep and her legs burned. She was winded from telling the story.

"If you keep talking, whoever is on the mountain is going to hear you coming from miles away," Jerome said, covering a smile with his hand. "Then it won't matter what Swan did."

"You like her, don't you?" Lilly asked.

"Who?"

"Don't act all innocent. The swan girl at the soda fountain."

"She has nicer hair than yours."

Lilly put her hand up to where her hair sat like a broken bowl on her head and felt its blunt edges. "Don't be mean."

"Why'd you do that anyway? Why didn't you just let Anna cut it?"

"You keep talking and they'll hear us for miles, Jerome West."

"I like her, but you are my best friend," he said, covering the smile again, "and I'd much rather be out here searching for killers with you than drinking sodas in town with her."

This time Lilly was the one hiding a smile. She didn't want him to know that he mattered so much to her.

They drank water and ate rationed bits of bread each time they stopped. The bear grass had wilted and died, leaving long stalks tilting toward the ground. Once Lilly and Jerome moved out of the trees, long grasses, dried from the summer heat and the fall wind, swayed in the breeze. Bear scat and autumn wildflowers littered the open fields, stubborn against the frost. Small patches of snow from the early storm hid in the shade of rocks and stunted pines. A small creek trickled from the larger snowfield high up on the mountainside.

A loud cracking sound, like a branch breaking, stopped them both in mid-step. A growl filled the air as a huge hump-backed bear stepped out into the grass in front of them. He swung his full head, sniffing the air. He swung his head up the mountain and back toward Lilly and Jerome, his paws clawing the air. Pearl appeared just over the bear's back. She trilled and Lilly looked at Jerome to see if he heard her. His eyes were wide, the pupils large and dark.

"Do you see her?" Lilly whispered.

"Hard to miss a full grown grizzly."

"Pearl. Do you see her?"

He tilted his head and looked back toward the bear. He didn't see her. Although Lilly didn't know what it meant, she knew it was not good. She watched the bear. He followed Pearl into the field of dried flowers, far from Lilly and Jerome. The bear dumped two boulders and dug up a rotten tree stump. In moments, he shredded it, throwing off pieces, the pieces cutting right through Pearl as if she was invisible. Lilly followed Jerome as he quietly moved up the mountain, never taking her eyes off the grizzly.

"Over here," he said, pulling her behind a small wall of rocks where they could watch the bear from some kind of mock safety. Bears run thirty miles an hour and dump boulders like fallen leaves. If the bear came after them, no quick place would be safe.

"It's OK," Lilly told Jerome, keeping her voice low and quiet. "He doesn't want us. He'll be much happier with an old deer hide. If we don't bother him, he won't bother us. Pa taught me. Stay alert and watch for signs."

"Like live bears right in front of us," Jerome said.

"Smarty pants," she said, undeterred. "Especially, keep alert for any dead carcasses. If we see one, it's a really good idea to go the long way around, far away from the spoiled meat. That's one time a bear will attack a human. Bears don't see really well. But they have a strong sense of smell."

"I say let's just get out of here." He started up the mountainside away from the bear and stopped. "Look." He pointed to the entrance to an old mining tunnel, open mouthed, right behind the bear.

Before they could even move toward it, Drake sauntered out of it and, watching the bear, hiked downhill. Lilly heard some rumbling and an animal nay. The bear lifted his head and looked in Drake's direction. Through the trees she could see a small corral where Drake kept his mule.

After he rode off, and after the bear had moved on, Jerome and Lilly went into the mine tunnel. It was dark and musty, and she could just make out a fire ring. The rank bear smell permeated the tunnel and Lilly finally located the source. In a reckless pile near one wall was a bear hide. Next to it something white glittered in the tiny sunlight that broke through the darkness.

When Lilly got closer she saw several white feathers spilling out of a small bag. Over on another wall, a canteen and a set of tin pans for cooking were stacked neatly on a makeshift shelf. Beyond the shelf sat a bedroll and next to the bedroll sat Pa's missing camera.

---

Drake was there when Lilly got home, waiting on Nell like she was a queen, or like she was just a little girl who couldn't do one thing for herself. He cleaned out the cook stove, brought in wood to cook dinner, and cut up a chicken, all with his face shaved clean and his hat left at the door. Lilly could feel him watching, yearning to know how much Lilly knew. She thought of the bear hide and the feathers and wondered if he could smell his hideout on her.

"Where's Anna?" She asked.

"Over at George's house," he said. He looked at Nell for verification and she answered him with a little girl smile. Her eyes looked wary though. Lilly hadn't seen that caution on her since before the shootings. Her mother shifted her eyes to the gun tucked into Drake's belt and then to the bottle of whiskey on the table.

"Your mother's worried because I've been drinking," he said. "But no never mind to me whether I been drinking or not, I'm the same nice fellow that loved you all those years ago."

Nell nodded slowly and her shoulders relaxed some.

Lilly didn't believe him, though, on either account. The gun and the raised hair on her arms told her something was amiss.

Outside purple asters poked through the grass. Huckleberry bushes had turned fire red. Way too soon pine drop stalks would reach their rusty, dry fingers toward the sky. Clouds settled over the mountains and the marshes in the foothills, where swans readied to make their way south, and all was as it should be. But here, in Nell's kitchen, something was terribly wrong.

Drake had lost the near-innocent look he'd had last time he'd made dinner for them. A certain knowing lit in his eyes.

Lilly's stomach tightened. Her breath caught in her chest and paused before making its way out. She wondered if Nell was onto him, if she was wondering what she'd seen in him, why she ever loved him at all. Lilly could see it in the glint of her eyes, as she looked toward the fire, that her love for him had turned to something else, caution or concern, disgust even.

But Lilly also knew that in an instant the crow that was her love for him could swoop back in and pick at her heart. The tears in her eyes told Lilly that she was torn. She was scared and she still loved him. Nell looked at her with determined eyes she hadn't seen in over a year. Those eyes said she'd put that love away, if it meant their safety, and she would never again move toward him. Lilly saw something flutter across Nell's face and heard a soft moan pass her lips.

Lilly moved closer to her. "You want to speak," she said.

"Don't be making her feel bad for things she can't do." His voice was tight.

"I'm not making her do anything. She wants to say something."

Nell made the sound again.

Drake had the chicken frying and the house smelled good. He'd let it cook a little too hot and opened the door to let the smoke out.

"Be a good girl and set the table for your ma."

"Will Anna be home for dinner?"

"I hope so. We got plenty. Ask your mother."

And just like that the moment of wariness passed from Nell. The warmth of the fire settled on her face and she gazed lazily at him. She nodded yes, that Anna would be there. Then she got up, handed four plates to Lilly, and motioned for her to set the table.

If she'd told her mother about finding Drake's den that afternoon, Nell would have said it was innocent. A man has a right to his privacy. He has a right to hunt in this country—not swans, but other things. Feathers proved nothing.

But Jerome had taken Pa's camera to his father. He would know how to salvage the film and get it developed. Even if the film was ruined, there was still hope. Lilly had the photo of Pa clenching his fists at his side and the photo of Drake standing, grim-faced, ready to drop the cage into the mineshaft. She had the letter that Pa had written, warning Drake to leave the valley. She knew where Pa had stashed a bag with something besides a gun in it.

---

Jerome refused to go up to Pa's cave with Lilly. He wanted to be sensible and give his father a chance to get the film developed. She supposed it made sense to have his father take care of it. Maybe in another year when she was older Lilly would have listened to him and stayed home. But she was, after all, twelve. Twelve had its own kind of wisdom, both good and dangerous. She went without him.

She left early and hiked most of the day to reach the snowfield that crossed the mountain to Pa's cave. Straight ahead of her, where the snowfield began, she saw a bullet casing. Next to it a set of large boot prints crossed the dirty white field, turned, and climbed the pass.

"Someone else is here." She smiled to herself. On the other side of the pass, a trail of heel steps punctured the glacial drop to the cave. As Lilly started down, she twisted her ankle, her foot slipped, and she did the splits for a few seconds before sliding down. The ice cold burning heat tore her sweater up to her neck and her back caught fire. She flipped over onto her belly and tried to dig her toes in. She gripped the snow with her fingers, but the snow burned fire into them and there was nothing to hang onto.

Before she hit the rock outcropping at the bottom, Pearl flew in and wrapped Lilly in her wings. Lilly floated in the pure white world of swan feathers, soft and warm. She looked around, her mouth trembling. Beyond the bushes that stopped her fall were boulders, hard rock, bound to break a bone or two. Like good soldiers, the bushes had protected her from the boulders and when she stopped sliding the calm and silent air encased her.

She wanted to cry. She needed to cry. But the tears froze inside of her, locked in her chest right where her missing heart should have been. God was watching over her this time, she thought, once she realized she hadn't been hurt. She collapsed and finally the tears came, soaking the snow. When she was all cried out, she wiped her face, looked around where she'd landed, saw Pa's cave, and hid behind the bushes. A man moved around in there.

After a while Drake came out cursing, empty-handed. He wore his pistol at his side and he looked mad. Once he was gone, Lilly went in, right to the spot where she'd watched Pa hide the pack. She dug it out and opened it. Pa's pistol was wrapped in a rag and tucked neatly in the bottom of the pack. The box for bullets lay next to it. On top of them both sat a cotton bag. The bag was filled with pictures.

Lilly took the pictures, left the pack in it's hiding place, and scooted to the front of the cave where she could look at the photos in the sunlight. One of the photos was of Drake pointing a gun at a dark-skinned man with dark hair. He looked a lot like a young Running Bear and she was sure it was Jimmy Joseph, Horse Child. The next photo was of Horse Child lying on the ground, the life gone out of him.

Someone other than her father had taken the next two shots. The first one was of Drake pointing the gun at Pa as he held Horse Child. On the back of the picture Pa had written "Horse Child, after Drake killed him." The second photo was of Pa writhing on the ground, his knee at an odd angle. On the back of it Pa had written "Me, after Drake shot me."

The light in the cave darkened and Lilly turned to see Drake standing there, holding his gun. "Give me the photos and you and I can put all of this behind us," he said. "That's what families do. They forgive each other."

"You're not my family."

"I will be soon enough."

"No. You won't." She tightened her fists around the bag of photos and got ready to run. Pearl put out a wing, encouraging her to stop and think, encouraging her to play dead. That new part of her brain worked fast and Lilly considered her options. "Not unless Nell takes you in," she added cautiously.

A smile lit across his face. "She's already clearing off shelves for my things. We're talking a real wedding."

The thought flipped her stomach right over her head. "Here," she said, handing the bag of photos to him. "No hard feelings." She was a pretty good actress. Maybe she belonged in the movies.

"None at all." He took the photos, turned on his heel and, without offering any help to Lilly he climbed up over the pass.

She jammed a walking stick into the hard snow and followed his heel steps up the mountain. On her way down the other side, she could feel her back burning from the slide down the hill. Sounds echoed off the rocks like something following her. Was Drake tracking her, like a mountain lion, all stealth and hidden danger, ready to pounce if she caused him trouble?

Thunder filled the sky and Lilly saw lightning spread out across the mountains. The rain came down heavy and she held up under a large spruce tree next to a creek. Pearl had already faded into the clouds but when she squinted she could make out her lofty shape. When the storm passed, Lilly caught that dreaded, familiar smell and she heard footsteps.

"Who's there?" she called, thinking how stupid the question had sounded when she'd heard it in her father's stories. Who would answer? Oh, it's just me, Richard, I'm just breaking in to rob you blind. "Answer me. Who walks there?"

But no one answered and the footsteps faded.

Pearl returned and floated on a slow part of the creek. She stretched her long neck into the water and tilted her bottom up, spreading an array of feathers toward the sky. When she righted herself, riverweed hung from her bill.

"Go ahead, get your belly full," Lilly said, feeling the empty ache in her own. "I'm out here hungry, while you eat like a queen." She cupped her hands in the cold water and drank. She was so thirsty. Fear filled her. Drake had killed Horse Child. He wrecked Pa's knee. He was a dangerous man. She pushed at the fear, knowing she'd be no good if it paralyzed her. Trying to get the fear away, as if shoving it into the mountain creek, she began walking.

———————

By the time she got to Jerome's ranch her calves ached. Her blistered feet stung. Everything hurt. Thinking of Nell, Lilly watched the rescued swans on Charlie West's ranch. They tilted their tail feathers to the sky and scoured the pond bottom for food. Water beaded on the wax-white feathers of the large ones. The downy gray of the younger swans seemed to absorb the water. There were nine of them in all, three adults and six cygnets.

She knew the fledglings would eventually migrate. The marooned parents would be left alone, which was not at all the swan's natural way. In the wild, an injured swan would simply die without help. Charlie had saved the swans, but he had also tied them to a life of captivity.

"You went up there by yourself, didn't you?" Jerome came up behind her.

Lilly nodded.

"Find anything?"

"I did," she said, turning her empty palms toward the sky, "but I lost it."

———————

Lilly was eight years old when she first heard her father scream from his bedroom. She opened the door and saw him in tremors on the floor, his skin the color of a bruise. Nell had come in moments later with a dry washrag and hot tea, which Pa spilled all over the floor when he tried to drink it. She wiped the sweat from his brow. When he shook, she sat behind him and wrapped her arms around him to quell the tremors. She motioned with her eyes to the towels set aside for Pa. Lilly picked up a wet towel.

"Not that one," Nell said. "It'll send him into the shivers. Take the dry one and wipe the sweat from his face."

Pa's grimace tore across his face from the inside out. If Lilly hadn't known that he was her father from the way his knee bowed out, she wouldn't have recognized him. This shaking, sweating, foul-eyed Pa frightened her.

"Go on," Nell said.

Lilly wiped his forehead gently, like she might've done with a very young child. When he went into another set of convulsions, Nell tightened her hug around his shoulders. Later, when Pa slept safely, Nell said he could've died. Alcohol was bad, she told Lilly, but Pa was good. He always did the very best he could. "Remember that," she said, "he's done his best. We both have."

Lilly thought of Nell's courage as she took a step toward Jerome. "Me and you are going to Drake's hideout to recover my things."

"What things?"

"Things he took from me today. Things I'm going to get back."

"Lilly," Jerome said after thinking for a moment. "He's dangerous. I'll go with you on one condition. We tell my father and he goes with us."

"You know Charlie doesn't believe a word I say."

"Tell me what you're missing, maybe we can convince him."

She was afraid to tell Jerome about the photos and Pa's letter, as if telling him would somehow put a hex on Drake's capture. Or that Drake would burn the photos and she'd be made to look like a liar again and he'd get away, and Pa would still be dead for no good reason. And Drake would walk right into their house and marry Nell. "Can you keep a secret?" She asked.

"You know I can."

"We can't tell your father, not yet."

Jerome looked from the mountains to the ground and back to the mountains again, as if searching for the right thing to say. He shrugged. "Go ahead."

"Pa hid photos in that cave the other side of the pass, pictures of Drake pointing a gun at a man, the same man dead, and then Pa lying on the ground next to the first man, with Pa's leg splayed out in a weird direction. His knee injury was no accident. Drake shot him. Drake killed Pa's friend."

Jerome bit his lip and put a hand to his forehead. "You saw these photos?"

"Yes, today. I was with Pa the day that he hid them."

"Why didn't you say something sooner?"

"I didn't know what was in the bag until today."

"How did Drake get the photos?"

"He was there, looking for something. I thought he'd gone and I went into the cave. I was looking at the pictures from Pa's pack when Drake came back. Jerome, he's practically living at my house. He plans on asking Nell to marry him and the sad thing is, she just might do it. The injury has done something to her brain. She doesn't think right. She thinks Drake is a good man coming around to help out now that Pa's gone. He even told her he'll find the man who shot them."

Lilly could see fear crawl across Jerome's face. "I can't imagine you giving the photos to him."

She bit her lip. "He had a gun."

"How are we going to go up against a man with a gun, Lilly?"

"We're not," she said. "He must have hidden the photos in his hideout. We'll go when he's not there, get the photos, and bring them to your dad."

"They still won't prove that he shot your father."

"There's more. Pa wrote notes on back of two of the photos."

"What notes?"

"One said it was Horse Child after Drake killed him and one

was Pa after Drake shot him." She still didn't tell about Pa's letter.

"We have to go to my dad with this."

"No! Not till we get the photos."

Jerome blew a whistle out through his teeth. "OK, but if he's there, we abandon the idea and come straight back here and tell my father. Agreed?"

"Agreed."

———————

The next morning, Lilly wore Sam's sweater. She put her father's folding knife in her trousers' pocket next to his letter and the photos of him and Drake at the mine in Butte. They spent the morning and most of the afternoon climbing up the trail toward the pass. When they arrived at Drake's hideout, the sun was high in the sky and voices floated out to the boulders where they hid.

"And it paid good," Drake bragged to another man sitting at the mouth of the tunnel with him. He threw back a shot of what might have been afternoon whiskey. "The man was trying to set up the Company. Taking photos of injured miners. Some folks don't like that kind of thing, scared he might blackmail them or go to a newspaper."

"I know. We hired you." The man had short dark hair and wore a canvas coat. He was the same man that had been with Drake that day two years ago when Lilly followed her father to the cave. "You have the photos?"

She looked at Jerome and raised her eyebrows. Drake was talking to a Company man about her father.

"Hardworking men could lose their jobs." Drake slurred his words, a sound Lilly remembered from Pa's drinking days. "You wanted the photos stopped, wanted them to disappear. I didn't mean to hurt anyone. I was just after his camera. But he got in my way. The Indian kid, he was in the wrong place at the wrong time. Those photos were bad news. But now they're all mine." He poured another whiskey for himself and one for the other man.

"Give them to me," the man said.

"Not so fast. I'll hold onto them until I get my money."

"Give them to me, that way we know where they are." The man stood up and started pacing back and forth in the tunnel's entrance.

"I'll keep them nice and safe here till you bring me the cash. That was the deal. The photos are not the problem; it's the girl that's the problem now. She saw me in the swamp the day her father died and she won't let go of it. Now she's seen the photos. She's gonna keep causing problems till one of us is gone. And I'm going nowhere."

Lilly took a breath, put her hand in her pocket, and ran her fingers along the smooth edge of the letter. She touched her father's knife.

She pulled out the knife and went after Drake. A black crow spread his wings out from Drake's ears and cawed, flapping his wings against her attack. The crow disappeared and Lilly saw Drake's hands were up in the shape of an x, protecting himself.

*Put the knife down. Justice, sweetheart, not revenge.*

She suddenly saw herself, a phantom Lilly, standing down the mountainside, next to Pearl. That ghostly girl cried huge tears that ran down her face.

Lilly stepped away from Drake, dropped the knife and ran.

Jerome followed her. "What the hell was that?" he asked when they were halfway down the mountain and certain they weren't being followed. "We had an agreement."

Lilly gripped the letter and the photos in her pocket. She gripped them as tightly as she had gripped the folding knife moments earlier, her insides burned up, a hollow shell of a girl. With the fire inside of her spent, she sank into the pine needles on the forest floor and wailed.

When she couldn't stop crying, Jerome took her home and told his mother the whole story. She insisted that Lilly spend the night with them. Charlie wasn't due back until morning. She agreed that they'd talk to Charlie about it when he returned. For now, she'd send word to Anna and Nell of Lilly's whereabouts.

When Lilly started for Pearl's pen, Lenore stopped her.

"I have bad news," she said.

Lilly's throat filled with feathers and she couldn't breathe. All news lately was bad news. Was Nell sick again?

"Pearl died today." Lenore's eyes clouded with tears. She took a step toward her.

"What?" Lilly's brain jumbled and twisted around in her head.

"She was doing so well, and then she just took a turn for the worse. Charlie doesn't know why. He buried her over in the old pen we never use anymore."

"No. There's a mistake."

"I'm sorry, Lilly."

"No, you're wrong. She's not dead." Lilly ran to her pen and found it empty of everything but droppings and straw. In the old pen, Lilly found the newly dug grave and the pile of rocks on top of it. She lay down on the soft dirt, near the rocks, rubbing her face into the ground, no tears left inside of her. When she refused to go inside, Lenore brought a tan quilt out to the pen and covered her with it while she slept.

# 25

Late that night, Lilly rose from a deep sleep, waiting for Pearl to show up. And she did. She came back from the dead. Lilly heard her in the ponds with the others, the sound of her great wings reaching up and flying, arcing against the night sky. She knew that if she stayed where she was, by morning Pearl would be under the quilt with her, curled up at her feet, her long neck stretched over her wing and tucked into the back feathers.

Lilly smelled autumn leaves and pine needles touched by fresh rain. A lightning storm had come and gone while she'd slept, the sky barely weeping, leaving the quilt damp but not wet.

Pearl flew over and edged close to Lilly in the gateway of the old pen. And Lilly let her get close knowing she had to go. Lilly had barely thought the words and she was up and out of the pen, past the house, and walking toward the mountains. An owl called across the branches. I'm here, she answered. The words fell and dried up. She had to get the pictures so she'd have something to show Charlie West. She meant to stay on the safe side of the mountain, away from the cave where her father had hidden a gun.

Her head filled with images of dead swans and the last look

on Pa's face in the marsh that day, lying in the water, eyes that looked out nowhere at nothing. An acid wind blew up her spine. Moonlight edged between the clouds. Dark shadows clutched their fingers around her neck. Like the killer's hand, the shadows covered her eyes, ears, and mouth. She walked and walked, lost her sense of time and balance, regained it and pushed forward. At times she ran hard, her bird legs pushing the ground away in a sure steady rhythm, her knees lifting toward the sky, her body feather light.

As she left the damp smell of cedar behind, she was transforming, her supple neck stretching to her head and out to her dark, flat bill, her belly round and smooth. The muddy ground squished up over the edge of her shoe and slunk down under the arch of her foot. Bushes scratched at her ankles and reached up her trouser legs scratching her calves, like fingers that would drag her back to the wetlands if she'd let them. She wouldn't let them. Not now. Not with Drake somewhere on this mountain with her father's photos. Gurgling sounds of water reached across the forest and encouraged her.

Run. Run. Fly.

She came out of the thick forest onto the grassy slopes. Pearl spread her wings across the sky. Her long neck curled and straightened. Her huge body turned the world white for a moment until, across the naked night, she disappeared. Lilly charged forward, woozy and thick, breathing hard. In the moonlight she spotted the white carcass of a dead swan. Maybe it had flown into a tree, or perhaps it was carried up here by a bear. But most likely it had been hunted down by Dean Drake and dropped without mercy on the side of the trail.

Suddenly Lilly was eleven years old again, near a marsh of brilliant white trumpeter swans. The gunshots rang out, turning the swamp crimson red and pink. The birds fell. Her parents fell. The world changed forever.

Pearl swept in beside Lilly once more, moving her swiftly up the mountainside where the dense timber thinned and led to Dean Drake's hideout. A feather fell into her hand and she put it safely in the pocket of her trousers, next to the photos and Pa's letter.

Pearl flapped her wings and swaddled Lilly in them, the down soft and warm, the last vestiges of night cool to the touch.

---

Lilly looked into Drake's hideout and he was nowhere in sight. He was probably down at the house with Nell. That thought punched at her chest where her heart should've been. The moon gave off enough light so that she could see shapes inside the mine tunnel, all still and solid. To one side, along a damp wall, was Pa's white cloth bag.

Pearl trilled. Lilly hushed the great white bird and grabbed the bag. Suddenly, out of the still night, she heard a jagged breath. She looked toward the sound and saw a blanket move as Drake sat up from his bed. Pearl covered Lilly with her wings as she ran away.

Drake went after her.

Running harder than she'd ever run in her life, Lilly's legs ached. Her throat burned. The blisters grew on her feet and her mind turned numb. Time slowed down. The moon set and the sky turned misty pink as the sun rose. Pearl flapped her wings under Lilly, closer now, nearly lifting her off the ground. She gave Lilly the strength of her own wings, the power of the wind, the power of love.

A grizzly moved carefully across the mountain. Lilly thought of the story about the bear and the swan. She'd had a choice to be the hunter or the protector. She had chosen both. It was the wrong choice, but it was the only choice. Dean Drake had presented only wrong choices.

Nothing could be made right.

If any of them could've seen into the future they would have seen the fallen swans. They would have seen Nell with her lost voice. They would have seen Pa die.

Stopping to catch her breath, Lilly held a hand above her eyes, palm down, and looked—but for what? Nell? Anna? Jerome? The terrain became steeper and she put her fingers into a crack between the boulders to pull herself up. She placed her feet carefully and her webbed toes caught the ridges. The higher she climbed the closer Pearl stayed.

Stopping again, she leaned on a stunted pine. Her over heated chest puffed out like the swan's chest, Pearl's feathers oiled and light, Lilly's feathers soft and elegant. Her lungs ached in agony, the air too thin to fill them. Her legs dragged, heavy with fatigue.

Even as Lilly's head pounded in her ears, she heard the swan killer getting closer. He was after her, mean and dangerous. She ran, stumbled, and ran again. The wind pasted itself to her back.

Drake gained on her. He laughed a dark laugh that she heard over the surge of blood in her ears.

Overhead, she heard the trumpeters' trill. In the distance she could see the flock in uneven lines above her. Pearl led Lilly, nearly lifted Lilly, her legs light and strong again. She shut her eyes tight and felt Pearl's breath. She opened her eyes. Something pure white flashed and a rush of cool air flowed past. The next breath was easier, and the third breath was easier still. The coolness in Lilly's lungs spread over her body and her chest feathers fluttered. She kept moving upward, up the pass, far up the snowfield.

Lillian. Elizabeth. God Has Sworn. She ran hard. Drake yelled her name. His voice hurt her ears. He was there, just behind her, kicking steps into the snow, climbing the pass with a mighty fury.

But it didn't matter. She put on a terrible Strength. She put on the power of Heaven, the light of the Sun, the grace of the Swan. At the top of the pass she lifted her arms and felt the flow of cool air on her fingertips. Her feet barely touched the ground. Faster, faster, she moved. The sounds of the world faded into the distance. The air rushed against her face. Another flash of white moved swiftly towards Lilly. Great wings cut through the air. She bounded across the top of the snowfield. The ice moved swiftly beneath her. Out of the corner of her eye she saw the hunter. She no longer saw Pearl, but she felt her where she lived, where she'd always lived, inside of Lilly. Lilly clutched the bag of photos in her webbed feet. She lifted her great white wings to the air that rushed in under them.

She jumped off the cliff.

The wind pressed against her feathers.

And she flew.

# Landing

# 26

There was a moment before Lilly landed, when the earth reached out to greet the breaking sun. She looked down on the tiny toy-like trees, boulders that looked like pebbles, slabs of boulders that jutted out into jagged peaks, peaks that rolled down into mountain lakes and soft meadows filled with dying wildflowers. She saw Nell standing on the porch, her gaze wandering out among the wilted glacier lilies, gazing out on the clouds where Lilly's father and his twisted knee had disappeared.

George was a tiny doll selling lumber, Anna a miniature sister making the bed and propping a toy swan up by the pillows. Jerome stood tall, a palm shading his eyes, his dark hair crossing his cheeks. From up here, even Drake was a sad little puppet, simple and strange, no more powerful than a broken down fence.

Lilly saw herself too, a discarded feather hat, soiled and wet, lost to its own beauty, ready to stand and brush down its riled plume. She heard tiny voices, little laughter, and saw eyes twinkle like morning stars. There below her, the world stood exactly as it always had been: full of love and grace, sadness and anger. Full of hearts swollen with joy and pride, hearts that shatter into a hundred tiny pieces. Her body occupied that little space at the bottom of the snowfield, pushed up against the boulders and huckleberry bushes. The wind blew life through her hair, and she belonged.

She saw the lakes on the eastern side of the mountains flowing one into the other, and she knew that hatred was contagious. She'd gotten hers from Dean Drake. It had filled her up and spilled out. It had spread like fire, cutting a black path before Lilly. Hatred had no resting point, flooding and burning and pushing on everything until everything good was gone.

Nell had told Lilly once, long ago, that love was contagious. You caught it from the eyes of another person. Lilly wondered if this was true. Someday, if she ever got off this mountain, if she had a chance to find the rest of her life, she would try it out on Jerome. She'd put her pride aside and find the courage to tell him the truth. And this was the truth: Lilly loved Jerome West. A shimmering warmth flowed through her body, melting the old and turning Lilly like taffy, waiting for her true self to take shape.

The voices of Jerome, Pa and Nell floated through the air and she knew that they had come to take her home. She reached out her hand and asked for help.

When she woke, she was alone, clutching the boulder like a rag doll, acting like the child she hadn't yet outgrown.

She looked toward her father's cave and listened. The voices were gone. The withered leaves of rosebushes stretched out their earthly fingers, telling Lilly that something else was missing. She looked around for it. She smelled the air for the scent of it. She listened in the wind.

Sorrow reached down into the deep pit of her stomach. A magnificent gathering of trumpeters flew in the sky above. That ghostly mass of white birds had lifted up from the wetlands and turned the sky into a shiny bright heaven. And there, in one of the jagged lines, flew a lop-sided swan, her great expanse of wings filling the sky. Pearl had joined the flock.

She had left Lilly in a crumpled mess at the bottom of the snowfield, left her to fend for herself. She'd brought Lilly safely back to

Pa's cave and now her job was done. Lilly stretched her frozen legs and wiggled her toes and fingers. She checked her pained head for blood. Finding none, she drew in a breath and stood up.

The sun lit the fall leaves and each detail on that mountain brightened and became clear. Near the mouth of the cave was a group of rocks, which she hadn't noticed before. They were piled high, something from a previous rockslide. Or maybe Pa had cleaned them out from the cave.

Among several dried branches brown pine needles had gathered into tiny anthills, nature's fuel for the next forest fire. A few clouds floated across the sky. All of this Lilly took in like grace. Heavy breathing brought her back to the reality that Drake was nearby. The good feelings evaporated. She told her legs to go but they wouldn't move. She looked down to confirm that they were still human legs, not swan legs, and that they still belonged to her. They did.

Lilly looked back at the snowfield and saw that other set of steps kicked into the snow. A patch of brown moved through a small stand of serviceberry trees.

Pa's cave was only a few feet away and she scurried to it, willing her muscles to work. Inside was damp and it smelled musty. Light came in on shimmering slivers, the wings of insects or bright angels, each one opening a hole in the darkness. She let her eyes adjust, welcoming the tiny shafts of sunlight that glittered off the rock walls of the cave. Feeling along one wall, she lost her balance, stumbled, and fell. Fatigue dropped on her like a boulder, it's rock solid center pressing down on her chest and pushing her into an anxious search for Pa's gun.

Drake had said that Lilly was his problem.

Feeling around behind a large boulder for a small loose rock, she pushed the rock and it rolled. Underneath it, a dusty cloth covered the pistol. Another rag held several matches and a handful of photos that she must have missed when she first found the photos. She put the matches in her pocket, took the gun to the front of the cave and stood to one side where the light glowed and faltered.

When she opened the gun chamber, it was empty. She found

the box of bullets. It rattled and Lilly thought she had plenty of ammunition. But when she opened it only one bullet and several small rocks in it were enclosed in it. No matter. She had one bullet, if she knew how to use it.

She tried to remember how Pa had loaded his guns. She'd seen him do it half a dozen times, but had never loaded one herself. She knew nothing about shooting something. Someone. She put the bullet in the chamber. But she knew luck would definitely have to be running toward her in order to stop Drake with the gun.

The stench of bear announced his presence. A spider crawled across Lilly's neck, sending an icy river down her spine. She quelled the urge to throw the spider off and run right out of there. Instead she slid her back against the wet wall and became a shadow in the cave's entry.

"I know you're in there," Drake said. "I can hear you breathing."

Lilly thought he was bluffing, since she could barely hear her own breathing.

Suddenly the other side of the cave exploded into a thousand white-hot splinters. Her senses shut down. Lilly couldn't see or hear anything. In that white-hot world, she wondered if she was dead. This must be what her father felt, completely purified, not a single molecule of his being left to determine right from wrong, everything bright and wide open, the trail cleared forever.

The first thing to come back was Lilly's sense of smell. Sulfur and dust became the very air she breathed. When her vision cleared, tiny particles danced across a beam of sunlight like high wire acrobats. Her brain was on high speed, sharp and determined.

She threw a rock from the bullet box into the far bushes, and heard Drake's footsteps quickly follow. That was when she slipped out of the cave and hid in another set of bushes. To cover the sound of her movement, she threw three rocks into the cave and watched Drake quietly make his way through its dark mouth, sneaking up on the Lilly that wasn't there.

Once he was inside the cave, she tiptoed as quietly as possible as close to the cave as she dared, and shot the gun right into the pile of rocks beside it.

The gun jerked back, bruising her palm and sending her shoulder into convulsions. The explosion deafened her. Even the wind went mute. As if in slow motion, the rock pile toppled down into the dark opening, trapping the swan killer.

A rock exploded on the far end of the pile. Tiny shards of it hit Lilly's arm just above the elbow. Red welts rose out of her arm and her skin wept bright red tears. For a second, she lost her hearing again, but this time she knew what had happened. She wasn't dead. Lilly lived, and she would make this right.

"Put down your gun," she said, "and I'll go get Charlie West to clear these rocks so you can get out."

Another shot skinned the bark off a fir tree. A black barrel poked out of a small opening at the top of the rocks. Lilly surveyed the rock pile for other holes that he might shoot through. There were two or three openings about the size of her fist. As soon as she saw them, a rock moved and the hole where the gun barrel had been got bigger.

"You get me the hell out of here and I won't kill you right now," Drake yelled. He hollered a lot more things, but Lilly's suddenly rational mind closed him out. She didn't care to make sense of his words. As fast as she could, she stacked branches in front of the rocks. She lit them on fire, and quickly built a stone barricade at the edge of the branches so that the forest wouldn't burn. She piled on more branches so that even if Drake managed to squeeze out one of the openings, he would have to walk through fire to get free.

Lilly watched the branches catch flame, smoke billowing out dark and sticky, scorching the air with its plumes.

As if from a magician's hat, voices popped up out of nowhere. She whirled around to see Running Bear and a group of his men step off the snowfield and walk toward her. Behind them came Nell, Anna, Jerome and Charlie West.

"Did you see the smoke?" She asked.

"Only moments ago," Running Bear said. "We heard the shots. I figured you'd be here. Two Sons and Horse Child came here often when they were young." His black hair glistened in the sun. He looked down on her with gentle, concerned eyes and a questioning half-smile. It was an expression she knew from Pa's face.

"How did you know to come?"

"Your mother, the one we call Flying Girl, came to my lodge to say you were in trouble, that the man named Drake was after you and you were out here searching for proof that he killed your father."

"She said?" Lilly repeated, disbelieving.

"Her mind is back. She remembered your father saying he'd put the photos in a secret place, that he'd had you with him at the time. She'd disapproved of him taking you with him and their talk turned to a fight so fast she never learned where he hid the photos. She thought I would know."

"My mother is talking to you?"

Charlie West came up. "You have quite a fire going there. Gonna burn the damned forest down to prove your point?" He smiled at Lilly and pointed to the row of rocks, her attempt to keep the fire contained. "That's some smart thinking. Is Drake in the cave?"

She nodded.

"Hurt?"

"I don't know."

Just then another shot rang out and nicked a pine tree. Everyone turned to look at the tree, as if it had the answer to Charlie's question.

"OK, Dean," Charlie said. "I've got a whole group of men out here to take you in. You can shoot one of us, but you can't kill us all. You'll go down for murder for certain in that case."

"She's the one you should be arresting. She damned near killed me, trapping me in here and then starting the damned forest on fire."

"Here's what we're gonna do. We're gonna let this fire burn down and then you are going to gently slide your gun and any other weapons you've got out on top of the rocks. Then we'll get you out of there and take you in. You'll get a fair trial. We'll make certain of that."

"Like I should trust you. I didn't do anything. That girl's after me because Nell loves me and she's jealous. She's crazy and jealous."

Nell stepped forward then. She wore a blue dress over long johns and a thick button-down sweater. The back hem of the dress was wet where it might have dragged in the snowfield. She opened her mouth and words came out.

"Dean," Nell said. A holy silence covered the land. Even the fire went calm. "Come on out of there. I already lost Sam and both of my parents to needless tragedy. I know you've done wrong."

"Nell?" His voice sounded ghostly white.

"I saw you stand aside when my parents went down in that river. I tried to get to them, but I couldn't. You had a rope you could've thrown to them, but you didn't."

"I was scared, Nelly. I was scared they'd pull me in too."

"I knew you were scared. It was the only way I could forgive you. But Dean? Now is the time for courage. Now's the time for you to come out here and face what you've done."

"Your parents were an accident."

"I believe that. But Sam?"

"From the very beginning he wanted to ruin me."

"Come on out, Dean," she said.

"Nell?" Lilly asked, her lips quivering. "Have you been able to talk this whole time?"

She looked at Lilly, a light in her eyes that Lilly hadn't even realized she'd missed. "I don't know. Maybe it took the thought of losing you to bring me to my senses and help me find my voice again."

Lilly put her head on her mother's chest, soaking her dress with her tears. She kept it there until Drake came out of the cave and Charlie tied him up and marched him up the snowfield and down the other side toward town.

---

Jerome went with Lilly to get the last of Pa's photos from the cave. She brought them out into the light, pulled the protective rag from them, and looked. On top was a photo of Drake holding a gun. Under that, one of Drake pointing the gun at two men on their bellies, their hands tied behind them. Every photo left in the cave was of Drake hurting or threatening someone.

Jerome lifted his eyebrows and nodded. "You were right," he said. "I thought he took these from you."

"I guess I missed some. These were still in there. I went to his hideout this morning and got the others back. I dropped them in the rocks at the bottom of the snowfield. They should still be there."

They found the photos and started for home. By the time they began the descent through the trees to the valley floor, the sun had crossed into the western sky. They picked their way through lilted bear grass, careful not to slip. Lilly heard the howl of a coyote, the trill of a trumpeter, and the growl of a bear and wondered if she was just imagining things. She heard Nell, Anna and Running Bear, who were just ahead of them on the trail.

When they reached the bottom of the snowfield Nell wrapped her fingers around Lilly's hand and pulled her into her chest.

"Baby," her mother said and nothing had ever sounded so good.

———

The idea of talking with Nell again both thrilled and terrified Lilly. She wanted to know what her mother had been thinking that last year, what it had been like for her in that other world. A small, quickly fading, part of Lilly wanted to tell her how angry she'd been. More than anything though, she wanted to tell her mother how much she loved her. "Thank you, Mama," she said, "for coming to get me."

They sat on a log and tossed pebbles into the water.

Anna soon sat on the other side of Nell and they all tossed rocks into the water together. Such simple gestures.

Jerome sat on the log next to Lilly.

"Dad took your father's film to a friend in Mission to have it developed," Jerome said. "When I woke up this morning, and you were gone, I knew you'd gone after Drake. We searched the woods all the way to his hideout. When we couldn't find you we went to Nell. She took us to Running Bear."

"Did he get the film back from his friend?" Lilly asked.

"He did."

"The film told the truth I'd been telling."

Jerome took hold of her hand. "It did," he said.

Lilly smiled at him. Her arm ached. Her legs ached. Her whole body ached. Her back still burned from where she'd slid down the snowfield and hit the boulders. Across the vast sky the clouds turned bright where the sun tried to shine through.

"Why didn't your dad show the pictures to my father?"

"He might have been about to when he was killed." Lilly took Pa's letter out of her pocket and showed it to him. "I think he didn't give it to your dad because Drake seemed to have left the area that winter. Maybe Pa thought he was gone for good."

"Maybe so."

"Jerome?" Lilly asked.

"Yes?"

"Do you think it's good for a man's soul to admit his wrongdoings?"

"I don't know much about the soul."

"But to stop a man from doing wrong, that's good, isn't it? Even for the man, himself? It's got to be good for him to be stopped."

"I'd say yes, although it sounds like a question for the priest. You can ask him when we get back to Mission. Right now, let's get off this mountain." Jerome put out a hand to Lilly and pulled her up off of the log. Her mother, Anna and Running Bear joined them. Lilly took her mother's hand again. She held it tight like it was the best thing in the whole wide world.

―――――――――

That was what Lilly wanted, when it was all over, for things to return to normal, for her mother to scold her for misbehaving and put her to bed at night, for Anna to do her chores while dreaming about George James King, while Pa pulled a saddle off of the brown mare, to be back in Mission with her parents and Anna, talking about frogs, giants and angels. For her and Jerome to go back to the kind of friends they'd been before: him thinking he knew more than Lilly, Lilly working hard to prove him wrong.

But Lilly was older now. That time had come and gone.

Still, she felt happy being there with her mother, Anna and Jerome. She felt so grateful to Running Bear for guiding her mother back to them. She felt happy in her heart, her heart beating strong and steady.

God had, after all, seen fit to give her back her missing heart. As it turned out, He hadn't taken it to make Anna happy, or to fix Nell, or to bring Pa back, or to put things back in order. He'd taken it for Lilly. He'd made it bigger and strengthened the walls to hold something beautiful and free, to hold sorrow and transform it.

When they reached Jerome's ranch a light rain rippled on the pond. Young trumpeters ran, flapped their wings, paused and ran again, trying to fly. Two adult trumpeters fluttered their injured wings and settled. They dropped their necks toward each other in the shape of a heart, telling each other secrets. The injured trumpeters trilled notes so sweet and soft, the world turned radiant. Even the fall leaves turned their faces to the sky.

Above the cooing swans, Lilly saw that great mass of white birds again, crossing the sky toward the clouds where the angels lived. Maybe Pa lived there too—content now that justice would have a chance. And she knew that it was true, in spite of everything, the stars of eleven had filled her heart. She held them there, close and precious. One day they would rise up and shine. Above her, near the brilliant sun, the flock of trumpeter swans disappeared into the clouds.

# Author's Note

As of July 2015 the Confederated Salish and Kootenai Tribes Wildlife Management Program's Flathead Indian Reservation Trumpeter Swan Reintroduction Project had released 258 captive-bred trumpeter swans into the wild. Those birds resulted in at least 294 fledged cygnets, with the numbers increasing every year. These swans have been seen in Canada, as far south as Utah, and near the Washington coast, although many of them have stayed in Northwest Montana. *The Swan Keeper* is a work of fiction and I have taken great liberties with the geography of the Mission Mountains. Any mistakes in fact or representation are entirely my own. All characters are figments of my imagination and are not meant to portray any actual persons, alive or dead.

# Acknowledgements

Thank you, first and foremost, to John Jarvis and the Montana Waterfowl Foundation for introducing me to and teaching me about trumpeter swans, and for working so hard for these amazing birds. Thank you to Dale Becker, CSKT Tribal Wildlife Program Manager, and the Flathead Indian Reservation Trumpeter Swan Reintroduction Project. Thank you to the many people who have taught me about trauma, grief, courage, and recovery, deeply touching my heart and enriching my life. Thank you to Maggie Plummer for her editing, encouragement, wisdom, and support through the years. Thank you to Cindy Williams for proofing *The Swan Keeper* and liking it. I am ever grateful for the Wild Horse Writers' Group, especially Maggie Plummer, Phyllis Walker, and Gary Acevedo for all of their comments and suggestions. They were all there when *The Swan Keeper* first took flight. Thank you to Judith Bromley for her photos and enthusiasm for this book. Thank you to Christy Dodson Kearney for her faith in my writing from the beginning, and to Jan Myers for her photos and videos. A huge thank you to Kelly Huddleston and David Ross at Open Books for their wisdom, guidance, and support. I am forever grateful to my family and my long time friends. Without their enduring love and generosity none of this would be possible.